9/4

———— TO AN

1964 · NEW YORK · SIMON AND SCHUSTER

EARLY GRAVE

WALLACE MARKFIELD

For Anna.

1 ———————————————————

THAT SUNDAY, when the phone began to ring, Morroe Rieff was dreaming what he had not dreamed in many months. Somehow, he was in a subway. He was on his way to a ship, a huge blue and white thing. To make time he ducked under a turnstile, got onto an escalator. But somebody on the platform next to it made a motion and cried, "Off, off." He wondered who this fellow was, where he got his authority. He looked more closely, and he saw it was his old dean of men, Carmody. "This is very stupid of you," Carmody told him. "You know we can't let you on, fellow, never in a million years." Carmody was wearing a gym outfit, with sneakers and shorts and a white T shirt. He took hold of Morroe and started to pull him off the escalator. And Morroe raged and warned him to keep his lousy hands to himself, telling him he would complain and make trouble. But Carmody dragged him over to a desk and said, "Fellow, you'll have to forget about the ship. You didn't take your required year of math. You cut every single one of your classes." Morroe argued and wheedled and sought to charm, but he was forced back under the turnstile again, pushed and harried up an escalator and sent reeling into the streets.

At the first peal, Morroe awakened to find tears running down his face. He felt an overpowering relief, as though something had been hanging over him and had passed away, spared him. Yet he knew that if he could ignore the phone, if he could keep himself for a moment, only a moment more at the fringe of sleep, a mystery would be revealed, a marvelous truth brought closer. The ringing stopped suddenly; a wrong number perhaps, or the caller had changed his mind, realized how early it was. But it started up again, persistent, powerful, banging away at every wall.

"I'll get it," he said, turning so violently his shoulder struck the night table and sent an ash tray toppling. "I'll go," he added, though his wife, Etta, had given no sign of rising. He worked his broad flat feet into carpet slippers and tightened the tape of his pajama bottoms. Then, lifting the receiver, Morroe wagged a finger at Etta, pointing to the cigarettes near her side, implying she should light one and pass it to him. But she mumbled something he could not make out and tunneled under the covers.

"Yes," he said tonelessly. His voice was smothered in

hoarseness and he nearly gagged from the foulness of his morning mouth.

He heard, "This is Inez. Inez Braverman." And though he sensed her nervousness, he deliberately permitted the silence to lengthen, forcing her to rattle on shrilly. "Were you sleeping? Yeah, yeah, yeah, you were sleeping!"

He said, finally, "Oh, Inez. Well, so how have you been?" He was precise and formal; he had that right after a year, make it a year and a half, of silence, after God knows how many calls to her office which she had lacked the decency to return. "Yes, we were sleeping. We had a kind of late night, some people over. If you want to know, I think we're not used to those hours any more." This was to put her on notice that he had no lack of friends, that he was part of other groups and other circles.

She said, "Look, baby, I have some very, very bad news."

"Whoosh! What? Inez, what's the matter?" He began to pace as far as the tangled wires would permit, and a terrific throbbing started behind his eyes.

"I got this call from Leslie's father. . . ."

Though it was his own little whimper he had heard, Morroe nevertheless begged Inez to put herself under control, saying, "Go ahead. He called you, Leslie's father. . . . Go ahead." Meanwhile he bared his teeth at Etta, who had hustled out of bed, and waved away her questions with frantic hands.

"Leslie's dead."

"Whoosh. My God." He groaned with sorrow and

rage and smacked his forehead. "Inez, oh, Inez, do you know what you're saying?"

"Yeah, yeah, yeah." Her voice shot up, dwindled. There was noise in the background—the kids, maybe static on the line—and he could make out only "coronary" and "Brooklyn." "Slow, slow, Inez. I don't get you." He remembered, with a sinking heart, that Leslie owed him a hundred and thirty-seven dollars. Oh, goodbye now my money. Down, down under the earth. With Leslie together. "You're all right? All right, Inez, tell me slowly. What happened?"

She gave out a wild, panting laugh, a trifle overdone, almost theatrical. She said, "Listen, you know what's so funny? Listen, listen! He was over a couple of days ago with a big bottle of wine and a new story. He starts reading it to me, but he really wants to screw and I said to him, 'Drop dead.' "

"Yes, but what did you say before? Did you say it was a heart attack, a coronary?"

"I didn't mean drop dead for *dying*. I meant drop dead for *screwing*...."

"And where does Brooklyn come in?" He covered the receiver and raised his eyes to the ceiling. "It's Inez Braverman," he hissed at Etta. "Hold on . . . one minute . . . dreadful." Then, to Inez, he commented bitterly, "Was he in Brooklyn? All this time in the city? Then how is it he didn't call me? Surely, that's the very least . . ." He was ready to say something about "owing" and "obligations," but checked himself.

"He didn't call? I bet he tried," said Inez. "Yeah,

yeah, yeah, he called, you were out. Because he told me you're the only one he was going to call, the only one in the bunch he had any use for, the only one he considered a person."

She's starting again, Morroe thought, those cute little ways, those snow jobs. Yet he was deeply stirred, and he smacked his forehead again and cried, "Whoosh. It doesn't register yet. It's impossible to believe. Poor little . . . *schnook*. We were just talking about him— honest to God, yesterday, or whenever it was, it's not important. How we were all in Washington Square, and how Leslie had a sudden yen, he had to have an egg cream. He was going to drag us all down to the East Side, he claimed—"

But she would not hear him out. "Yeah, yeah, yeah, he and his egg creams."

"It's funny what a person remembers. A million images to choose from. All right, not a million, but still, plenty. . . ." His voice trailed off. "Yeah. You think of it. What the human being is, the human life."

"Yeah, yeah, yeah. Life." He could hear the rap of her knuckles against the receiver and the sharp intake of her breath. "Look, baby . . . I'm imposing. . . . Am I imposing? But I have nobody . . . so come over . . . go to the funeral . . . you'll call the boys . . . do me that favor."

"Well," Morroe slowly improvised, "there's a little problem. We were supposed to go to Queens, to my father. You didn't know he's had this kidney condition for the past few months. In and out of the hospital."

11

"Aw, gee, kidneys. That's no joke, you don't fool around with kidneys. Take care of him, be nice to him, because he's such a sweet little guy."

She cares a lot, Morroe thought, she gives a damn. Why there isn't a true word out of her, a sincere word, there isn't a moment when she isn't spinning, planning. "I don't know what to tell you," he said, stumblingly, shutting his eyes against Etta, who had seized a scratch pad and scrawled a furious "WHAT?" "I'm not dressed. . . . I'm not really *up*. . . . I haven't even had my juice yet."

"Worrier. Pest. *Nudnick*." She lashed out at him, violent, delighted. "What, I can't squeeze juice? I can squeeze juice. And you don't like my pancakes? Not much! You'll be over. . . . You'll have breakfast. . . . I'll make and you'll eat. . . . It's not coming to me. . . . I don't deserve it. . . . I stink."

"When is the funeral? And what about the parlor, the chapel? You'd better let me have directions." Morroe frowned and nodded grimly, as though to say, All right, I'm your fool again, your sucker, your errand boy.

"I'll call. . . . I'll find out. . . . And tell me what you want for breakfast. . . . You want eggs? . . . I'll send out for eggs. . . . Or should I make French toast? . . . Yeah, yeah, yeah, I'll make French toast. . . . You like it. . . . I remember. . . ."

She was the old Inez, the charmer, the wheedler, the one who could promote and operate and take good care of herself. Derisively, he said, "Come on, come on, stop. . . . Breakfast! Worry about more important things, now."

12

"Never mind. I'll prepare. . . . You'll enjoy. . . . Yeah, yeah, yeah. . . . Like the old days."

"Like the old days," Morroe replied, fighting down an unexplainable surge of elation. "Give me an hour, make it an hour and a half, and I'll see you."

"I'll see you. And God bless you, baby." Inez blew him a kiss and hung up.

Now Etta came upon him as he crossed and recrossed the bedroom on trembling legs. "Did I get it right?" she demanded. "Leslie died?"

What little he had gotten from Inez he now gave to Etta as she fell in step with him, adding miserably, "It's so crazy, really crazy. All the time you think you're going against the rules. Momma, Poppa, Society, the good God in heaven. You think you're a big shot and a wise guy because they say 'Hay' and you say 'Straw.' When the whole time you're getting away with nothing. Absolutely nothing."

"Who would dream? So much energy. I used to envy his energy. He reminded me of a Russian peasant, with that ruddiness, that stockiness, the kind who lives forever. A muzhik."

"A muzhik was not a peasant. A muzhik was a member of the middle agrarian class which Stalin wiped out by the millions. The millions!"

She disconcerted him by saying, "Never mind. One thing I'm telling you, once I'll make my stand. You are not going to the funeral."

He turned toward her and warningly said, "What, what's this? You're giving me orders? Fiats? Ukases?"

"You are a stooge. You are a born stooge," she said

with great distinctness. "A good word from her and you still go crazy. You baby-sit, you help her move, you lug five hundred books up and down the stairs—and this, this I'll never forget: the time you left me alone with fever and swollen glands to fix her hi-fi."

"I changed a cartridge for her. I saw the needles were shot and I changed the cartridge. To you everything is *fixing*."

And, as though mocking his own mortality, Morroe posted himself near the air-conditioner, taking its full blast upon his overheated back. "Anyway," he said, momentarily reflecting on the patterns in the parquet floor, "besides, that was the period, that was the Village. What's the matter with you? There was coming and going, there was tumult and shouting, and when you could you did a favor. You got favors and you gave favors. Yes." His voice vibrated. "Why, God almighty, it was marvelous in a way. Okay, not *marvelous*, but very nice. Everyone was always in the streets. Always, any hour. Whomever you knew, bingo, you'd bump into him. Casual, free and easy. You needed a job? On Eighth Street somebody would tell you there was a job on . . . Tenth Street. An apartment? The same thing. Today you've got to plan and invite and make phone calls weeks in advance to get somebody to drag uptown."

"Ooh, faker, phony-y-y!" Etta jeered from the bed. "You loved the Village so much, you miserable hypocrite; then tell me who forced you to move? Don't give me that 'tumult and shouting' stuff. My memory is just a little too good. You were the one, Buster, you! You couldn't take it any more—the lousy shopping, and whenever we took a walk, bumping into somebody you couldn't stand. You outgrew the Village. You wanted to run, to fly, to kiss them all goodbye—Leslie and Inez and the boys."

"Whoosh!" cried Morroe and, "Yippee! You've made a point. Congratulations." But she had him off balance. For he, he had been the one who had chosen the West Nineties, who had searched out the apartment, made the deposit and overridden Etta's protests, he who had dwelled and dwelled on the long hike up the firetrap stairs, the peeling laths, the lousy wiring, the walls that couldn't take a nail. And if he had wept along with her when the time came to pack their books, well, so what? He had no regrets. Why, the same apartment would run twice and three times as high in the Village. Where did you see six rooms like this any more? With a doorman. With a tremendous kitchen. With closet space and brand-new fixtures and a super who came to do his fixing ten minutes, make it a half-hour, after you called him.

But, still in all, he heard words like "crap" and "shit" banging away in his head.

He took four big strides, plunged down on the bed and from time to time released a pent-up breath. Yes, oh, yes, he would be in the Village to this day, climbing those stairs, hauling the agent to the Rent Commission over broken windowpanes and running toilets. Only, he had fallen out with Leslie. Well, not fallen out, exactly. Say rather, something in a person suddenly strikes you, sets you back, puts you off: a continuity is broken, a current interrupted. Oh, there is rapport, there is warmth and love and openness, but it, it strikes you. You catch a

15

phrase, a tone of voice, a special wrinkling in the eyes, and he becomes repugnant to you, and everything is finished. Then and there, finished.

So it had been with Leslie. Once, on a Saturday night, when Morroe had made plans for a Chinese meal and a movie, Leslie phoned to announce a gathering. Morroe was annoyed; something almost as deep as instinct told him he had been the last called: somebody's afterthought. But he could not bring himself to refuse. And for no good reason he had decided to wear a new suit of fine Irish linen and a long-sleeved shirt with a knitted tie— despite the oppressive heat and the muggy, motionless air. "It's going to have to be cleaned anyway," he had insisted to Etta. "And even if it's wasted on them, I feel like getting dressed up. To please myself."

A mistake. From the moment he arrived he could see he was in for it; they would come down upon him, hot and heavy, from all sides. First, Leslie. Sweaty and *shlumpy*, in the foulest of polo shirts, he had bumbled over. He rubbed Morroe's lapel, he prodded at the collar and yoke and, falling to his knees, made an imaginary adjustment of the cuffs. "A *m'chyah*," he said, finally. "Look at the quality. Look at the tailoring. Look how nice it hangs."

Then Barnet Weiner rose from a sling chair, grabbed Morroe by the shoulders and shook him like a child. "By you this is, gaah, goods?" he howled tragically.

To which Leslie made reply, "By me this is goods. What's the matter, by you is no goods?"

"By me—" Weiner paused and moved his fingers like a pair of shears—"is no goods. By me is the lining no

16

lining. By me—you should pardon the expression—is a piece toilet paper!"

They carried on with their razzing, pretending to trade blows, hauling Morroe this way and that way, whooping and stamping around him like tribal dancers. At last he broke away, muttering, "Cut it out!" and thrusting with his shoulders. He gave notice, by a bray of laughter and a wink of complicity, that he bore no malice, that he could hold his own when it came to horseplay. But he was annoyed, and more than annoyed.

During the hours that followed, a peculiar crankiness settled over him. He sat with folded arms, unsmiling, unconciliating. When he spoke up he was somehow off stride, he labored for words and could not clarify his thoughts or bring them into focus. He argued Marxism with Norbert Amsterdam, who knew the subject backwards and forwards and put him in his place. Though he was aware that Benno Buchalter was entering his eighth year of psychoanalysis, he announced loudly, stridently, that he had seen no cures, that the analysts he had met were fakers and confusers. And when Etta pooh-poohed this he glared at her and made so snappy a comment she turned scarlet and pale and rose, in a kind of flight, for the kitchen.

Later, he told a joke. There was this Jewish businessman who each day has his lunch in the same dairy restaurant: Ratner's. As an entree, he orders matjes herring. Day after day, month after month, year after year, he begins his meal with matjes herring. Once, running into a friend, he confesses that he has begun to find Ratner's herring tasteless. His friend tells him there is another

17

restaurant, known far and wide for herring. So he makes it his business to try the place. He goes in, he sits down, he asks the waiter for a piece, a nice piece of matjes herring. It comes, on a little plate, with a snip of lettuce. He picks up knife and fork. He gets ready for the first slice. When suddenly the herring opens its mouth and says, "What's the matter you don't eat no more at Ratner's?"

Of one thing Morroe was certain: he could tell a joke. He had an ear, he could command all accents and intonations. Yet there was no laughter when he finished. "Gaah, you ruined it," Weiner said, "that one you ruined." And, as though by common accord, they passed on to another topic. Then it seemed to Morroe that Leslie, on the sly, had given him a look of peculiar disfavor, taking him in with a shrewdness that was almost killing, inhuman. Under that gaze, so palpable, so like a weight, a . . . pressure, he became weak-headed and confused. He saw himself being sized up and all at once recorded as something dull and flat and ordinary, an outsider, a *nachshlepper*, a bourgeois, one who held a job and carried a briefcase and set too much store by appearances.

A look, that was all. But he could not shrug it off. He could not escape the belief that he had been told, once and for all, who he was, what he wanted and where he stood in the world. Even now, the memory of it caught and tore at him, so that he pummeled the mattress with both fists and swallowed and tasted first one lip, then the other. Dry of mouth, he turned to Etta, muttering, "Squeeze some juice. Or, better, let me have some of that cantaloupe."

"Go to hell and squeeze your own lousy juice!"

"How's that?"

"You heard."

"I see something. For the first time it dawns on me. You have no feeling, you have no compassion." He turned his wedding band slowly clockwise, then counterclockwise. "A friend is dead. Let's even say, not a friend. An acquaintance, all right? A figure, a talent, an original. And in a little while there'll be nothing left. Before the day is finished he'll be closed over, covered up and that's it." He saw Leslie in a casket, going into the grave, taking the weight of earth full on his moon face, on his peeping, despairing eyes, on the snub nose where the glasses bobbed. Silent, silent forever, the one who could talk you deaf and dumb and blind. And, whoosh! Without clothes! The way the Orthodox send you off.

He said again, "Make me juice."

"A person without compassion is not a juice-squeezer."

There was rumbling in Morroe's stomach and a huge pocket of gas was expanding through his chest. In a quivering, vindictive voice he told Etta, "I give in too much to you. You know? On everything. When it comes to your family, your *meshpuchah*, it's all right if I run around and put myself out. It's all right, you know, to give your cousin Maxie my insurance—though I'm losing a good eighty dollars a year. And *bar matzvahs* and birthday parties for their brats and family-circle meetings. People I can't stand. Yes, for you and yours it's all right, isn't it? So don't you dare tell me I shouldn't go to Leslie's funeral. Because that—that, I assure you, you will not get from me."

"He is such a mourner." Etta's lips began to curl; her eyes shone at him with reproachful irony. "But when my cousin Harris died, that was another story. He was too sensitive. He couldn't take funerals. He didn't believe in the rigmarole."

"Drop it, change the subject." He made a pass at her like a magician.

"The only one who couldn't pay that last little respect. And it was coming to Harris, I assure you, more than to a hundred Leslies." She hunched forward, tendony, pinched in the neck. Tears sprang into her eyes and she whimpered, "Who—whom—have I got? A mother? She wouldn't let anyone touch my little slips or my dresses. She used to boil a special starch for them while my father laughed and said, 'Lena, Lena, *du bist eine eisel.*'"

And rocking and rocking, this small, dark, pretty girl, whose absurdly large breasts he could stroke and pet by the hour, who, for all her graying bangs, read movie magazines and hummed to foolish radio music as she did her kitchen work, blurted out again the story of her afflictions: how there had been department stores in Cologne and a houseful of servants (a pastry cook, the pride of the Hapsburgs); how her father had ignored warnings and portents; how he had packed her off to an older sister in Liverpool; how he and her mother both had one morning been moved to a convent outside of the city ("Take only toothbrush and a change of underwear"); how before long, the chimneys of Buchenwald had belched forth their blood and bone.

And though he was swept through and through by a

20

surge of love for her, Morroe said nastily, "Stop, stop the Ingrid Bergman stuff. And don't embroider every time. Because from my understanding there were no department stores. And how did it suddenly get to be servants? One, one broken-down day worker."

In the pain of the moment, she was almost speechless. When she replied, her color was very high and she looked dazed. "You know what you are? I will tell you what you are. You are a *schmuck!*" She heaved herself off the bed and out of the room.

And Morroe let himself fall back, onto the pillows.

And a "Doo-doo doo-doo-doo-doo" bubbled from his lips.

And he stiffened and arched two fingers and walked them, rocked them, danced them down chest, belly and thighs and leaped them daringly across the abyss between his knees.

And into the circuits of his mind he fed GO and DON'T GO, and also profuse memory and complicated doubts.

And when it came out a clear and simple DON'T GO he roused himself, cast a desperate glance at the clock and hurried into pants, shirt, jacket, deciding against shave and shower and, finally, tie.

"I'm going. Honey, I am going," Morroe bawled, lagging near the kitchen door, ready to trade a pleasant goodbye for half, make it a quarter, of an orange. There was only the ferocious running of water and the banging of bottles in the refrigerator. Good, he thought, very good. I'll pick up the paper, I'll grab a bite in the B & J or the Sabra, I'll do some of the crossword puzzle. Nevertheless, while he let himself out, while he twisted both keys in both locks, he was far from pleased; these were not his habits in the morning, and holding to small habits was a weakness with him.

Near the incinerator he saw Toego, 5K, whom he couldn't stomach. "Howdy like our landlord there, Mr. Rieff?" Toego asked, advancing upon him. His mean, greenish eyes watered for a moment, and he turned away, racked by so many tics and spasms he seemed uncertain which to suffer first. In bathing trunks and felt slippers he seemed all gristle and vein and crabbiness.

"I have no opinion," Morroe said distantly. "Since I live here I've seen him twice: when I signed the lease and when he came to inspect our paint job."

"Yes, but you got the form, didn't you?" There was a resonance of horror in Toego's voice. "He wants fifteen per cent. Hardship. My, my, my! Oi-oi-oi! Hardship!"

"Well, we didn't get one."

"Oh, I see you must be among the favored. Burke, now, he got one. And how is it Lang got one? *And* Volkening? *And* Maggrett? *And* Baerst?" Toego winked, or twitched.

"I wouldn't know," Morroe curtly said.

"Of course, and how would you?" Toego paused, cracked a few knuckles. "The things you see you never saw under the old management. God rest him, Mr. Carmichael had a Christmas tree up every year and a lovely little crèche in the lobby. A wonderful man. Old New York type. Straw hats and bow ties and very gruff

22

in his manner of speaking. 'Youse' and 'dems.' Oh, but a gentleman. Honor, integrity. And service—my Lord! He *ran* the building!"

Morroe began a protracted study of his watch, saying, "Look, today everything is sky high. Whoosh! Labor, materials, whatever you touch. And this is an old house. It's falling apart, it can bleed you of every penny." He turned, rang for the elevator. But Toego followed, raising his hand in the gesture of one about to enter a plea. "They're driving us out," he said. "Oh, it's fifteen per cent now, Mr. Rieff, and then one of these days we'll get a notice. 'Clear out! Go! Never mind where, the building is being torn down.' And it's not even that! The city—why, the whole city is impossible. I'm a native New Yorker and I say that. Like the dirt. Every morning my nose is clogged; I wake up choking. Or you walk around a corner and your nails are black. And you're always smelling that garlic frying, and when it's not garlic it's marijuana or—"

Morroe cut in with, "I have a funeral. People are waiting."

"Oh, say, say." On either side of Toego's face veins tapped. "Family? . . ."

"A friend."

"I hadn't seen your father around."

"No, knock on wood, he's fine. Oh, not *fine*, but—"

"Good news!" Toego stepped halfway into the elevator with Morroe. "That friend . . . how old?"

"Forty." Morroe fixed a finger on the lobby button. "Maybe a big forty-one."

"Lord, Lord, younger and younger and younger. My father made eighty-four. And I'm not sixty and I had my first stroke." He gave a nicker of high glee.

He stepped out of the elevator, closing the door carefully behind him. But then his voice was floating down, down the shaft after Morroe: "Hardship. My, my! Oi! ..."

2 ———————————————————

THE FIRST IMPRESSION Morroe gave was one of intense redness. To his family, he was still *"der Royte,"* not so much for his hair, which, at thirty-nine, was brown and heavy as beaver fur, but for his temper—at four or five, he had launched himself against an older sister and dealt her a scratch that needed stitches and injections. His large glasses shrank his eyes and, with his way of squinting—as though for him all things were in gray outline—gave him a bluff uncomprehending look. When he walked, he bent forward slightly, his arms stiff, with the no-nonsense air of one who is wise to the complications of the city, who can find a subway seat and a restaurant table during the worst hours, a taxi in the rain, a wholesale outlet that beats even discount-house prices, one who kept an electric razor in his desk, Pream for his instant coffee, deposit and withdrawal slips to beat bank lines, sent personal mail through office meters, sneaked home envelopes, clips, pencils, staples and carbon paper, saw that his resumé was up to date, his connections solid.

All the same, he was a latecomer to New York. When he was ten his father, a small, harsh pepperpot of a man who could not bear working for others, moved from Cleveland to Norfolk and opened a laundry near the huge naval base, believing that a good living could be made from the sailors. At four in the morning, in all weathers, he would park his truck and take his stand before the huge sheds, jockeying for position with his rivals, between whom not a look or word passed. Then the sailors would come, by the hundreds, lugging their sea bags, and the line of laundrymen would stiffen and surge forward. They could not solicit; the rule was strict and the smallest infraction got you declared off limits for a week.

But they would call attention to themselves in other ways. They would paint lavish nudes on their doors and fenders, they would bang drums and blow whistles and pitch pipes, they would fire cap pistols and set balloons floating out over the harbor.

And each with his own costume.

There was Leo the Lumberman, taking listless swings with his heavy ax.

There was Hershel the Hawaiian, decked out in leis and hula skirt.

There was Moishe the Mexican, in his Sam Browne belt and *huaraches*.

And there was his father, Cowboy Joe, the last to give in, sullen and unconciliating under the weight of his Stetson hat.

Later, when it was impossible to compete with the laundromats, his father decided on New York, where, after taking heavy losses on a commission bakery and a milk route, he found a gold mine in a candy store near Washington Heights. And though Morroe did his share, his father stubbornly refused to give him more than the dollar and a quarter a week which barely covered the cost of milk in the high school cafeteria and the outlay for G.O. fees and books and gym outfits. Then, in his senior year, there was a terrible quarrel: Morroe had brought friends into the store, gone behind the counter and dished up egg creams, frappés, malteds. His father, in full view of all, fell upon him with fearful curses, letting him know that he was not in business for love, that, like it or not, his friends must pay. They raised hands to each other; before the night was over Morroe walked out for good, moving in with his Uncle Lazar.

If he did not prosper, exactly, during the years that followed, he nevertheless came through better than some. He registered at City College, with the idea of studying medicine. But he had no aptitude and, besides, he could not bear the night students who jealously guarded their lecture notes and would not give you so much as a cigarette; inside of a month he dropped his science courses. He settled, finally, like most, on English literature, taking just enough education credits to qualify for the public school system. For a while he tied bundles and stacked remnants in a dress house. Later, he landed something with the Hollis Protective Agency, going around to the smaller chain stores and cafeterias to make sure the help didn't hold out on the cash register or serve double portions to friends. The job kept him out in the air, he could charge off meals to the agency and make a little besides by adding fifteen minutes or a half-hour to his time sheet. When it folded—once too often he had taken pity on a shortchange artist—a friend wangled something for him in the college library. There he stayed for over three years.

Morroe graduated into a gloom of a time, when all the civil service lists were closed, when you knew better than to argue with a snotty receptionist and read great promise into the personnel man's fish-eyed grin, when the strongest pull and the best of connections left you no better off than the next fellow, the one who shared your waiting room bench and made sure you got no inkling of his stale leads. Finally, his Uncle Lazar had spoken to a rabbi. Who held out little hope, but nonetheless made a few calls. And referred him to a Brighton Beach yeshivah, which needed someone for English studies; here Morroe had his mornings free, to say nothing of the Jewish holidays and Fridays, when he got out before sundown.

It so happened that the yeshivah held a bazaar, and the principal turned to Morroe, asking his help with a few fund-raising letters. Though he was at first wary and disdainful, Morroe soon found he had a knack for the stuff. He talked a printer into making up some posters, he sent out press releases, and the *Brooklyn Eagle* ran a small story on the day of the affair.

The principal, though generally petty and stingy with praise, was pleased, and steered Morroe onto something good: he had heard about this giver, Zeigler, a man who sat on every board and committee, a powerful *macher* in Jewish communal affairs, who had passed around word that he needed a speech-writer. There were other applicants, plenty of them, and Zeigler would be no pleasure to work with—the principal made this clear —but anyway he pressured Morroe to try, for the fun of it.

Thus, on a morning when he had other interviews set, Morroe received a call—a summons, really. He was to come to Zeigler's house, he was to bring along resumé and samples.

It was an insult, not an interview. Morroe was kept waiting a half-hour, and then, when Zeigler made an appearance, it was in a bathrobe, mountainous, slovenly, without the grace to offer coffee or rolls from the tray a maid bore after him. For several minutes he ate and drank, then fell back in his chair and crossed his hands over his belly.

He said, "So write me a speech."

Morroe started to say something, and fumbled in his pockets for the resumé.

"No, no, forget that stuff. Write me a speech."

"Well, what do you mean, 'a speech'?" Morroe's voice was congested by rage.

"Do I know?" Zeigler shouted. "A speech. With words. It should move and sway people."

Praying for restraint, Morroe pointed out that he would have to know something about the subject. "And how long should it be, and for whom is it meant? Otherwise I'm completely in the dark."

At which Zeigler laughed and laughed and threw up a pair of meaty hands. "Only one thing I'll tell you. Israel is the subject. Money is the theme. Giving is the idea."

And he shook a little silver bell for the maid, who came on crepe soles and led Morroe to the door.

Morroe was all set, later, to write Zeigler an angry note; such phrases as "impossible conditions," "ordinary decency" and "contempt for people" ran in his mind. Once at the typewriter, though, he fell into another mood. He was overtaken by an enormous confidence, by the belief that whatever he put his hand to would at this moment work in his favor. Without conscious thought, without even knowing whether one sentence followed another, he turned out a shrill, high-pitched speech. Which he sent off without even reading.

In two days Morroe was hired, making more money than an assistant principal or a welfare department supervisor. And if Zeigler took handling and pestered at all hours, he knew, at least, what he wanted; they got along. Profoundly grateful, Morroe did not spare himself, making sure to come up with fresh approaches, digging up pointed jokes and newspaper items which he wove into the speeches. He was certain his luck had turned. Till the following winter, when Zeigler suffered a diabetic coma in Miami Beach, and was warned to give up absolutely all outside activities. But by then Morroe was known in the field, he had made contacts. Shortly before the New Year he was hired by a medium-sized agency which raised funds to train Israeli farmers in the agricultural sciences.

Meanwhile, he had found himself a cold-water flat near the Village, and he began taking adult education courses and attending forums on Marxism and psychoanalysis and creative writing. So he met Leslie. It was at the Everyman School, on a night when, for the first time, Leslie had given high praise to some little thing he had written about Anna Karenina, and how it had been needless for Tolstoy to kill her. Morroe, a bit shyly, went up to him after class; without ceremony, Leslie took him for coffee, reaching him quickly, talking and talking of things that mattered. When the restaurant closed he dragged Morroe to his place, where Inez, despite the hour, rose to make French toast and put out Polish sausage and a very nice eggplant spread. There was no holding back with them; everything that was his Morroe laid bare over the kitchen table: his father, the days of Norfolk, the yeshivah, Zeigler. He went on and on in a rollicking satire, mimicking and burlesquing with a deftness that was new to him and rendered them, at times, helpless with laughter. After he left for the office—Inez had insisted they stay up all night and await the sun— he was lightheaded, in a state akin to exaltation.

During those years Leslie and Inez gave party after party. Big names came, writers of much promise, people who were publishing right and left. And, always, some busted-up character, someone on the verge of divorce, someone who had the look of a potential suicide or an alcoholic. Wandering near one of the bedrooms you could make out the sound of his weeping, or Leslie's voice, soft, tremulous, counseling and cajoling. Later, Morroe and the boys would stay behind, a small, permanent cadre, while Leslie, spreading out on the sofa, gave them the full story. This bothered Morroe; not so much the betrayal of confidences—he loved gossip as well as the next man—but Leslie's studied Talmudic air threw him off and gave warning that it could be dangerous to put yourself under his power.

At one such party he met Etta. She had been brought by a girl friend, an annoying type, with pretensions to all the arts. Etta, on the other hand, was simple, straightforward, moving uneasily amid the talkers and drinkers. Morroe was greatly pleased by the light spicing of her accent, by her high color and drastic pigtail, by the pendant earrings which would have been vulgar on others, by her accidentally-on-purpose posing so that he could look either up or down her dress. Even her slightly crooked teeth, with their greenish roots, pleased him; and he would gladly have shared with her a common toothbrush. Morroe began to bait and tease her, rather heavy-handedly. This was his way with girls; but Etta took it well, giving as good as she got. They sang German *Lieder* together, while Leslie accompanied on his recorder, leering over them like a satyr. "Look, look, look," cried Inez, "aren't they cute together; don't they make a nice couple?" All night long she bumbled around them, and at one point beckoned Etta aside, talking to her heatedly for a few minutes, finishing up with a noisy kiss and a little push in Morroe's direction. To his inquiries, Etta, somewhat flushed, answered, "She said you were a guy with certain problems, and I should be good to you." He hadn't believed her; for that matter, still didn't.

Four days later Morroe made up an extra set of keys to his apartment. Yet he could not quite believe in his good fortune; and, sure enough, trouble came. There was a convention of Jewish agencies in Chicago. He spent a week there, increasingly disturbed when Etta failed to reply to the long letters he mailed out every night. On his return he rushed over to her place by cab, but her girl friend would not let him in and, when he made an uproar, picked up the phone and actually started calling the police. By the time he was home and unpacked, Etta had shown up. Half-drunk, her face white and straining, she confessed that from the moment he left she had been sleeping with someone: a West Indian who held down a stockroom job in her office while he studied modern dance. It had nothing to do with her feeling for Morroe, she insisted; she had had certain fears about sex, she wanted to prove herself with other men, and she had chosen this one only because he was handy. It was a piece of nonsense, *mishugass*, and the whole thing had only awakened in her hungry longings for Morroe.

Wild with grief, Morroe slapped her. Then he pushed her out the door. Afterward, he fell into a fit of uncontrollable trembling, and in the morning went straight to her office, dragging her out to the fire stairs, begging her forgiveness with all his might. They waited a month, till her birthday, and went by bus to Arlington, where they were married in a quick civil ceremony.

Not long afterward, his Uncle Lazar died. Morroe caught sight of his father in the chapel, but ignored him. Finally, when the grave was closed, a group of relatives forcibly drew them together, and they embraced. The old man took a liking to Etta and, winking at Morroe, invited her to the candy store. "I'll make you a malted," he promised. "Something special." And whenever he visited he brought a bagful of Hershey bars and Charms and sour balls and chocolate-covered halvah; it became a standing joke between them.

With its low morning lights, its coolness and organ-swell of Muzak, the B & J seemed more like a cathedral than a restaurant, and the bowed, hushed eaters, de-formed in the dark-tinted mirrors, a collection of peni-tents. His *Times* bulking in disarray under his elbow, Morroe ignored the host, who indicated the empty booths, and took a seat at the counter; he was in no mood to make a production of his meal. But when the waitress came he changed his mind, ordering a half grapefruit and scrambled eggs with Nova Scotia lox, helping himself to one of the horn rolls in the over-flowing basket. He had an idea—a premonition—that he would need all his energy, that this would be a day of days. "And if you don't mind," he said, while she filled the water glass, "some butter."

"One minute." There was brazen assertion, a tough-ness in her eyes. "I have only two hands."

Voice rising a notch, Morroe answered, "Whoosh, is that so? I'll tell you something: I'm not so sure."

Morroe started on the book section, but was diverted

by two men whose voices reached him from the cashier's box. One was dark and bony, with a long Nefertiti neck, and he was saying to his moon-faced little friend, "If it was on my okay I'd have the Czar back in a minute."

"The whole works? The serfs, the hemophilia, the corruption, Rasputin?"

"Right, right, absolutely right. And, for my part, with the pogroms, with the famines, with 1905."

His friend considered this gravely and said, "Part of the way I go along. But 1905, there I turn off."

"I'll split up the lot, you don't have to order the whole shipment." He took his friend's elbow and drew him close. "I'll tell you something. Last week I was looking at television—"

"I thought you couldn't stand it, that once the picture tube went, to hell with it, you'd never call a mechanic."

"For the cowboys, once in a while. Anyway, I tune in on something special, a program with old newsreels. And there's the Czar with his legs crossed, very neat you know, not to ruin the crease in his pants. Then the missus comes over from the garden with a picture hat and she bends down to give the kids a pat. Play nice she's telling them, don't get overheated. But you paid attention? That's how they paid attention. Like wild Indians they run down the stairs with this big ball—you don't see them that size any more—and they start playing a game. Bouncey-bouncey, one-two-three, so cute you could eat them up alive. All of a sudden one of the girls—I bet it was Anastasia—gets frisky. Zetz! the ball goes flying and nearly hits Poppa on his shoulder. What does he do? The little sourpuss, he breaks into a smile

35

that goes from one end of the Russian Empire to the other. He bends down. Up, up comes the ball, and now both hands over his head. He looks to this one, he looks to that one. He's going to throw, he's not going to throw. Meanwhile, the kids are jumping around, they're going crazy. And finally he gives the toss. To whom? Naturally. A father's heart. To the youngest, the boy."

He perched himself on his toes, unabashed by Morroe's delighted stare, and flung both arms out in a heaving motion. He said, "Do you know what my reaction was?"

"Come, let me hear. Tomashefsky number two."

"I cried. I said Nickie, Nickie, dope, fool, idiot, bungler, horse's ass, come back to us. Make believe it didn't happen, a bad dream, look away from it. You'll forgive and we'll forgive and we'll all have it good."

Giant brain, Morroe thought. Probably the first to shoot off a toe on the eve of conscription. He loved himself, that was clear—the haircut just so, the fingernails and cuticles taken care of. Which was nice in an older man. Not like his father, who wore the cheapest stuff and grudged himself so much as a clean handkerchief. And Morroe would have gladly gone on listening, but something else claimed his attention: two women in identical Paisley prints. Though the place was practically empty they took stools right next to him, and the older one tapped his shoulder, saying, "The paper . . . if you don't mind . . . it's right in the way. . . ."

She had a powerful hook to her nose, like a Renaissance pope, and there was something mean and hard, small and unrelenting about her concealed eyes. You saw her kind right and left; wherever you went on upper Broadway, they ruled the neighborhood. They double-parked near your car, they slammed doors in your face, they talked without letup in the movies. You had to give way to them on the sidewalk and in stores they sneaked their shopping carts ahead of yours and made the delivery boys follow them home with two containers of milk.

The younger one began to bleat, "Ma, Ma, he positively did not mean it that way. Believe me, there was no harm intended."

To himself, Morroe said, whoosh! Take a look at the harlequin glasses, with the sequins. Or those wedgies, who wears them nowadays? And that mouth, that mouth! She's telling you how well she's done, how good she has it, how pleased she is with herself. As he dug with trembling fingers into his grapefruit Morroe became aware of his own luck. And he gave silent thanks. That he had gotten away with it. That he had not fallen into such hands.

He heard the voices grow sharp, and then there was the mention of money. "I gave him plenty," the mother insisted. "Shirts and ties and underwear. Complete outfits. What I did for him his own mother didn't and wouldn't do."

"What does his mother have to do with it? Why are you bringing her in?"

"Because she's the troublemaker, the one who steams him up and tells him to take and take. And he listens. I wish you'd listen to me the way he listens to her."

37

"Ma, Ma, let's say, for argument's sake, you're right. So what? So *what?* Once, just once, forget an injustice. Look away."

"Look away, yes," her mother mimicked, vindictively. "Don't you worry, daughter mine. When it comes to looking away you're dealing with a real master, a professional. Yes, in fact I'll tell you something. Why not? After all, you're a married woman. I'll bet it's news to you that your father, rest in peace, was for years taking money out of the firm that Susskind didn't know a thing about. Not a fortune, but taking out is taking out. It doesn't add up to a profit."

But this did not faze the daughter, who said, "Well, all along I knew there was something. As a matter of fact I figured, like, marital problems. Because it struck me so odd, that time you ran out and bought a whole new bedroom set. Twin beds, all of a sudden."

"Nah, nah, nah. Foolish child. Didn't you wonder what happened to my rings—the big solitaire I was saving for you from the day you got out of high school? Whatever I could get for them I took. On top of it I had to go over to Susskind and plead with him. He was talking about connections, gangster friends. For a couple of hundred he was going to have somebody break both your father's legs."

"Oh, Ma, that's so ridiculous. Farfetched." A tongue-tip flicked out between the hard little lips. "It's not twenty, thirty years ago. They don't go around breaking people's legs. That's all Susskind would have needed."

"What did I know? Was I experienced in those

things? Susskind was a wild type, he ran around with all kinds when—" She swiveled around suddenly in Morroe's direction. "Excuse me. Are you enjoying yourself? Can you hear good? You, you, mister! If not I'll make sure to talk a little louder."

Morroe uttered a low, unwilling laugh. He pointed out that the restaurant was far from overcrowded, that it was his privilege to sit here and hers to move elsewhere. Furthermore, he had heard, in his time, more interesting conversation.

"Ma, Ma, don't argue with these types. You don't get any satisfaction, you only demean yourself." The daughter put a finger to the side of her head and rotated it significantly.

Now Morroe spoke up sharply. "What's my type? Come, tell me, I'd love to have your . . . analysis."

With a distended face the mother answered for her. "I, I would definitely call you a moron. My honest opinion, mister. You get your pleasures not only from overhearing but peeping, too." She began to address the waitress, who had taken a neutral stance near one of the coffee urns. "Did you ever see anything like it? Everything collects into this neighborhood. You walk out any time of the day and you think you're in wacktown. I'm not exaggerating. Last night I was looking out of the window and saw one fellow kiss another fellow smack on the mouth. And all of them with dogs. One animal is bigger than another. Like ponies."

"I think it's time you moved away already. You ought to look in Far Rockaway," the daughter advised. "Even if you had to pay a little more it would be brand-new, on top of which you wouldn't have to travel for a dip in summer."

The mother smiled and once again addressed the waitress. "See, see. The best of daughters, it doesn't matter. They don't want you too close to them."

She fell into silence and her daughter put on an expression of suffering tolerance. Neither one reacted when Morroe hoisted himself off the stool, and bowing slightly, murmured a flamboyant "Pardon me." He left his paper behind, and a rather large tip, far more than the waitress had merited, with that sullenness. Standing before the cashier he laughed aloud and said, "What a pair. What a combination."

From under his eyeshade the cashier scowled, insinuating, perhaps, that such remarks were out of order. Then he shoved over the change and hid himself among the shelves of cigars.

Morroe flinched as he stepped into the white metropolitan morning. The sun was out in full force now, overpowering, and where it fell upon people they reeled like drunkards or moved with utmost slowness, undeviating, as though through mine fields. Then, squinting out into the street for a cab and about to try his luck on the other side, Morroe was hailed with an "Oh, mister, oh, moron . . ."

He made a thrusting gesture with his elbows.

". . . get hit by the next car."

And, as a matter of fact, before he flagged down his cab, he nearly was.

3 ────────────────────────

No MATTER where he lived, no matter how much it annoyed visitors, Leslie Braverman would never put a nameplate over his bell. "Why should I?" he would say. "Why should I make it easy for them when they come looking for me?" By matchlight, Morroe hunted and hunted, till finally, losing patience, he pressed one whole row of bells on the top floor. With the first clicking of the lock he sprinted inside, taking the steps two at a time. "Who is it?" someone called down. "Hello." He froze against the landing and fought down an impulse to reply, to make some apology. Then, after he heard doors slam, he continued his climb, breathing heavily, feeling an unexpected tickle of nervous excitement. The Village, he decided. No matter how he knocked it to others, the place gripped and held him. This kid now, brushing past him with her armload of groceries. Where else could you see her kind? She glowed, she positively twinkled and shimmered. He could make out the point of a long Italian bread sticking out of the bag and smell the odor of sour pickle and maybe corned beef or ham. On Sunday morning the Village delicatessens were filled with young people, paying unbelievable prices and taking the kidding and the pointed remarks of the clerks who knew the source of these big appetites. And Morroe chuckled to himself, and as he followed her up the flights he wished long life and good years to her breasts, belly and behind, to her Keds, Amazon belt, copper bracelet, beaten silver ring, to all her parts and all her accessories.

But when he stood before Leslie's apartment his mood evaporated. The chink in the peephole was still there; if you leaned and listened you could make out a few words amid the hubbub. Many times Morroe had done this, wondering if he would hear his name, perhaps some comment letting him know whether or not he was welcome. And seconds later he would enter, bearing his pack of troubles, dimly aware that he was talking too much, that Leslie and Inez were not to be altogether trusted. Mind you, he wasn't the only one. Far from it. Why, the very walls dripped troubles! You could peel them off with the laths and tiles, they hung from the clothes dryer in the kitchen, they stuffed up the drains, they killed the plants, they brought in roaches! Every bedspring sang of shack up and abortion and breakdown and louse up and bad ball!

He took a handkerchief and mopped his face. All sorts of things churned in his mind, recollections from which he shrank. "So?" he grunted in annoyance at his clammy hands, his parched throat. "What are you afraid of? What? You've learned a few things, you're a match for her. What you were then, you're not now." Resolutely, he knocked.

Pilar, the older girl, let him in. Still on the small side for her eight years. And chubby; it looks like she'll have Leslie's build, Morroe reflected, though I hope not. She smiled, but her expression was guarded, suspicious, and Morroe hastened to say, "I guess you don't remember me, eh?"

"Well, should I?" There was a certain charm in the way she said this—Leslie's charm, Morroe reflected— which softened what might have been snottiness in the mouths of other kids.

"Whoosh, I think so, I honestly do." He started toward the living room. "Where's your mother, honey?"

"She took Sister to Mrs. Falvey. Dolores is too young to go to funerals. You know, I have a story all made up for her. She's going to ask where Leslie is, and guess what I'll say."

"What? What's that?" He drew up a hassock and sat down heavily, his hands joined over his knees. With silent repugnance he looked around the room. Inez had never been of the housekeeping breed, but this—this was something! The couch looked as if it had been gored by bulls. There were burns on the television cabinet, and a fat grease mark near the center of the screen. And wherever you looked, bottles and cups, and magazines from the year one.

"I'm going to say . . . I'll say . . . Leslie went to . . . Africa. On a safari. He heard drums. Boombala, boombala, thump, thump, thump. Miles and miles away. The natives didn't want to go there. 'No go, white chief!' They were very, very scared. But Leslie wasn't scared. Guess why he wasn't scared!"

Morroe looked at her high, wrinkled forehead and conniving eyes, seeing Leslie, only Leslie. He said, "I'm waiting, honey."

"Because . . . Because . . ." She uttered a bark of laughter. "Because he was a . . . *braver* man."

Morroe pretended to shudder. Then he drew her close and rubbed his nose against hers. "You are a character, all right," he informed her gravely. "But continue, proceed."

"Oh, there is no more. I had an idea for a witch doctor, but I'm going to put him in my next story." She pulled away from Morroe, but gently. "You know what?"

"Let's hear."

"When I'm sixteen, I'm going to get married."

"Hey, is that so? Who? Would you like to tell me who you've got picked out?"

"Oh, I don't know yet." Suddenly she appeared to be somewhat depressed. "Only . . . only I want him to have . . . a drugstore."

"A drugstore? Well, how is that? Wouldn't you rather

marry a, well, a writer?" Wrong, all wrong, he realized. Bite your tongue, fool!

"Nah." She was annoyed—Morroe could tell from the way she blinked and averted her glance. But otherwise no sign of what was going through that old little head. Which didn't surprise him. In this house you learned how to hold back and dissemble. From experts.

Nervously, he said, "Say, look how late it is. It's nearly ten o'clock, and where's your mother? I'll give her a ring, I'll tell her I'm here."

"I can go bring her." Pilar scooted to the doorway.

"Well, wait, honey, I'm not sure she'd want you to leave the house. Just while you're out she might—"

But Pilar was in the hall, her footsteps clattering over the tiles. "If that was mine," Morroe reflected, "I would take a little better care of her. At least, brush out her hair once in a while. And that blouse, it looks like an iron never touched it."

Suddenly restless, he got up and took a look out the window. In the courtyard below a shirtless Negro was hosing down the furnace-room stairs. He seemed to be raging over something, muttering crazily and shivering, though the sun was directly upon him. "Hot shit!" Morroe heard him cry, and then was roused by pink-and-whiteness, by nipple-brown and pubic-black. Two flights up, a young girl opened a medicine cabinet, dusted her skin with talcum. Morroe stooped, squinted. In a few seconds, though, she had passed beyond his line of vision. Which was just as well. For when he turned, Inez was in the room. How long, he could not be sure.

In a cracked voice Inez said, "Hi, baby." She was heavily made up; under the layers of lipstick her smile was hard and professional, like an airline stewardess or a chorus girl.

Morroe extended both his arms as she came forward, and they clasped each other.

"Inez, Inez, what can I tell you, what should I say? We should meet, next time, under better and happier circumstances."

"Yeah, yeah, better and happier." She wheeled swiftly and began to clear off the couch, saying, "Look, look at him! What's the matter, you're no stranger here. You don't have to wait for me before you sit. Did you eat? I bet you ran out without. Dope, come on, I have so much in the refrigerator. I shopped yesterday for the whole week."

"I ate, I ate," he protested. "Honestly." He sat down beside her, trying to keep himself impassive while he took in her getup. Whoosh! Where had she picked it up? Gold earrings, so heavy it was a wonder she could lift her head. And in this weather a black taffeta dress. What his father called a *shiksa* dress. Yes, but she *was* a *shiksa*. Easy to forget. Her ways and mannerisms were Leslie's. And she could speak Yiddish with the best.

"So tell me what's happening," Inez demanded. "You put on some weight I think, but it doesn't hurt. How's the job? You're still doing . . . the fund-raising work?"

"Still in the Jewish business. Still with the speeches and the releases and the letters. Did you hear we moved? But, of course, that you know."

"And how's Irma? Did she finish that thesis finally?

46

Ooh, what a mind on that kid, I'm telling you!" She gave an ecstatic little shiver.

"Hah?" Morroe's lips stiffened, and he said, a trifle bitterly, "What kind of an Irma? I think you have your signals crossed."

With shaky fingers Inez began a drumming of her brows. She shut her eyes tightly for a moment, then opened them to the full. "Etta, Etta, Etta!" she shouted. "I was thinking of—oh, sure, you know her—the one with the bone condition. Every other day she'd be in the hospital with a fracture."

"Sure, a bone condition." There was a ring of exasperation in Morroe's voice, but he pretended to make the connection. "Yes, definitely, I have that one placed. Anyway, never mind. Let me hear about Leslie. You know how it is over the phone. A million questions . . . and especially when you get up from sleep . . . a person is still groggy."

"Wait, you'll hear, you'll hear!" She sprang up from the couch. "Sweetie!" she called into the kitchen. Pilar entered, chewing a slice of dry white bread. "Look, you'll do me a big favor, yeah? You'll go downstairs. You'll go into Dienstfrey. Make sure *he* waits on you, not the wife; she's a terrible bitch. You'll tell him, 'Mr. Dienstfrey, my mother wants two iced coffees and two— better say four—of the prune Danishes.' You'll bring down some of the deposit bottles and the rest he can charge. Okay? You got it, chutzie?"

Pilar gave her a wise little smile. A sign that she was accustomed to stranger errands and dealings.

"Hey, don't bother," Morroe protested. "It's so fierce

out, don't send her up and down the stairs." Then he checked himself as he caught Inez gritting her teeth and flaring her nostrils. She had things to say; she wanted the kid out of the house. Dumb and heavy he sat, watching her zip around the room, bending and hauling and shoving, while bottles chimed over her footsteps. Whoosh! Grief had made her radiant, positively radiant. And that energy. She looked capable of tearing down walls, wrecking entire civilizations. Yet by the time she returned to the couch she had altered herself, collapsing on the cushions like an accident case, too far gone to worry over a hiked-up skirt or the abandoned spread of her legs.

Again Morroe said, "Let me hear now about Leslie. Fill me in."

"Okay, all right, sure. You know we were all set for a divorce?"

Working his feet back and forth on the thinned-out carpet, Morroe said, "I knew and I didn't know. I mean, I ran into Harvey Katzman about a year ago, and he dropped all sorts of hints. Of course, who could be definite? The person isn't alive who can get a direct statement out of him."

"Yeah, yeah, yeah, that louse, that cheapskate! I hate his guts!" But she said this without interest or feeling. "Oh, it was building up for years. I think he lived only to punish and needle me. That's how he got his kicks. If I was a fly he . . ." One shoulder quivered, as though from the tearing of a wing.

"Hey, hey, come on, he wasn't *such* a monster,"

Morroe contended. "And by talking this way you only do yourself harm."

The look she shot him startled Morroe, filled him with a peculiar dread. "Sure, who am I? What do I know? I was only the coffee server. He was the big-shot intellectual, the profound personality and I was the coffee server. He was the intimate friend of Kafka and Kierkegaard while I was rattling cups in the kitchen and making dialogue with the other broken-down wives about wee-wee and formulas and vaginal cream and spaying cats and where do you get the best grated parmesan. Yeah, yeah, yeah, grated parmesan."

In affable, even-minded fashion Morroe said, "Honestly, you're not being fair. He was a writer, a creative person. You couldn't think up his stories and he couldn't make your coffee. And those other things. Tolstoy's wife could make almost the same complaints. Except vaginal cream . . . I don't think . . . in those years . . ."

"Ah, go 'way. You're talking to the little gal who slept with him. I couldn't get him to take a bath, you know that? His feet stank. 'Leave me alone,' he'd tell me, 'that's the odor of sanctity.'"

"Oh, now, come on, Inez, come on." Morroe gave way to a short laugh. "What's so terrible? It's far, far from a revelation. Believe me, nobody ever said Leslie was the cleanest person in the world."

Inez turned down her underlip, and flecks of blood appeared in her pupils. There rose to Morroe's mind images of harpies and witches . . . haters and eaters of men. "You want revelations?" she demanded, speaking with enormous pleasure. "Yeah? Well, one Saturday he gets up, he wants a Pepsi. 'Where is the Pepsi?' 'No Pepsi.' 'No Pepsi?' 'No Pepsi.' He sees I'm not going down, so he goes down. A half-hour, three-quarters of an hour. I grab myself a little snooze. I wake up, it's four hours now. I feed the goldfish, I make a few *latkes*, I paint the kitchen chairs, I stuff the hassock Morty Zelenka got me from Tangiers, I *potchke* with my pottery. Cut a long story short, you know when he came back? Ask me when he came back?"

"I'll bite." Morroe showed teeth. "So when did he come back?"

"I forget. Okay, you no-good, miserable bastard, where were you? Oh, he's amazed that I'm sore. After all, we're modern, ain't we? We don't have to account for every little move. He just ran into Tillie Dreyfus—"

"The dancer? The one who was always telling you how she was going to put out a little magazine?"

"She dances like I dance. But it was a big coincidence. In fifteen years neither of them had been to Steeplechase. Whee! Let's take the subway down, let's get hot dogs and custard and let's go on the rides. Oh, he gave her a ride all right. He probably screwed her ass off."

"Ucch!" said Morroe, and "Whoosh! Tillie Dreyfus! You'd think . . . I don't know. Anybody could hop into the sack with her. Take my word for it and without going into detail, I had plenty of opportunities. Plenty!"

"Look, kid, maybe he had standards in literature, but when it came to you-know-what it was just a question of what could fit on a mattress. If Greta Garbo came along—fine! And if Rose Dreckfresser turned up—also good!" She abruptly laughed. "Did you hear how he carried on at Bentley? All those sweet, juicy little things. He came back with a prostate—"

"Bentley?" cried Morroe. "Where did he come to Bentley?"

"Manny, Manny Ribalow is up there. They were looking around for somebody to give a popular culture seminar and he pushed hard for Leslie."

God almighty, thought Morroe!

From each Leslie had taken and gotten!

Wherever there was a foundation.

Wherever there was a grant.

Wherever there was a publisher to hand out advances.

And he, he himself, out one hundred and thirty-seven dollars. Who would go blocks and blocks to save eight cents on a bottle of shampoo.

His heart quickened and a great roaring started in his ears. "Please," he wanted to tell her, "enough already," while she plunged on and on, carrying him along in the swell of her grievances. Mama, Mama, was this a Leslie! He was her enemy, even as Hannibal was enemy to Rome. If he had been better in the sciences he would have extracted the calcium from her bones. Once he had forced her to wear a crucifix in bed. Unto her ninth month with Pilar she had worked for him. Her stomach dropping, her legs swelling like hydrants. He had a habit of helping himself to whatever was in her purse. He grudged her an old razor blade to shave her legs. No library would issue him books, so he took cards out in her name and in the name of her Bessarabian grandmother. He peed in the sinks. He would go to movies in the afternoon. He would demand all kinds of crazy dishes. He sat in the toilet for three hours at a time. He held on to no jobs. He farted away golden opportunities. He met no deadlines. He could be your best friend and, overnight, disappear like Job's boils.

There was no end to it. There were no words for so many sins and abominations. The human mind could not order or contain them.

To shut her up, he said, "Let me ask you this. What was he doing in Brooklyn? Or maybe I misunderstood. Though how can you misunderstand Brooklyn . . . ?"

In a firm matter-of-fact tone Inez replied, "I threw him the hell out."

Morroe dropped his eyes as if to spare her.

"Yeah, yeah, yeah, I took all his things, I put them in the hall."

"In the hall?" Morroe's voice rang. "Oh, you're kidding!"

"He was going out on a date. I didn't say anything, not a word. I figure, baby, you're going to play around? You want dates? Fine, fine, fine! You fat little slob, I'll give you dates. I ran downstairs, I went to all the stores, I got a bunch of cartons. Whatever he owned I put in. I locked the door from the inside. And I hold my horses. Finally, finally, I hear him shnuffling around. He rings and he bangs and he bangs and he rings. He starts howling and calling me names. 'It's all right,' he tells me, 'tonight we broke up.' You hear? 'We broke up!' Then he starts bringing his stuff downstairs. A dozen trips at least. That I feel guilty about. For all you know he got strained, he damaged his heart."

"Very doubtful," said Morroe. "I would guess it was the least of all the contributing factors." And he began to muse. Leslie should have called me. I would have certainly come down and given a hand. No matter what time, I would have overlooked it. Then a crazy night, like in the old days. Where he would talk and talk, and for all you know we'd make contact again. And I would have brought him home with me and put him up on the couch, or fixed up a couple of chairs with cushions. No matter how Etta carried on. I mean it.

Suddenly Inez ran to the door, saying, "Good, good, good! Here's Pilar, she's got coffee, we'll have coffee, it'll be nice." She hunted up the sugar bowl; the sugar was hard, encrusted and stained brown. As Morroe hacked and hacked with the handle of a spoon, Inez told him, "You know he started in to write smut?"

"Hey, now you're being silly." An astonished grin spread over Morroe's face. "I remember what Wilner wrote about his stories. Sure . . . 'The cerebral is carnal and the carnal is cerebral.' "

"I know what I'm talking about. He said so in a letter. You want to see, you'll see." She launched herself against one of the bookcases and started to drag it from the wall, meanwhile babbling, "It's behind here. . . . How do I know? Because I put it in my winter bag . . . and the lock is no damn good . . . Leslie's presents . . ." Books began to slide and spill from the top shelves, and though breakfast lay heavy on his stomach, Morroe sprang to assist. "Hold the bottom," she instructed, fishing with her hand along the molding. "Push a little more. More. Now give it, like, a lift." My destiny, my fate, Morroe thought, while blood pounded his temples. To *shlepp* for her. "Okay, okay, okay." She drew out a wad of paper folded down to matchbook size. "Now you'll read, you'll see."

The letter was typed on blank loose-leaf paper; there were no margins and the ribbon had given out near the end. Morroe drained the sweetened sediment at the bottom of his coffee and sank into the couch. His lips unwittingly moving, he read:

DEAR INEZ:

So where were you last night? I called and I called, to no avail. She's watching TV, I told myself. She's spread out on the daybed, shaving her legs or doing her nails, *fressing* away on ice cream and pistachio nuts, sprinting, during commercials, to the potty. In our Drawer of Love her pessary lies sealed and dry and talcumed between plastic covers. *O, sancta simplicimus!*

And what's doing with me? Well,

1) In four weeks I have copped only one quick feel. Even in my wet dreams I'm being rejected.

2) I have become, in a small way of business, a pornographer.

3) I have taken a room in Brighton Beach.

Number one I shall charge off to *Zeitgeist*. Number two —number two is the fate of the artist in mass society, the atomization of the individual, the quality of contemporary experience, the triumph of *kitsch*, the blight spreading over our moral imagination. All right, all right! One Saturday I'm passing by Marty Menashim's bookstore. I wave. He runs to the door and pulls me in. He's all around me like a warm bath. One of his biggest customers, a textile king who spends almost four hundred dollars a month with him, has a yen to help the young and promising talents. This poor guy, it hurts him, his disc is slipping because I have to teach and write reviews for two and a half cents a word. And he wants to do something about it, he would definitely like to help. All right, but how? After all, there are the foundations—God forbid he should start competing with the foundations!

He has conceived, therefore, the following proposition: He shall be my patron; I am to write for his eyes alone. So what am I going to write? Well, it should be realistic and, if it's convenient, here and there my characters should administer a little discipline. Stern, mind you, but nothing complicated—no Chinese boots or iron virgins. And, above all, no Jews.

Thus, once a week I deposit my manuscript with Marty, who solemnly delivers over the check. Ten cents a word—was there ever such a fee? The stuff flows, it pours out of me like curses from a Roumanian mouth. And do you know who serves as model, who it is that fevers my fictions? Give a guess! *Tsatskeleh meineh*, you have been housemaid and nun, overseer of a concentration camp, librarian, Hollywood starlet, lady editor, Eskimo woman. You have been ill used by Lascars, private eyes, prep-school boys, embassy officials, London bobbies and French *flics*, you have made whoopee with Great Danes and been dildoed by Eurasian midgets.

Which brings us, by commodius vicarius, to Brighton Beach. On that night of nights—and why didn't you close the top on my talcum powder? It spilled over everything—

I checked my stuff at Grand Central and wandered, in a state of holy madness, all up and down Times Square. From movie to movie I went, amid the living dead, the sleep-walkers, the Desdemonas and Othellos, the Pucks and Oberons, sustained by pina coladas and coconut drinks and the thinnest of Grant's hamburgers.

At Bickford's in the morning to search the ads. (Let none say a word against those oatmeal cookies!) One, one alone holds my eye. "A very clean room for a nice person." Here are no complex structures, no big deals, no mishmash. "A nice person." The phrase holds open a universe of fixed and eternal values, of certainties unfolding upon certainties. I *shlubb* down my coffee, I make a wee-wee and, forty-two minutes later—door to door—I present myself to Mrs. Holzberg.

But first let me tell you what a country I have entered. It lies between the heel and instep of the great boardwalk that carries you through the promise of Coney Island and beyond, to Sea Gate, watering place of the once rich. Here is a bazaar, a sun kingdom, here there is no humiliation, no indignity, here all things are endowed with grandeur and significance. (All right, the el can kill you with noise, the fancy-shmancy apartment houses are going under, the bungalows could cave in from a dirty look, the beach is a Castle Garden—never mind!)

Anyway, with Mrs. Holzberg I knew I had fallen into good hands. A few jokes, a Yiddish phrase, and identity was established; I had stepped off on the right foot. Before she even put out the honey cake she let me know she'd been on the Yiddish stage, a singer who had played second fiddle only to Jennie Goldstein. Her late husband, did I know of him? De Hirsch Holzberg. The last of the Yiddish Lears. Even Hollywood had grabbed him, and once in a while he still shows up on an old TV movie. A witch doctor, a mad scientist, a good-natured Indian who begs and begs Sitting Bull not to start up with Custer.

The room is in a back-yard bungalow; the shingles smell a little of *flanken*, the walls are covered with green oilcloth and the toilet doesn't let up for a minute. But linens like snow, towels upon towels, and over every door a *mezuzah*. There was a time, Mrs. H. assures me, when she could pick and choose, when people were happy to pay three and four hundred dollars over the summer. Now there's only myself and, two doors down, her son Chester and his wife, Evelyn. Chester is a big fellow who once did all right for himself in the Golden Gloves and still keeps fit with long hours on the handball courts. Every day he's *nuhdging* me to do some push-ups or to pace him while he runs around the block a few times. An intense Zionist; when he finishes up his dental mechanic's course he will settle in Israel. He talks of long sentry duty in the Negev, scaling walls, leaping ditches, hand-to-hand combat with Arabs. For which he'll be more than ready. And he pinches the roll of fat over my gut.

Evelyn is a kind of *gelaymteh*: whatever she touches falls from her hands. At Brooklyn College, where she will soon enter her senior year, the authorities are insisting it's time she picks a major. Between education and sociology she is going crazy, she is getting cramps. What do I think? Because if she takes education it's more practical; she can walk into a job; they're begging for teachers. Though she relates better to sociology, and would have received an A for the course if she had not been late with a term paper. She falls back into the beach chair, spent, inert. She can barely get up to go to the bathroom. But at night—ah, that's another story. Then it's pound and thump and huff and puff and zing-a-zing-zing. I lie and I listen. Please, I beg, have a heart, take pity. Then I can't stand it any more. I rush out of bed and I start scribbling my little stories. Which I shall do in a moment, when I have finished this letter. (There's a beauty in the works, about a Tibetan monk with an enormous dong.) And then off, off to the boardwalk, to hang around and watch the kids. Honest, you never saw such kids. Brown and round and mother-loved, fed on dove's milk and Good Humors. At night they pair off under the pavilions—Milton and Sharon, Seymour and Sandra, Heshie and Deborah. They sing stupid songs, an original word doesn't leave their lips and, clearly, not one will ever stand up for beauty or truth or goodness. Yet—do me something! I could stay and watch them for hours. I feel such love, I chuckle and I beam, and if it was in my power I'd walk in their midst, pat their heads and bless them, each and every one. So they don't join YPSL and they never heard of *Hound and Horn* and they'll end up in garden apartments, with wall-to-wall carpeting. What does it matter? Let them be happy, only be happy. And such is my state that I will remit all sins, even these:

That you have not read my work in three years.

That you do not utter little cries in sex.

That in company you will not laugh at the second hearing of my jokes.

That you have let the Chinese laundry ruin my shirts.

Of course, you know how long this burst of love will last! It'll start to diminish by tomorrow morning, when I get the first jostle on the subway. By the time I hit the city, by the time I search the kiosks for the new quarterlies, it'll disappear altogether. Rankin will have a review, Pankin will have an article, Rifkin will have an excerpt from a novel in progress—and right away I'll eat myself up alive. What can I do, *nebbach?* Am I the *primus mobilus*, am I more than a *nachshlepper* in the order of things? I'm not the owner, lady, I only work here! To love costs, and costs dear. Like my grandmother used to say, sometimes you kill three chickens for one jar of *schmaltz.*

Stay well. . . .

LESLIE

P.S. Do me a favor. Send some undershirts. You threw in only a couple and they're turning green already.

Morroe put aside the letter and sat stiff-backed, in a state of arrest. In his thoughts he begged, Leave me alone. I feel disgusted, I want to vomit, I'm sick and tired of everything. Where do I come to this? I have my own problems. First thing tomorrow morning I have to start on a new brochure, get a gimmick for the campaign theme. The fund-raisers are pressing and pressing. And there would probably be a showdown with Rugoff, the talebearer, the troublemaker, the Uriah Heep. So what kind of "love," what kind of bullshit? Yes, and blessing other kids. His own, though—his own he doesn't even mention.

After some time Morroe got to his feet and said, "I think we should start. Till you get a cab, and everything. Plus the fact that you should arrive a little before everybody else."

But Inez took hold of his arm and drew him back. She said, brooding, "What am I going to do with his clothes? He used to buy and buy. Sell and you get nothing. You want them? Yeah, yeah, yeah! You'll come later, I'll put them in valises, you'll take everything."

"They'd never, never fit me," Morroe protested. "Remember, he was on the broad side. And shorter in the legs. It wouldn't pay with alterations and everything."

"It's only right," Inez continued, unheeding. "Because he was so crazy about you. Because he'd always say, this is a real person, a human being, a *mensch*." She tightened her grip on his arm, then lunged up and kissed him violently on the lips. The drag of her weight took him off balance; he toppled to the couch, one knee folded clumsily under him. "I wished him harm," Inez said, tears running down her face, her mouth fallen, black and twisted. "I'm scared. Do I have to kiss him when he's in the box? That's how it is in my religion. My mother made me do it once to an aunt when I was a kid—the old bitch! You beg the dead: forgive, take my sins under with you."

"Foolish, foolish," Morroe cried, stretching out beside her. "I've been to Jewish funerals—too many in my lifetime. And they don't go through any of that stuff. You'll see how foolish you are." He squeezed closer and stroked her hair. "One-two-three. In and out, no big deals." As if by accident he lowered his hand down and down, till it fell near the ridge of her panty-girdle. Whoosh! It dawned on him that on this day anything was possible. But suppose Pilar walked in on them?

Never mind. It could be a quickie, sneaked in the name of compassion. Coolly, without caution, Morroe began to gather up the folds of her dress.

And the bell rang. Two short bursts, then a prolonged, tearing peal.

"Wait, wait, wait," Inez cried, deftly stiff-arming him and making for the window. "It's Falvey." She flung up the blinds and bent out. "One second," she howled. "I'll go to the john, I'll wash up and I'm ready." And to Morroe: "My earrings. Are they too loud? Eh, as if they'll even notice."

"Whoa," said Morroe, muddled and fatigued; he had broken into a heavy sweat. "What's the arrangements? I thought you and I would go together."

"I can't talk," Inez snapped. "He's double-parked and it's the beginning of the month. They're giving tickets right and left." She turned away and called for Pilar. Whose face, as she came forward from the kitchen, bore the same wise little smile.

"Then I'll ride down with you," Morroe insisted. "Just let me wash my face, that's all."

Inez gave a nervous shiver and wagged her head. "No room. Where's there room? We have to pick up Falvey's sister. And her kids, she can't leave the kids. We were so close. Could I say no to her, could I say don't come?"

"No room?" Morroe croaked. "That's nice, very nice. You couldn't make better arrangements, hah?" He was ready to say more, much more. But for Pilar's sake he dissembled his anger.

Once again Inez kissed him flush on the mouth, though

he shrank from the contact. She said, "You'll call up the boys. You'll let them know. You'll all come together. A big crowd. It'll be nice."

On shaky legs Morroe followed her into the hall. "You didn't tell me where the funeral is. Tell me!" he demanded.

"You know where Ocean Parkway comes into Prospect Park?"

"I think so. Yes."

"Near there. *Parkway Memorial,* or *Parkway Chapel.* You'll see, you'll find it."

"I'm not so sure. Hold it! There must be at least—" But he heard only the knocking of her footsteps on the landing and Pilar's quick-running chatter.

He went back into the apartment and began an aimless wandering of the rooms. Without knowing precisely why, he decided to clear away, straighten up. There was a small carton under the kitchen sink; into this he emptied some of the ash trays and discarded the coffee containers. He adjusted the blinds, climbing on a chair to do what he could for the fraying cords; he shut off the lights, he moved the bookcase back against the wall and, if he had been able to find the vacuum, he would have gone over the rugs. Though he was soon winded and overheated, the effort nevertheless had a settling effect upon him. He rested, smoked a cigarette and rose to make the calls.

His voice was pitched low, somewhat strained and unctuous. With each of the boys he dropped into the same phrases: "A little bad news . . . coronary thrombosis . . . not a bit of warning . . . lousy, rotten deal. . . ." In a few minutes everything was arranged; they were to meet at Sheridan Square, and Holly Levine would pick them up in his Volkswagen.

When Morroe hung up he remained at the telephone table. "Cry," he muttered. "Now cry a little." He bent his head and thought of his Uncle Lazar, of the slights he had suffered over the past month, make it six weeks, of Auschwitz and Buchenwald and the six million. But it was useless.

4

LATELY, death was a strong consideration in the mind of Felix Ottensteen. A little past fifty-eight, with a broad flat face and hair short and black as peppercorns, he loved and took good care of himself, and there were few cravings he could not still satisfy. But though he was no believer in evil eyes, though he was unafraid of making enemies right and left, he could not shake off the notion that somehow menaces were after his life, that he and his cronies, the vigorous, powerful and flashy who questioned God, man and devil, were going under.

True, he had just had a mild scare with food poisoning, and, on a hospital bed where lights and loudspeakers kept you from sleep and the nurses wouldn't take an extra step, it was no wonder that thoughts grew sour and ugly. But it was really at work that Ottensteen had fallen into his present state. He wrote literary articles for *Yetzt*, a Yiddish daily, and one morning, when things were slow, when he was brooding over the person his son Max had become, Shiffman, a proofreader, blundered into his cubicle, exclaiming, "*Gottenyu*, don't ask, Felix, don't ask!"

In the corridor the whole staff was coming together. One of the women had fainted, her head had struck the edge of a chair, and people were rushing for smelling salts and dabbing her face with strong cologne. For Gollowitz, the executive editor, was dead of a massive stroke. He had been washing up in the men's room, he complained over the quality of the paper towels, and all of a sudden he had reeled and sagged onto the tiles. Gollowitz, who didn't know how to raise his voice or say a harsh word, who had once wept while firing an errand boy. This pen, this voice, this monument, this influence, snuffed out, finished, vanished like a fog.

Then, in a few short months, Ottensteen was to hurl clods of earth into other graves. Schlossberg . . . Chaim Posner . . . Mendel Amsterdam. . . . Poets, sweet singers all, they had never been before and would never be again. Not like his Max, a complainer, a whiner, knowing only how to take and take, pinched and gray already, before he was twenty-eight. No, they were first human beings, laughers, drinkers, whoremasters, and because they could put a few lines down on paper they didn't take the attitude that the world owed them a living. Touch one of them and you touched a man.

And now, as he hung up on Morroe Rieff, Ottensteen banged his thighs with tiny fists and in his fashion prayed. "You, hey, You, please, please let up on us. We had our share." Angry tears approached his eyes, but he quelled them. "You are getting cranky and spiteful. Strange. Like a woman in her change of life. You couldn't leave Leslie alone? In what way was he hurting You? Such a wonderful boy, such a classy writer. And what kills me is the way You keep hands off all the lowest of the low, fifth-rate types. Who are no good to You and no good to people. Here, right here in this hotel, don't go any further than that fat lawyer. Katzka. When he has to look at his watch he makes sure to turn his back on you. And Nickie the elevator man. He gets his living from Jews, but the more you *shmeer* him the more he hates your guts."

Then Ottensteen went on to other reflections. He was putting on his special shoes with the heavy metal arches —he would need them for the hard cemetery paths—and with his knees locking his face, his belly pressing upward and hampering his breath, he suddenly felt in his heart one great desire: to take the life out of Max and bestow it upon Leslie.

All right, it wasn't nice, it was unnatural; other parents carried children on their backs, suffering and sustaining, letting themselves be clawed and torn and stamped upon, without end. But he, Ottensteen, could not see this. He was no hypocrite, he could not say, "You are my son, so I will judge you differently from the rest of mankind." Nothing doing! Where was it written that he had to love Max for his selfishness, for the way he antagonized you, for his habit of looking at you so painfully, so angrily, as though every minute you were killing his soul?

Last Friday they had come close to shedding blood. Max had called him for lunch, stammering and speaking so slowly you grew old between each word. He has something in the works, Ottensteen suspected, a fresh piece of business, and it's going to cost me. But when they faced each other across the restaurant table Ottensteen had been affable enough, saying, "*Nu*, sonny boy, *kaddish meiner*, what's doing and what's happening?"

Hanging his gloomy, narrow face in which Ottensteen saw nothing of himself, Max said, "It's getting quite unbearable in my place, Papa. I don't think I had a chance to tell you they got rid of one of the copy editors and loaded some of her work on me. By the time I'm home about all I can do is lie in bed and watch TV. Of course, I can't go near my own stuff. I'm pooped, I just don't have the energy."

"*Vei*, such problems, such a terrible and dreadful cross to bear." Ottensteen clicked his tongue. "I remember, once upon a time, there were poets who were as sensitive as you and, maybe, God forbid, as talented, who worked fourteen hours a day in shops. Fourteen? Sixteen! Where you had to keep a little water bottle next to you because the boss would look cross-eyed if you shut off the machine a second. And still—" he tilted his head and tapped his brow "—still-l-l they weren't, they managed not to be so pooped. They did their scribbling, they had energy, they even went out and tried to make revolutions."

Max grew sullen and droopy. He drank down a whole

glass of water and crammed his mouth with bread, tearing the soft white center out of the loaf. Then he said, "Papa, we see each other—what? At most, oh, once every seven, eight weeks. And you never let up. You belittle, you keep cutting me down." He began to cough and stammer. "It's not my fault if there are no revolutions to be made. Besides, the poet has a tough enough time today. He can't just put a word down and leave it at that, plain, simple, open to all. If he says 'grass' he has to make sure he shows off all kinds of history and physics and archeology and myth. He has to keep up with everything. If he can't, he's out of luck, he'll never get anywhere. Because there are hundreds and hundreds of other young poets who can, who are after the same few pages in the same magazines. On top of which the editors aren't really interested in verse. They keep you waiting for months sometimes before you hear from them. And they are doing you a big favor to print you, to stick you in somewhere to fill a hole at the bottom of a page. So don't talk to me about revolutions."

Flinging out his arms, Ottensteen said, "We drop the subject. Only answer one question. To ease a father's curiosity." There was repressed laughter in his voice. "Those poems you had in that—what?—with pink and green paper—"

"*Serpent's Tongue.*"

"Anyway, how is it—how *is* it—that a—you'll pardon the expression—a *cocker* like you comes to write a line: 'Let's sack the city, tear the lamp posts by the roots'?"

"*Pluck* the lamp posts . . ."

"Because I'd like to know what it is you have against the city, what harm it ever did you?"

"A complete misunderstanding, Papa," Max informed him. "Actually, I was mocking, satirizing the poet's attitude toward industrial society."

"You don't say!" exclaimed Ottensteen blandly as he cut away fat from his meat. "You know, I feel better. I was getting very, very worried."

Then in complete silence they sat and ate, crowding their food. And Ottensteen kept wondering, "When, when?" Any minute he's going to spring something. The way he sucks on his lips, the way the legs are moving, like he has to go to the toilet. He doesn't know how to get around people. Even as a kid, the same way. From the minute he walked into the class the teacher had it in for him.

He noticed Max stooping and scribbling on the back of an envelope and he said, "What, what are you doing there? Why don't you sit straight, nice, like a human being?"

"That's how I keep track of my poems," Max answered gravely. "I send out a dozen at a clip and I have to have some kind of system, since it's embarrassing if the same poem goes to one magazine twice." He handed over the envelope. "On one side I put the names of the poems and on the other side all the magazines. I give every magazine a letter and every poem a number and as soon as I mail a poem to a magazine I put the right number alongside the right letter."

Ottensteen went, "Tsooh-tsooh-tsooh," and, after a long

look at the envelope, said, "I'll advise you something: send this away to print for a poem. As is!"

Max retrieved the envelope. His jaw grew slack, his eyes lidded and he uttered a bark of senseless laughter, like a distraught parrot. "I guess to the next person it could seem . . ." He faltered, puffing out his cheeks in so repulsive a manner as to make him look like a mental defective, a glandular case. And, true to his nature, chose that moment to reveal what was in his mind.

Without preliminaries, he let Ottensteen know he had decided to go back to school. There was no getting away from it: he would be a hundred times better off teaching. Six or nine hours a week were not forty. To say nothing of tenure and vacation and sabbaticals. But you needed a Ph.D. No matter how well you were known, no matter how much you'd published. Plus two thousand dollars. At the very least. Aside from what he himself would earn from a part-time job. Because he would still work; he was quick to point this out.

When the two thousand dollars came up Ottensteen started to interrupt. He let Max finish, though, and reared back in his chair, staring at him serenely. Presently, he said, "You wanted your own place, I helped set you up. You wanted Mexico, it was Mexico. You wanted Paris, I financed you. Twenty dollars a week. From which I see very little in the way of returns. So without argument, without raising a voice, I tell you leave *der alte* Ottensteen alone."

With a moistened fingertip Max was carrying crumbs from the tablecloth to his mouth. "You gave me twelve dollars a week," he managed to bring out. "Not twenty. Boy oh boy, when it suits your purposes—"

"Excuse me. Twelve dollars a week for close to twenty-six months is not money." And Ottensteen flung down his napkin. "He thinks I piss and shit thousand-dollar bills. No, no, sonny boy, it doesn't come that easy. For a few extra bucks I stand on my sick feet and I lecture an hour and a half to the Hadassah ladies and I spend another hour answering their brilliant questions." He formed his lips into a cupid's bow and simpered, "Mr. Ottensteen, my Zelda wanted me to ask you about Philip Roth. . . ."

"You have it, Papa," Max said with great earnestness. "You have it and could spare it."

"Who denies?" Ottensteen laughed at his own irony.

"You spend it, too. But on strangers, not your own."

"What, what's this?" said Ottensteen, screwing up his eyes so that they completely disappeared. "Elaborate a little. Because I smell, like . . ."

"Drop it, Papa, drop it. You know what I'm talking about."

Ottensteen opened his hands in a movement of denial.

There was a pause; then Max looked at him searchingly and said, "All right. Essie Meltzer. How much does she cost you? I'll bet plenty. And not only her. You send the two boys to camp and you lay out—why, a small fortune—"

"Oh, is that so? Is that so?" said Ottensteen, astonished.

"—to straighten their teeth. I know. I also go to Dr. Kolodny."

Ottensteen's voice broke as he shouted, "Your own teeth should fall out!"

"You weren't really so different when mother was alive," Max said, once more puffing out his cheeks. "You had money for the whole world. Ottensteen the big shot! The heavy spender! When he comes, he comes like a sport. Oh, but when mother wanted—needed—a new winter coat, what a scene, what a cry of poverty. Yes, and even when she was sick, when it was a question of two weeks or a month at most, you debated a hundred times before you wrote the check for a private nurse."

With a thrust of his little arm Ottensteen cracked Max across the face. He said, "I wasn't too crazy about your mother and I like you even less."

In the sudden stillness of the restaurant Max's cry hung like a curl of smoke. He jerked his chair away, raised his own hand, then let it fall limply at his side. "All right," he said, dully. "I see where we stand. All right. And you know what I wish you? What mother had. No more, no less; I'm being fair."

And he walked rapidly away, while Ottensteen, for the benefit of the waiter, whistled a little tune between his teeth.

So it was no wonder that as he descended in the elevator with its dark paneling, its stifled light and rich red plush, Ottensteen saw himself in his coffin. His bankbooks would help irrigate the Negev; his shoes, in plain brown paper, Max would get. By special messenger. And since he was a sport, he would throw in whatever troubles he had not finished up in this life.

On his way out he checked with the desk for mail and messages. There was nothing, and he handed over his key to the clerk, Sobiloff. Who hissed and pointed to the elevator. Turning, Ottensteen saw a bunch of young girls in white uniforms, most likely from the beautician's school on the second floor. "Ummmm," said Sobiloff, licking his lips, laughing, then groaning. "Where are the youthful energies, heh? That's how it is, Mister O. When you're a boy, you say, Oh, did I have myself a good screw; when you're middle-aged you say, Oh, oh, did I have myself a good meal; and when you reach our years it's Oh, oh, oh, did I have myself a good crap."

To which Ottensteen, standing rigid as brass, made reply: "Sobiloff, I'll give you information. You're a dopey man. An idee-*yut*. A big horse's ass."

And linking thumbs behind the small of his back, his paunch upthrust, he strode slowly into the killing sun.

"The Bronx girl," said Barnet Weiner, poet, critic, contributor to the literary quarterlies, "is different from the Brooklyn girl."

And inchwise, on elbows and knees, he began to make his way across the bed like one covering a commando course. Then, far, far over to his own side, he rested: eyes filled with morning fluid and sediment, sighting along navel and big toe at the flaky imprint of a moth on the bedpost.

"The Brooklyn girl is tough, independent," he continued, "a terrific little dresser. In contrast, her Bronx counterpart will permit Momma to wash her underwear

73

and iron her blouses till age thirty-five. Or sex, take sex. The Brooklyn girl is frank, open, she won't make you feel like a murderer if you squeeze her tsitskies."

Drawing a Kleenex from under the lean pillow, Myra Mandelbaum blew her nose and blinked at him with lamenting Sad Sack eyes, her thin pale features coiling into a mask of infinite endurance. Which stirred him even more deeply against her.

And he said further, "Yes, but the Bronx girl, after a year of Carnegie concerts and New School lectures, becomes receptive, in her various apertures, to all manner of diddling and fingering. When you plead with her, when you pant with passion, when you swear to her that non-consummation is wrecking your nerves and ruining your health, she will only adjust her suspants and sneer, 'So why don't you see a doctor, then?' "

Her eyes wet and brimming, Myra Mandelbaum demanded, "Tell me! What did I do and what was so terrible?"

Weiner turned mute.

"Tell me!" she persisted. And she yanked at the stockings that lay in elephantine folds about her ankles. "Because I can't take it from you any more, you mad bastard, with your fake sociology."

He replied "Gaah!" and raised himself again for a swift assessment in the chiffonier mirror. It was all he could do to hold down a sob as he remembered his photo on the dust jacket of *New Critics: 1944*—the hard strong features holding back easily the encroachment of Semitic melancholy, the springy black hair needing a trim, the mouth soft, full, delicate, even with that cocky cigarette stub. Now he was bare on top, his scalp the color of an old callous; a cheap piece of bridgework had left him fallen in the cheeks, his nose was broadened, veined. And he had published nothing in years.

"Gaah!" he said again, recoiling in blind shock from his image. "I was willing to put up with anything. I might have overlooked the little coat with Persian lamb sleeves, the rhinestone jewelry, the Helena Rubinstein compact. . . ." He pointed a prophetic finger at her. "I could have found it in my heart to forgive the fact that we had cohabited—say, two point five times a week and five months, which makes it roughly, conservatively—gaah, maybe sixty times before you could be prevailed upon to stay the night."

"Was it my fault?" said Myra Mandelbaum in a small but staunch voice. "Because my hair is oily and I have to wash it every few days and you have such hard water?"

He got up, teetering a little on his feet. "But you're clever," he insisted, laughing a slobbish Harry Bauer laugh. "Oh, shortener of my life and devourer of my days, your Bronx peasant cunning showed you where I was vulnerable, where to put in the grijjies." With thumb and forefinger he clamped down on her long chin and waggled it back and forth. "Where did you get that gall, that effrontery, that *chutzpah* before? Where do you come off with that ass-heaving, that moaning and groaning, that ooh-ing and aah-ing?" He shut his eyes and went through a pantomime of shivering and ragged breathing. "Oh, baby, baby! I love it, oh I love it, I love it!" Then, serenely, "Where is the style, the sense of structure? Aren't you aware that the anticipatory 'it' heralds a deferred subject? Gaah?"

A lewd smile of complicity split wide over the face of Myra Mandelbaum. "Wise guy," she said, "big shot. He forgets I took a few psych courses in my time; he doesn't realize that maybe I have some insight into the source of his hostility. Yeah-yeah! Because I refuse to be a masochist. Because I refuse, in this heat, to ride an hour and ten minutes on the subway to his mother's house when it's positively not appreciated, when I get from her only digs and needles."

"Gaah! Digs and needles! She's crazy about you. She sees ketchup is on sale, two-for-something, one bottle goes to you. She grinds by her own hand top round for your stuffed cabbage. She saves little jars so you can take home apple sauce and first-quality chicken soup." He began to rock and sway and beat his breast.

"Stuffed cabbage, my ass. She talks a good meal, your mother. But all I ever got from her was hard-boiled eggs. No, no, no—excuse me, I won't lie, I won't distort. Because once, once upon a time, she actually did open a can of sardines."

"Stockings," said Barnet Weiner, "she gives you stockings." He returned to bed, fitting his soles against her soles so that they reclined like a pair of pornographic bookends. "Box after box. *Shnorred*, with cunning and craft, from tough-minded Cousin Schmeilick."

"Boxes? You case, you nut, you miserable liar! Three pair, three lousy pair. And seconds, to boot. Before I even had the tissue off, in my hands, they fell apart."

"*Shah, shah,*" he comforted, stroking her instep with his big toe.

"And by the way—once is a joke and twice is a joke. But I'm getting sick and tired of her cute little habit of calling me Mary Murphy. Or asking me do I know what Yom Kippur is. . . ."

"Gaah, that," Weiner crowed, "that's nothing. You should have known her when she was on top of her form. A name for everyone. Did I tell you that Hilbert Stein used to live on our block? Well, he did. And Momma couldn't stand him, even before he became a big-time hotsy-totsy critic. She called him by one name and one name only. *Pishteppel.*"

"You know something? You're losing money. You ought to write her up for *Reader's Digest.*"

"Don't be churlish, girl." He rolled over onto one elbow and with his free hand plucked the elastic of her garter belt. "One hour we'll spend with her. Come! Tops, an hour and a half."

Myra Mandelbaum blew her nose and told him, "Turn purple."

"She has sour cream. She has pot cheese."

Myra Mandelbaum feigned sleep.

"And onion rolls. The Bronx girl loves onion rolls."

"You're starting again?"

"Onion rolls."

"Once and for all you're going to learn. I'm going to teach you a little respect for—"

"You'll lick your fingers."

"—to find one or two other pleasures besides aggravating me."

"She'll cut up a cucumber."

"Turn blue!"

"Be nice." And Barnet Weiner began to pet her breast. "Ah-ah-bay-*bee*."

She slapped away his hand and cried, "Nothing doing."

He groped again for her breast, crooning, "There and there and there. Whose young Jewish intellectual is it?"

"Don't bother me." Yet her body was arching, her knees dividing.

"Whose?"

"Mine, mine! Unwillingly. . . . Grudgingly. . . . Mine."

"And who has talent? And who has promise?"

"You and you."

"And who will do the definitive piece on Lawrence?"

"You and you and you!" she ground through her teeth.

Then gently, almost abstractedly, he entered Myra Mandelbaum, heaving as she heaved, plunging as she plunged, matching thrust with counterthrust. And though he worked in feverish haste, he saved breath enough to mutter, "We'll spend one hour, only an hour . . ."

But before her answer came the phone was ringing and ringing. At the sixth ring Myra Mandelbaum gave in, pulling and tipping over the night table so that the receiver fell neatly into his hand. Before it was even at his ear he made out the idiot voice of Morroe Reiff.

"BarnIgotsumbanewsBarn . . ."

To own a car in Manhattan is like towing a camel across the Sargasso. It is a terrible weight to bear, a stupendous obligation, an absolute commitment, a piece of absurdity. No day goes by without unforeseen trouble and hidden expense; it will give you no rest. You must pay through both nostrils for insurance, maintain a small store of dimes for the meters, walk blocks and blocks to move it before eight in the morning. Vandals will strip your aerials for zip guns, your emblems for belt buckles, cranks and kooks will paint "Jesus Saves" on your windshield, police will find an excuse to ticket on the first and thirtieth of each month. From front and back bigger cars will box you in. Snow trucks will lay down special salts to corrode your undercarriage, pit your chrome, dull your finish. In the end the car is a metaphor for man's fate, the blind unalterable fact against which he rages in vain, the setting of his limits, the definer of all his terms, the objective correlative of the possible. . . .

Such were the thoughts that battered the spirit of Holly Levine as he darted an uneasy glance out of his window. When he had gathered the nerve he rapped on the glass and gave a lusterless smile to the bunch, the collection, the host of kids perched and prancing atop his frail Volkswagen bumpers. "Hello-oh," he sang, and "Ah, ah-ha, fellahs. . . ." One, one only took notice, with a look like a swift kick in the testicles. To him, Levine called, "Keep an eye on the car, will you do that, sport? Okay, *paisan? . . . Hombre? . . .*"

And, perspiring lightly, his teeth on edge, his ears freezing—a trick of nerves, a throwback (for this plus a recent instance of ejaculation praecox he blamed his analyst's too-long vacation)—Levine paced his den, his study, his writing chamber with slow steps. Then, by devious ways—tamping down the shavings in his pencil sharpener, giving a just-so twist to his gooseneck lamp, swabbing an ash tray, squirting the lightest of oils into his Olivetti and a few drops of Windex on the plate glass of his desk—he regained a measure of repose. He sat, let one more jittery moment pass, and with almost closed eyes picked up a file card and peered at his crabbed writing.

Cold War
meaningful
meaningful and integral
life
Life
LIFE
pages swarm teem burst with bearthevitalburstof
commentary—ironic, self-satisfied
Open Society, Closed Terrain

From the *n* of "Terrain" Levine began a spiral, let it rise and rise, halted it, subdivided it, modified it into a lyrical rhomboid enclosing THERMONUCLEAR.

From the *R* of THERMONUCLEAR Levine made a foetus, a snail, an egg, a cradle, a seal butting a ball, the ball enclosing "corruption" and "decline."

Then with a blue pencil he filled in every other letter.

Then with a red pencil he filled in the rest of the letters.

Then over each *i* he placed a dot, worked the dots into perfect little circles, and these circles he filled in also with blue and red pencils.

Then from the lower left corner of his desk he took up a book of paper matches, he twisted off one match and, with utmost delicacy, leaving the head intact and no end frayed or split, peeled it into four parts, and each of these parts he peeled into four more parts.

Then, then Levine judged himself ready.

So, sighing frequently, his eyes tied to the keys, Levine typed, fitfully typed:

Certainly, Professor Gombitz' essays, gathered together for the first time, yield pleasure of a kind, but a pleasure increasingly tempered by the realization that Professor Gombitz is not altogether his own man.

"Nice, ah, nice," he muttered aloud, his nostrils palpitating at the ease, the verve, the easy verve of that "Certainly" as it pushed the sentence along to its little climax. A bit of warmth returned to his ears, and he all but cheered as a wild rush of phrases stormed his mind: "the pressure of impulse; fierce and abrasive; polished and supple; merely to assert; keened edge; blunted perception; living stream; dry watershed." He thought, Poor Gombitz, and at once had visions of irony acting on coincidence to throw together the two of them. Between or after classes their heads would collide over water fountains. Their elbows would nastily rub at adjacent urinals, they would identify each other's shoes under toilet stalls and behind library stacks. By the parking field they would race without quarter for the last spot. Under chapel spires Gombitz would shake a palsied fist, he would thumb his nose.

But in afterthought he saw graciousness, mutual respect, himself peeping into Gombitz' office, Gombitz swiveling to face him.

He would say, with rueful smile, offering his charm, "I am sorry I did not like your book better."

He would quote Wordsworth: "I have endeavored to look steadily at my subject."

He would quote Goethe: "Against criticism we can neither protect nor defend ourselves; we must act in despite of it. . . ."

Later, but not much, friendship would flower like a Chinese bloom in a water glass. They would swap scholarly journals, talk of herbs, tobacco blends, bird life, compare dissertations, chip in for a hot plate, Earl Grey tea, Scotch shortbread, lighter fluid and flints. His acknowledgement ("I should like to express my particular gratitude to Dr. Horace Gombitz for his careful reading of a bulky manuscript and for his many cogent questions and observations") would blur the old gent's eyes. In time, in good time, he would inherit first editions of Edith Wharton, a colonial breakfront, two hooked rugs, six pieces of Venetian glass, a recipe for clam pie.

Certainly, Professor Gombitz' essays, gathered together for the first time, yield pleasure of a kind . . .

All at once Levine was curiously disappointed in that "Certainly." Chill, detached, bleak and glacial. It expanded without being open, absorbed without responding, offered insurgence but no heresy. It was a dim figure in the carpet, a face behind the curtain, a fly trapped in amber. It was a pain in his balls.

With hatred of self, then of Gombitz, he sneaked in the

"Certainly" between "time" and "yield"; it made stone of his ears.

He would have settled for the spot after "kind," but the droop of the extra comma fatigued him.

Using red pencil he tried:

An essay by Gombitz will clearly yield . . .

and:

Surely, essays such as these must certainly yield . . .

Using blue pencil he tried:

An essay by Gombitz will surely yield . . .

and:

Surely, essays such as these are bound to yield . . .

Then he went to the refrigerator and tightened all jars, twisted Handi-Wrap around half a tomato, two scallions, a tarnished wedge of Swiss Knight, and with moist toweling wiped a ketchup bottle and a butter dish.

Then he went to the stove and with a wire brush painted Easy-Off into the oven and put scouring powder, steel wool and dry paper toweling to the jets and burners.

Then he went to the garbage pail and lined the bottom with aluminum foil, and with Scotch tape fixed a plastic bag to the sides.

Then he went to the sink and stooped amid the pipes and set up a milk carton that it might be handy for coffee grounds and grease.

Then he went to his bookshelves and at the bottom of the vertically stacked *Kenyon Reviews* found the one

Playboy and, though fighting not to, shook out and inspected from many angles the center fold.

Then he sat.

Then he took up his match again and peeled four more perfect strips.

Then he hummed, hummed and clapped hands to "The March of the Movies."

And he hissed softly, "Trilling . . . Leavis . . . Ransom . . . Tate . . . Kazin . . . Chase . . ." and saw them, The Fathers, as though from a vast amphitheater, smiling at him, and he smiled at them.

And he typed, with a smoking intensity he typed:

Of course, Professor Gombitz' essays, gathered together for the first time

Taking a relaxed position in his chair, Levine warned himself not to be too pleased. Still, withal, nevertheless, the "Of course" was a piece of the greatest good luck. The linkage, the irremediable coupling of the small syllable and the large—Bloom and Dedalus. "Bloom and Dedalus," he murmured, "Dedalus and Bloom." It warmed his ears.

. . . yield pleasure of a kind . . .

This was muted yet menacing: mutedly menacing. He was all in favor of letting it be, but nonetheless tried out and was deeply affected by:

. . . yield a kind of pleasure . . .

Who could doubt that a tough no-nonsense mind was at work here, here at work? Not, certainly not Fendel.

He would gnash his teeth. Rosner would be displeased Greenfeld would be enraged to fury. Tabak stunned. Wilner—Wilner would positively *cholish.*

. . . but a pleasure increasingly tempered . . .

Levine drew back, desolated at the thought that he was not, by any means, the first man to use "increasingly tempered." Fool, plaster saint, whited sepulcher—would any know the difference, he asked himself.

He gave unequivocal answer: Only you, Levine.

And let it stand.

He was pacing about, every so often peeping at his *Playboy,* when he suddenly stiffened and with his every blood cell listened to what drifted up from below: the wild thrashing of many voices, the whoops of mean laughter, the cadence of cheers and razzing, the pummeling, as of bone upon skull, the clank, as of hubcap hitting pavement, the wheeze, the wheeze and sob as of air leaving tires.

To the window sped Levine, leaning out as far as he dared. His neck craned, his elbows lacerated by the stone ledge, his entrails crowded toward his chest, and choking somewhat, he had the impression that his car was gone. For a few dreadful seconds he debated between one great powerful shriek and a quiet stroke.

But then tears of deliverance sprang to his eyes.

And he waved and showed a happy face to the troop, the mob, the horde of kids who bounced balls off his doors and fenders, who tried his locks, who tormented his windshield wipers and his side-view mirror.

And to him, that one, that mass man, that totalitarian

type, that *momza,* Levine said a hearty "Hi, guy" and "That's the ticket!"

And a moment later, while freshening his bathroom with Air-Wick, Levine gave thought as usual to the idea of a garage or a lot at least. But he was determined to meet and master the city on its own terms, to defend his little vested interest before its monstrous complications, to keep wit and nerve intact against the inexorable megalopolis. Besides, he didn't want to spend the money.

. . . is not altogether his own man . . .

Once more The Fathers smiled at Levine and Levine smiled at them. And his underlip was still curling, his teeth still bared as he hopped up to silence the phone.

His first thought after talking to Morroe Reiff was of annoyance with Leslie; he must now, now he must go elsewhere for entree to *The Naysayer.*

His second thought was shame for his first thought.

Then he poured talcum under the arms of a once-worn sport shirt, whisked clean a lightweight suit, washed with Tide-and-water his desert boots, and dressed.

Then he closed and locked all his windows.

Then he turned down his refrigerator from five to three.

Then he set a fresh paper match on the lower left-hand corner of his desk.

Then he made a mental, then a written, note to restore that first "Certainly."

5 ———————————————————

FEELING EMPTY and ill used, Morroe Rieff waited amid
the brazen pigeons of Sheridan Square.

He was watching Jack Delaney's electric horse leap the
neon stiles when a man came reeling through the thick
of traffic and sprawled out under the shade of his legs.
Almost at once Morroe was flanked by a crowd; from the
benches and the subway stairs people yelled advice or
made wisecracks. And though he had little heart and no
stomach for it—in the office he kept jealous guard over
his soap dish—Morroe stooped and forced himself to slap
the bum's cheeks, saying, "Get up, there! Don't you want
to get up?" To those nearest he grunted, "I'll tell you, he
doesn't look so good. Drunk or no drunk."

The bum turned his dark swollen face toward Morroe. He gave a gap-toothed grin, he opened his eyes, made a wild effort to focus and shut them with a huge sigh. A thin stream crawled along the cheap stuff of his pants and down his broken shoes, widening out along the curb.

"We should raise him up just a little bit. And I'll open his collar. See, notice how it's choking him. . . ." Morroe spoke clearly, quietly, with an impressive air of competence. He called to someone to fetch him a newspaper, and when it came he cushioned it neatly under the bum's head.

Then a cop came forward, laying hands on shoulders and elbows and thrusting roughly. "Come on, come on," he chanted, "let's go, folks, let's take a walk." He scowled, he threw out a "Jeez" and a "Crap," he nursed the tip of his club. Yet he did not seem to mind that only a few drew back. "Up, up," he ordered the bum, playing to the crowd. "We're going to make it. We can do it. For me, little buddy. Try for me." And he squatted on huge haunches, turning toward the gapers his hearty beefeater's face whose florid cheeks seemed to give off the heat of the day.

"Say, how about an ambulance?" Morroe spoke up, straining forward. "Maybe he's an epileptic. Maybe he's in a coma. You can't be sure."

But the cop only gave him a sideways look, putting him on notice that it would be dangerous to interfere, and Morroe concealed his annoyance.

Now the bum coughed and heaved and jerked and cried like a patient who has become immune to anesthesia. He nestled against the curb, so that the cop, to get at him, went on all fours, crouching until their heads almost touched. "Friend, hey, friend, don't make me get rough-rough," he pleaded, thumbing back one of the bum's lids and engaging the lusterless eye. "What have you got against me? Don't you like me? I like you. Hey, little angel, hey, sleeping beauty." Next he grabbed and hauled, holding up all the while one macelike fist. "Is this what you want?" he inquired with grating, provocative pity. "I like you. Honest to God, I'm trying to give you a break. Only you got to give me a break, little friend. I'm your pal, you be my pal."

"Mommy!" the bum squealed.

Whereupon the cop, wasting no more time, gave his jaw a good bang against the curb. Then he clamped a hand like an electrode on the top of his head and raised him by the short hairs.

"Now, button your fly," the cop instructed, shaking his club at the dark gap.

The bum burst into tears.

"This minute, Bumhead."

Lacing fingers, the bum made a fig leaf.

"You want valet service?" said the cop. He stamped his foot twice, as though scaring off a dog, and moved in fast upon the snarled zipper.

Then the bum let out a high, soulless, unreasoning roar. He kicked, he spat, he called dirty names into the heaving crowd, and his skimpy arm came down upon the neck of the cop. Who seemed to gasp, not at the blow so much as the idea of the blow. He turned toward Morroe and whispered despairingly, "Son of a bitch . . . You *got* to be a son of a bitch. . . ."

He grabbed the bum by the waistband of his loose drawers as with the other hand he cracked him across the face. They wrestled furiously for a moment, till the cop, using his bulk, carried him forward to the ground, trapping his head and punishing him neatly over the kidneys. When the bum was thus quieted and made mild the cop took him by the hair, jerking his head back on his neck, then bowing his back, then bringing him up. And for no good reason dealt out a backhanded slap that opened up the bum's lip, saying, "Wait, little friend, I'll show you what my good arm can do."

From the buzzing circle of spectators Morroe came forth. "Okay," he said, in a mild piping voice. "You've made your point. He had enough. Enough already."

"Take a walk," the cop told him, gripping Morroe's shoulder and applying pressure with a fat thumb.

"Not with the hands," said Morroe, reeling back. "*Not . . . with . . . the . . . hands!*"

He squared himself, resolute and ready, then and there vowing to join a gym, to work out at least twice a week with medicine balls and weights. But the cop was already crossing the street, steering the bum toward a chained-off subway entrance.

"Know what he'll do?" Morroe met the slitted eyes of a dark Mafia type who seemed to speak out of some secret knowledge. "He's not going to no fuckin station house. He's gonna give him a Chicago rubdown. Ribs, gut and dick."

Imagining how this would be—the cop doing his cop's work, cutting knuckles on the poor croak, whose bones would give like a cheap pencil—Morroe's heart picked up

90

a rough beat and a light of hatred entered his eyes. He said, "I want to see that. I want to see him just try."

With a crazy rush he started into the street and after the cop. "One minute" he cried huskily.

The cop stood still and studied Morroe silently. Then, pinning the bum to his side, he started to walk off.

"I said wait a minute. . . ." Morroe circled the cop and moved his shoulders up and down like a wrestler. "What's happening? You're bringing him in, preferring charges? Or what? I mean . . ."

"Take a walk, Charley."

"I'm talking to you, officer."

"You gonna get the hell away from me? Because I don't give a shit. You're wise, I take ya in. For blocking traffic."

"Don't get so tough," Morroe answered. "How about not getting so tough? You want, take me in. I'll have a thing or two to say to your superiors." If he forces it, Morroe thought, I'll put up a fight. But shame was blunting the pure edge of his hatred, and he began to regret that he had not hit out blindly before, when hands had first been laid upon him.

"Let's go, let's go, let's go," the cop chanted. "Come on, four eyes; walk away, four-eyed jerk." And he hefted his club delicately and blew at the tip.

"Somebody, I want somebody to give me a pencil," said Morroe, casting a glance behind him. "I'm going to make sure about his number, I'm going to mark it down."

The crowd drew a few steps nearer; a bald, stocky man, cautious and worried, flung Morroe a stub, saying, "You can keep it, Mister; it's all right."

Almost at once the cop had a hand over his badge.

"I want that number. Let me have that number!" Morroe demanded, searching his pockets for paper and bringing forth an ill-used snip of dental floss and two salt tablets.

The cop laughed, as if at the greatest of jokes.

And Morroe hoarsely declared, "There was a four and a two on your badge. The rest I'll check—don't you worry. This is not . . ." He was going to say something like "Hitler's Germany," but held back and finished off with ". . . a police state."

"Goombye, comrade," the cop grunted, pressing a palm against the bum's back and moving him inexorably toward the subway stairs.

"Take a good look. . . . Our defenders . . . guardians . . . one of the finest . . ." Still more ferocious phrases rang with a nice ring in Morroe's mind, but the cop was already beyond hearing, and he was not altogether sorry.

Reflecting on the nature of physical violence (how dangerous is the human being, how a touch or a jostle, a look or a word brings him down with the lowest of the low, the meanest of the mean), Morroe resumed his post among the pigeons. Two kids passed him, sucking cups of grainy ices. Looking around, he saw a runty Italian wheel his cart near the fountain and dip a scoop into the water that ran sluggish and with a smoky glint. In no time a line had formed, and Morroe joined it. "Lemon," he called out, frowning, "you got any, or pineapple?" And he pressed closer, to see for himself. As he did so he was elbowed aside, and a man said, "You got a line here, where you *shtupping?*" "Excuse me," Morroe haughtily replied, not bothering to turn. Then he heard the man come out with something like "These *Yidlach!*" Despite this, Morroe kept his face averted. But a moment later the back of his jacket was lifted and he got a stinging pinch on the behind. Wheeling swiftly, he clutched at an arm. And, with a wild pipe of glee, saw Barnet Weiner.

"Hey!" cried Weiner, "People's Hero. *Shtarke.* Benya Krik."

"Then you saw? Whoosh, I'll tell you something, I—"

"He would have rendered you like a chicken."

A trifle sullenly, Morroe said, "Maybe. He had the height and weight on me, of course. But I used to put on the gloves at City. I can handle myself."

"*Maronne!*" And Weiner spanned Morroe's biceps with mock reverence.

"Whoosh, stop, come on, nut!" Morroe began to grin. "Hey, ices. How about some ices?"

"So you are buying?"

"I'm buying, I'm buying."

"So I am having."

"Two large lemon," Morroe ordered. He watched the Italian artfully pack the cups so as to leave plenty of air at the bottom. The stuff was second-rate, oversweetened, but he welcomed it after that spicy breakfast.

"Eat, eat," Weiner urged, as they headed toward a bench. "It costs enough blood." Then, with a chiding gentleness, "How is it you never called back? I waited and waited, only the phone booth was getting crowded."

"Sure, get away. My big friend, my ass-hole buddy. Who called last? Remember? You were going to come, we were going to prepare—chopped liver, sour tomatoes, big fat specials. Sure, and you're still coming." Oh, you two-faced hypocrite! You crap artist! You phony baloney! Morroe reviled himself, even as he worked Weiner over. Who wanted him? Who needed his visit? To suffer his shafts at the lobby, the carpeting, the teakwood stools and the marble-top coffee table? God bless him. Let him stay well, let me hear only good things about him. But from a distance.

They found a shady spot commanding Seventh Avenue, where they could keep their eyes open for Ottensteen and Levine. From time to time Morroe studied his watch or went to the corner and scanned all approaches; not a sign of them. "We should have been halfway there already," he told Weiner, who was concentrating only on the ices, his tongue systematically burrowing into the crevices of the torn cup. Whoosh, thought Morroe. Look, look at him *shlubb* away! Eyes bulging, spittle flying! Go figure him out. You read his prose and you think you're in the presence of absolute intellect. Inverted and ironic, finicky and fastidious. He did articles on modern dance, he used to correspond with Gide in French and call him *Cher Maître,* and I'm not positive but I think once or twice he wrote the Art Letter for *Horizon.* Only to look at him—pure *bulvan.*

He was on the point of going to the corner to check for the boys when Weiner seized his jacket, crying, "Quick, quick! The one on the left!"

Two girls flashed by, high-breasted brats, white and pink and tender.

"That little *tochiss*. I could bite into it like a piece of hot pastrami."

Making no answer, Morroe deliberately fixed his eyes elsewhere.

Weiner continued his rapturous ogling till the pair were out of sight. Then, pulling himself erect, in a sudden change of mood, he raised a clawed hand, as though against fate. Somehow, to Morroe, at least, the wrinkles between his eyes and under his closely shaven neck seemed ludicrous; he looked like a Baby Leroy ambushed suddenly by middle age.

At last Weiner said, "Gaah!"

And Morroe answered, "Whoosh!"

"It still doesn't register. Leslie dead; it's like a Jewish joke. Any minute I expect him to come *schlumping* along. You know how he used to walk . . . a little *bubbe* loaded down with shopping bags."

"Perfect, you got him perfect," Morroe cried wonderingly. "A *bubbe* . . . Like he's going to offer you a glass of tea or a lox wing, maybe."

Weiner laughed and laughed and fell into a fit of coughing. He sighed, wet his lips. And then, strangely deadpan and formal, said, "Tell me. When you called . . . before. I wasn't clear. Gaah, where were you exactly?"

Perplexed, Morroe frowned and looked away. He finally said, "Inez. Where else? I'm positive I mentioned it. Though, of course, by the time I called you I didn't know whether I was coming or going, I could have—"

"Speak up, boy! I've been meaning to discuss with you that morbid City College whine."

95

"Inez, Inez, Inez!" Morroe twisted around and shouted into Weiner's ear. "And I'm sorry if my education wasn't fashionable enough for you."

"Gaah, good for me, good for me. I deserve it. It's coming to me," Weiner gave out in rich singsong. "Because I took you into the group. Because I raised you from a middlebrow. Because I gave you your first copy of *Partisan Review*. Because I weaned you away from the art films, showed you the difference between the Western as mass myth and mass rite." He was smiting his chest.

"You know . . ." Morroe floundered for the proper pitch of righteousness. "There's a time and a place for that crap. You're not sitting across a cafeteria table."

With a "Shah!" and a "Shush!" Weiner forestalled argument, saying, "When you're right you're right. Only—" And he fell into an attitude of deep brooding. "—I'm a little surprised. I didn't realize you were with Inez."

"So?"

Weiner gave no sign he had heard.

"So? Make your point."

Weiner's eyes gleamed into his as he said, "In other words she gets the news and right off the bat she contacts you. . . ."

"Right, right. Therefore . . ."

"Therefore nothing. Therefore she *shlepps* you from all the way uptown when I live—what?—three and a half blocks from her. That's all."

What is he so sore about, Morroe wanted to know. Because Inez called me first? Well, he could have had that honor. With the greatest pleasure. The way he fumes and pouts. Really, I let him get away with murder. Saying he, he brought me into the group. That remark I absolutely should have taken him up on.

But he answered very mildly, "You ought to know Inez by now."

Weiner let out an affirmative "Gaah!"

"Does anything ever come easy to Inez Braverman?" he continued. "Are things ever simple for her? She could be going downstairs to the A and P and before she's finished she's . . . on safari. In darkest Africa. Why? To get in touch with the old woman who used to do her windows."

"Ye gods!" Weiner cried, almost with a sob. "Look, listen who's telling me about Inez. He's telling me! You think she's something now? Hoo-hah, then you should have been in the group when they were living on Leroy Street."

"When I met Leslie they had just moved. Just!"

"In which case," Weiner pounced, "you must surely remember Kaplan?"

Morroe bowed his head.

Then Weiner's hands flew up in an epic gesture and he stamped his legs and blinked his hot dry eyes. "The whole world has dogs," he crowed. "Big and small, cute and ugly. After all, what can you say about a dog? Four legs, a head, a tail and a wee-wee maker. Right? But you're dealing with Inez. And Inez goes to a chiropodist. Who has this super, see. Who is a moron for the little girls. Who has been carried off in a paddy wagon as a consequence of once, or once too often, playing doctor with Zelda, nine years going on ten. Whose dog remains yet in the cellar, taking food from no man's hand, making outcry by night and by day. Meanwhile, what do I know? I'm going up to their place. Innocent, open. I have just sold a little piece, I feel like celebrating and so I am bringing a salami from *Schmulka Bernstein*. I ring. I hear a 'Come in.' I open the door. I start walking through the foyer. When it is upon me. Made crazy by the salami smell. Drooling all his juices over my socks. Clamping paws over my knee and rubbing away like a subway queer. It, it! The abomination! Kaplan!"

"Who names a dog Kaplan?" said Morroe, fighting down a surge of despair as he scanned his watch.

"Think. Think! You should know. You should recall it." Weiner's voice was kittenish, but by the arch of his brows and the span of his mouth he seemed to announce how much longer and deeper ran his memory of the Bravermans. "Leslie's parable. 'Marcus Is Always Willing.' About the Jewish intellectual who goes to the Midwest so he should feel alienated. Where he has this line: 'It may well be that God is listed in the telephone directory under the name of Kaplan.'"

"I read it. It just so happens," said Morroe, a shade roughly.

"You don't want significant detail? By you is the quality of experience strictly nix? Very good. Anyway-y-y—" Weiner stretched the word as with a shredding tissue he wiped his mouth, his neck and each stubby finger —"anyway, Kaplan was the single most disgusting thing I have ever seen in my life. And I throw in, for good measure, Tessie Lepinsky, the crazy girl on my block who, for a George Brent movie and a frozen custard went

98

under the Steeplechase Pier with me two months after my fifteenth year to heaven. Picture! Part spitz and part spaniel. With a nose like George Arliss. With a bark that could chill mother's milk and grow hair on palms. Also, you think you could just open a can for him? *Bald.* For Kaplan, it was nothing less than boiled spring chicken. Pullet he wouldn't go near. Let it be summer, the middle of the afternoon. Leslie is finished with his classes, it's a nice day, he's feeling *lebedig.* A good time to knock off a quickie, no? Zip-zip, he's in bed with Inez. Hutz-hutz, she's mounting the pillows. When all of a sudden there is a yap and a yip. Kaplan is climbing in between them. He is lying on his back. He is wriggling his dwarfish legs and his tongue is going like a metronome. Nor will all their blows and buffets budge him. Gaah, mind you, this is only a sample. It gets worse and worse. Every time they want to make whoopee he sets up a scream and a holler. He snarls, he shows his teeth to Leslie. He chews up his books. All right, let time pass. Calendar leaves exfoliating. Pilar has been born, an easy delivery. Leslie is taking Inez home from the hospital. Kaplan is waiting by the door. He looks up, he sets eyes upon Leslie's tender little bundle. And his spirit gives out. Slow, grieved, majestic, he takes one last leak on Leslie's jockey shorts, he toils up the stairs, he's on the roof. And without a farewell, lets himself tumble the five and a half flights."

Then Morroe whistled and laughed immoderately. "Are you finished?" he said. "Or you're planning sequels? *Bride of Kaplan? Feigenbaum, Son of Kaplan?*"

"Maybe I embellished," Weiner conceded. "The

chicken—okay, so you could fool him with a piece of pullet. And I won't swear he went all the way up to the roof. But for the rest—" he actually crossed his heart —"may I forget my grounding in the New Criticism. May my landlord install an inside john and demand a professional lease. . . ."

"Meanwhile," cried Morroe, jumping to his feet, "it gets later and later and we sit here like dummies. What do you say I call Holly and you call Ottensteen?"

"First of all," Weiner told him, bowing his head and assuming a mild rabbinical manner, "it stands to reason they've started out already. Therefore it follows we won't reach them. And then, let's say we leave here, we go to call them and, ut-ut-ut, the second we're dialing is the second they arrive."

"I'm going to take one more look. One more . . ." And this time Morroe darted into the center of Seventh Avenue, peering into the fiery mouth of midtown till his eyes teared. But no Holly, no Ottensteen.

When he returned to the bench Weiner was proffering another cup of ices. He waved it away with a "Whoosh!"

To which Weiner made reply: "Gaah!"

"Forty-one. When you think of it . . ."

"It fits in with everything else. From all sides we're getting it."

"True, that is so true."

"And wherever you look they're taking over. You know what I mean?"

"I know. Oh boy, do I know," Morroe responded with all his might.

"The middlebrows. The fats. With their grants and their fellowships."

"Don't knock them for that," Morroe reprimanded. "Leslie got his share."

"All right. Except there was a difference. He was no *tsatskeleh*, Leslie, he was in certain respects far from being trustworthy—and some other time I'll tell you a little thing he pulled on me—but he had . . ."

"Like, integrity."

"Exactly." Weiner spoke with a gentle glow in his eyes. "He didn't want it, he didn't ask for it. But he had it. The way some people have B.O."

"Two days he could spend over a sentence."

"Because he had such respect for the printed word. Unbelievable. A guy who must have published—gaah!— an easy two hundred pieces in his time. And he'd have a conniption, a nervous stomach, every time a set of galleys came in the mail."

"So? So what did it get him?" Significantly, Morroe patted himself on the chest. On the left side. "All alone —that's what I can't get over. A guy who could call up six people when he wanted to take in a movie."

"Isn't that funny? You should mention movies. It happens Leslie was the only person I would go with. Bad movies, especially. And always in the front. If he was able, he would have burrowed right into the screen." Weiner paused, then turned and pressed upon Morroe's knee. "They're after us, *boichick*, they're after us."

And Morroe with a heartening rush of feeling, nodded and nodded, and thought, "He's one of my own kind.

We're on the same wave length. He and the boys. I forget sometimes."

To Weiner, he said, "Soon . . . when this is over . . . Etta and I were talking. We'll have a party. All the boys. Everyone. A real wild night."

And he would perhaps have said more if, at that moment, they had not spotted Holly Levine cutting a dangerous curve around a bus. "Hey *vaglio!*" screamed Weiner, while Morroe beckoned and waved. But Holly, intent on the business of parking, took no notice.

6

"KEEP GOING. . . . That's good. . . . Back . . . Back . . . More . . . More . . . And a little more . . . Now! Now cut sharp!"

There was the buffet and clash of bumper against bumper.

"Any more orders?" said Levine, clasping hands over the wheel and turning upon them a look of barbarous abuse.

"Didn't I tell you cut?" Weiner poked at Morroe. "What did I say?"

Morroe waved him off, and in a voice smothered by hoarseness said, "In case you don't know, we're waiting and waiting and waiting. Where the hell were you?"

But Levine was paying no attention. As if in prayer, he lowered his head, fumbled with the gear stick and shot halfway into the street. Then back and back he inched the car, chanting like a muezzin over the infernal engine grind, "Slow and slow and slow yet and fine fine okay you're okay fine and in. IN!"

"A classic parallel park," he informed them gravely.

"A *m'chyah*," Weiner cried. "If you could write like you can park . . ." And he thrust himself between Morroe and the door, saying, "Gaah, let me sit with Holly, okay? Since I was a kid . . . carsick . . . They had to take along a vomit bag for me."

"You can sit, you can sit," Morroe told him, gesturing expansively. Climbing into the back, though, with the sealed windows and the baking upholstery, his stomach lurched. Every part of the car seemed to press in and weigh upon him, and he was half-maddened by the lack of air. Soon his handkerchief was too wet to deal with his face any longer.

He said, "A little room. Please, can't you make a little room? A person can die here."

"Certainly, certainly." And Levine began to pull and probe under his seat. "Good gosh," he chortled, "there are fourteen—fourteen!—different ways to adjust these seats. Tilt *and* rake. In addition to which you have far more head room than in the average American canal boat." He made a final elaborate adjustment. "There. There we are. Cross your legs. See, see? No banging of the knees. And support, true support from these springs."

"Not bad," said Morroe, feeling as far from comfort as he was from the equator.

"And now . . . now . . ." Levine clapped hands lightly, "now let's have, engage in, some good conversation. Make significant dialogue!" He winked broadly at Morroe. "How have you been? And how is . . . your wife?"

"*Etta?* Oh, *Etta's* fine, fine." Jerk, pompous jerk! Morroe inwardly called him. What's the matter, you can't remember her name? It escapes you? You should choke on every dinner she ever fed you. Retroactively.

He groped for something subtle and infinitely malicious to say. But by the time he had dredged the past and seized upon one of Leslie's old cracks—"Bend over and I'll drive you home"—Weiner had begun to pinch Levine's cheek and grab at his shiny black hair.

"Look, take a look at him!" Weiner groaned. "You *pascudnyak*, lose a few hairs already, get a day older!"

Pleased and a little incredulous, Levine pulled away.

"Honest to God!" Weiner patted and patted his own few hairs. "It's unbelievable. With that dimple yet. The truth, tell the truth, doesn't he remind you a little bit of Vidal?"

"Vidal?" Morroe pretended to peer closely at Levine. "Yeah, yeah . . . definitely . . . Izzy Vidal . . . his father used to have the chicken-plucking concession at the Essex Street Market."

"Or Tony Curtis," Weiner persisted. "An avant-garde Tony Curtis."

With a benevolent chuckle Levine said, "Well, now, since you speak of, mention, the avant-garde, I shall pass on a rather significant tidbit." He gazed off abstractedly, as though allowing them time to take notes. "You are, ah, aware, gentlemen, that for some fifteen months *Portent* has been hunting, seeking an, editor."

Weiner's nostrils grew wider.

And Morroe snapped, "We're aware, we're aware."

"Very well, then," said Levine, slowly stroking his ears. "Now, please bear in mind the fact that thirty-two, yes, gentlemen, thirty-two top names were considered. My own among them. It would seem, however, that someone—and, ah, let him be nameless—someone on the publications committee had the impression I was a wee, wee bit too partial to Leavis. It goes, of course, without saying that Leslie was out of the question. Unreliable, not quite the hearth-and-home type. The same reason you"—he indicated Weiner—"were turned down. Coupled with your rather . . . spotty list of publications during recent years."

"So who?" Weiner begged, panting a little. "Give a hint!"

"It would do no good," said Levine firmly. "I have the greatest respect for your wit, your essential grasp of the absurd, but—"

"Shah, shah!" cried Weiner, and "Gaah, gaah! An idea is coming, a picture, a picture is forming." He half-raised himself in his seat, then sank down again. "No and no and no! I would say it, I would utter the name, only I'm afraid it would mean the final refutation of God's existence."

Giggling, Levine beat a little tattoo on the horn.

"Brrr!" said Weiner, doubling up and hugging his belly. From his mouth there issued burps and growls and a high lyric wheeze. Then, in another voice, a voice strangely high and uncertain: "B-b-b-but Leslie . . . the p-p-plight of the Am-muh-muh-rican intellec-ch-ch-ch-ual . . . doesn't it g-get you sometimes? In the d-d-dark night of the s-s-soul?"

"Please God, nah! Not him! Him not!" Morroe reared back and stamped his feet like a frightened horse.

"None other," Levine affirmed. "Bruce Siskind. And may I say, Barn," he added in a dry lecturer's tone, "that in acuteness and perception, in inflection and pitch, you have surpassed even your take-off on me last New Year's Eve."

"*Vei! Vei-vei-vei,* I'm sick!" Weiner hollered. "Bruce Siskind! Remember what we used to call him? The name Leslie, *alev hasholem,* gave him?"

"La Pasionara!" Morroe screamed out.

Clearing his throat, Levine announced, "He has asked me for a piece. Well, not a *piece* exactly. More an omnibus review of some Nathaniel West-iana. Now, I am momentarily, at the moment, overcommitted, but you, Barn, you . . ."

"Gaah, gaah!" Bugging his eyes and slowly passing a stiff hand along the length of his face, Weiner did an Edgar Kennedy slow burn. "I should give him the satisfaction of calling? So he should play big-shot editor with me? He can cock so!" And he broke into hacking and sputtering. "Furthermore, I once . . . it wasn't nice, even I have to admit . . . but I couldn't resist. You wanna hear?"

Levine cackled.

Morroe whinnied.

"Well, I'm coming home from my mother's house—

you remember when she broke her hip—and from shopping and straightening and up and down the stairs with bundles, I am pooped. So instead of the express I grab a local, and even then I barely get a seat. One station goes by, two stations, three stations, and I'm beginning to get this feeling. Like I'm in the presence of evil. Sure enough, I begin to hear, from right behind, that terrible, unmistakable Siskind laugh. 'Choopie-bar-choopie!' I give a look and he's sitting there, like a Modern Library Giant. I say to him, 'Harya, Brucie, how's it going, Brucie?' 'Oh,' he tells me, 'I am doing a piece on Melville.' And without a what's doing, what's new, how's your mother, he immediately gives me the lowdown on how what's all along been fucking up Melville criticism is that nobody knows anything about fishing. Then he offers me a Chiclet. *One* Chiclet. He says, 'Do you know, *chaver*, I haven't chortle-chortle, choopie-bar-choopie, gotten or been laid in nearly three months?' Then—God forgive me, but he was begging for it—he starts telling me how tough it is for him to break in another nookie, how he's tired of having to make up reading lists for them and giving out all kinds basic instruction in literature and art and on what really went wrong with the Bolshevik Revolution. All in all he's irritating me, he's working on my nerves. First I figure—gaah!—I'll kid him along a little. But I am seized, I am possessed. Something marvelous and mysterious happens. 'Brucie,' I say, 'I have someone definitely in mind. Except I gotta know —you like big tsitskies?' He doesn't commit himself, except that in front of my eyes his beard shoots out a half-inch. 'Another thing, how are you on Zionism?' *Nu, nu!* It takes him from Eastern Parkway to Brooklyn Bridge to cover just the destruction of the Temple. Then I order him to make a muscle. 'She'll like you,' I tell him. 'Especially those pectorals.' And I really start in. Mind you, from one word to the next I'm not sure I'm making sense. Also I feel mean, low, contemptible. Only I can't stop. Like when you start eating polly seeds. Lie upon lie. I invent a girl. Shoshana Shunra, by name. A special agent for the Israeli secret service whose mission is to kidnap Bernard Baruch, David Sarnoff and maybe Jacob Blaustein and get them to ante up enough loot so Israel can buy Poland and that way, that way, get a foothold in Eastern Europe. I warn him, though. How he will be dealing here with a very tough cookie. How during the Sinai campaign she beat two Egyptians to death with a *Mogen David* she herself welded together from a pair of captured gasoline drums. And I'll tell you something else: the more he doubted, the more I believed. Why, when he cocked an eyebrow at a little detail—I claimed she had a Turkish lover who taught her the secret of unendurable pleasure indefinitely prolonged—I got up from the seat and I was ready to walk away then and there. Till he apologized. Wheedling and groveling. No, no, please, Barney, he didn't even want to see the snapshot I made believe I had. I finish up with her generosity. After all, didn't Ben Gurion himself hand her a blank check, she should have what to hire a couple gunsels? So that in the middle of the night Brucie can expect to be sent out for a bottle of celery tonic and told he can keep the change from a hundred-dollar bill. By Astor Place it's settled. I give him a number—a real one. Only it belongs to Fat Gittel, my appetizing-store lady. Then a week passes and the whole thing has left my mind. Till, suddenly, three, four in the morning one day, the phone rings. I pick it up. Am I crazy? Because it seems to me the party on the other end is saying 'C-c-c-carp.' Followed by 'W-w-w-whitefish . . . sturgeon . . . sch-sch-sch-schmaltz herring.' Then a snatch of 'Hatikvah.' And when I start to bang down the receiver it comes floating, gaah, vile, vicious and vulgar over the ether. 'Choopie-bar-choopie . . . Choopie-bar-choopie.' "

"Oh, God! Oh, God!" Levine seemed to gather all his energies for the assault of laughter which spun him, weeping and shrieking, into Weiner's lap.

"W-w-w-whitefish!" Weiner choked out. "Sch-sch-sch-schmaltz herring! C-c-c-carp!"

And Morroe, after looking at his watch, cried, "Choopie-bar-choopie! Choopie-bar-choopie!"

"You have ruined me," whimpered Levine. "Ho-ho! I have a pain over, in the area of, my liver. Ha-ha! W-w-w-whitefish!"

Teeth set in a sadist's grin, Weiner said, "C-c-c-carp!"

Too spent to laugh, they sprawled in their seats like sunbathers.

Till Weiner, the first to come to himself, flipped out a "What else is new?"

"There is a possibility . . ." Levine pressed his right side and blew a tormented breath, ". . . well, a strong likelihood, that I shall be giving a popular culture course this fall. From 'Little Nemo' to 'Li'l Abner.' "

A stir of unbelief went through Weiner.

"Something wrong, Barn?" said Levine, with a sudden

tightening of his lips. "You are, ah, perhaps, displeased, old sport?"

"I? I?" Weiner said softly. *"Nahrisher kint!* Except . . ." He scratched behind one of Levine's ears. "Gaah, I don't know. Is that for you? Is it, like they say in the quarterlies, your métier?"

His color deepening, Levine answered, "My piece on John Ford has been twice anthologized. Twice!"

"Granted, granted. Your grasp of the gap between low-middle and high-middle culture—perfect. Your cinematic depth analysis—I don't think I would want better. But when it comes to comic strips and such—unh, unh, man, you doan know shit!" And Weiner shook his head in the slow mournful rhythm of an old darkie.

Levine pursed his lips, as though sucking through a straw.

"Maybe I'm wrong," Weiner placated. "Maybe I am being less than fair. In which case, answer me this: Who used to say, in moments of *Angst,* 'Golly Moses, I got the whim whams all over'?"

"Rooney, Rooney, Little Annie Rooney!" Levine looked around as if for applause.

"Don Winslow of the Navy—his rank!"

"Commander!"

"Now the nemesis of Bim Gump!"

"Wait, wait! She wore a veil . . . she would always drug him . . . MADAM ZENDA!"

"And the protectors of Daddy Warbucks?"

"Punjab," Levine said, delightedly. "Punjab and the Asp."

"The Rinkeydinks," Weiner came back, relentless. "Who and from where?"

"From 'Winnie Winkle.' The club. And there was Perry, the little brother. And there was Spud. . . . There was Chink. . . ."

"And who else?"

"That's all."

"That's all?"

"I give up."

"Come on," Weiner exhorted. "One, one more. The most important one. With the hat. With the moron face. Who would always say, 'Perry, youse is a good boy'?"

"Ah, ah, I remember," said Levine, a sorrowful sweetness passing over his face. "I recall and recollect. Denny Dimwit. Bear in mind, however, that he was the last arrival, that his position with the Rinkeydinks was essentially a fringe position."

"If you get this one . . ." Weiner mumbled, squashed and submissive.

Beaming, Levine braced himself.

"I . . . want . . . the . . . name . . . the name of . . . THE GREEN HORNET'S DRIVER!"

Quietly, without fanfare, Levine answered, "Kato."

Then, drawing Levine's head down and dragging it from side to side, Weiner murmured, "*Ah leben uff der kepele!* Everything he knows, everything he remembers!"

"What is more," said Levine, far gone in triumph, "furthermore, I believe I am one of the few who is able yet to remember the 'Jack Armstrong' theme. In its entirety!"

"Gaah!"

"Rah, rah . . ." Levine began, a little flustered.

Whereupon Morroe offered up a "Boola boola boola boola."

Which Weiner matched with a grudging "Rah rah rah."

And drumming on the seats and slapping their thighs they joined voices:

"Wave the flag for Hudson High, boys,
Show them how we stand.
Ever shall our team be champions,
Known throughout the land!
  Rah rah boola boola boola boola!
  Boola boola boola boo rah rah rah!
Have you tried Wheaties?
They're the whole wheat with all of the bran.
Won't you try Wheaties?
For wheat is the best friend of man.
They're crispy and crunchy the whole year through,
Jack Armstrong never tires of them
And neither will you.
So just buy Wheaties,
The best breakfast food in the land!"

As they uttered a last "Boola!" and a burst of "Rahs!" there was thumping and thumping on the sun roof, and then the face of Ottensteen darkened a window.

He said, "Such sweet voices, such marvelous mourners. *Yoi*, Leslie, Labeleh, I envy you your friends."

A stillness descended over the car.

At last Weiner broke the silence with a "Harya, Reb Felix!"

"Look who's here, look who is here!" Levine chanted foolishly.

"Felix-*el*, Felix-*el*, what's doing and what's new?" cried Morroe in a rush of good feeling.

"You really want to know?" Ottensteen said, telling him with a frown that he would not be happy with the reply.

Morroe gave a submissive shrug.

"Because what's doing is that you're a big *yolt*. What's new—what's new is you sent *der alte* Ottensteen on a fool's errand to Washington Square Park, where, on his sick feet, he had to stand for thirty-three minutes by the clock until he realized he's dealing with a party that has very few brains and no common sense. That's all. Period."

"*I* misdirected? *I* told you Washington Square Park?" Morroe trumpeted.

"A mistake," Weiner said. "It happens."

"What then?" demanded Morroe, consumed with the injustice.

"Naturally, naturally . . . the tension of the moment . . . the bearing of bad news . . ." Levine was all moderation and easy affability. "And now let's give Felix room. Let's make him comfy-cozy and let us get started."

In a broken voice Ottensteen said, "Don't put yourself out, please. For *der alte* Ottensteen you're not going to have to bother."

"Gaah, Felix! Felix, gaah!" Weiner grabbed Ottensteen's arm and drew him half in through the window. "Honestly, I am surprised and ashamed."

"You're surprised?" With both fists Ottensteen knocked away Weiner's hand. "You don't need to be

surprised. And when it comes to shame—*der alte* Ottensteen isn't ashamed. *Der alte* Ottensteen is a simple,
simple person and individual. He knows how to love, he
knows how to hate. Thusly, when a Sholem Asch turns
M'shimid and no-good bastard, he don't talk to Sholem
Asch. And if the Germans kill six million of his people—
his people—he don't ride in German automobiles."

"On the face of it," interposed Levine, "flawless logic.
And yet . . ." He pretended to puzzle over the point.

Ottensteen peered at him as though through frosted
glass. He said, at length, "There is an old, a very old
saying: 'Who is a hero? He who keeps down a wise-
crack.' " He wheeled and strode away, his pants bellying
at the knees, his feet, in the high orthopedic shoes, turning out.

"*Shema Yisroel*," said Weiner.

"Let him go," said Levine.

"Whoosh, please, call him back," Morroe exhorted
them. "Aw, look, he's older, he's been sick. Call him
back, let us be the good ones."

"Gaah, sick, sick!" Weiner answered him coldly.
"He'll outlast all things, all systems. He'll—"

But Levine had already started the car, working wheel
and gear stick in abrupt jerky movements, racing for
the corner and jumping the light to scrape the curb
alongside of Ottensteen. Who played dumb at the in-
sistent croaking of the horn.

"Felix! Yay . . . y . . . y! Ottensteen . . . n . . . n!"
With the last air in his lungs Morroe cried into the confusion of the street.

Cupping his ear, Ottensteen went through an elaborate pantomime of looking and listening for the voice.

"For Leslie. Is it nice for Leslie? It's not nice!"

Slow, stooped, as though hindered by underbrush, Ottensteen trod to the car.

He said, "Only for Leslie."

"Only for Leslie!"

Then they moved and maneuvered and half-lifted Ottensteen into the car.

"A wonderful little automobile," he said, fingering the upholstery. "I bet they used here only the finest human skins. The finest!"

"Felix, Felix," Morroe scolded mildly. "*Yoishe*."

"No more," promised Ottensteen. "No more. Leslie already it can't help."

"Does anybody else feel hungry?" Weiner asked plaintively. "I had almost no breakfast."

Before they could reply Levine had broken into a fit of giggling. "Hoo-hah," he gasped. "I can't stop it. Help me. . . . *Aidez-moi!* Oh, choopie-bar-choopie, choopie-bar-choopie!"

7 ————————————————————

As they climbed the bridge to Brooklyn a train ground by with steel sounds, throwing grit and sparks. On the upgrade it labored, lagged, fell behind, and when they drew even Morroe saw a man raise a hand in silent greeting. He touched his forehead stealthily, holding the salute till his gaze was drawn elsewhere. To a face that somehow made him feel his heartbeat in his teeth and enraged him to fury. There was a likeness, but to whom, from where? Then, after a short tormented time, it occurred to him. The complexion, the beefiness, the look of command. And the way the fellow reclined, spreading over more than his share of seat. Why, put a badge and a gun on him and you'd have that cop from before, so free and easy with his hands!

And in this state Morroe saw other resemblances. As though, say, a half-dozen faces were allotted to each man's life, and these, suffering only the changes of race and style and tribe, follow him through every place and condition. So never mind if that little gent by the window wore a hearing aid and a pince-nez; give or take a feature, this was his father. Two cars down his Uncle Lazar opened and closed a small carton. And gross and mountainous in a housedress, Etta laughed at someone beyond his vision. While Landau, his boss, held a thermos jug and beach toys and danced a little girl on his knee. But what a child! What a sweetness, what a butterball, what a set of healthy cheeks on her! She waved, or seemed to wave at Morroe, and showed off her little play suit. Melting, he clapped hands at her, banged the window, made funny faces.

For which he drew the wrath of Ottensteen.

"Stop the jiggling," he was told. "You don't sit still for one second, you're getting me dizzy."

Swaying and swaying on the wire-mesh surface, with the wind beating like wings on the sun-roof folds, they made the descent to Brooklyn. Where Morroe got the momentary notion that the sun was hidden, the air a good ten degrees cooler. So a fish must feel, he thought, as it leaves its native water. They passed a movie house. Posters from his father's time. The marquee flashing only half its bulbs. Then a Spanish grocery, with green bananas. Then gypsies, mocking and mimicking behind a storefront. Then a block of sailor bars, where television was going full blast. Then whoosh! Under an el they turned against four-way traffic, punishing the tires. And again a turn. Into a country of churches. Minarets and cupolas. Angel armies over the doors, and every kind of Christ. The little shepherd smiling with prissy mouth. The athlete, powerfully muscled, trained for the burden of the cross. The Negro-headed, with his crown of thorns like a sharpy bowler. The wise-guy son, cool to his Mother Mary. The anatomist's cadaver, eviscerated, drained. And left and right, what cemeteries! The bitter green pallor of the trees. The birds, like clusters of fruit, weighing them down. The gates and the padlocks upon them enormous, as though to keep the dead within.

Now sickly pink housing projects. Brand-new, still with ground to be filled in. But already, bedding on the terraces, beach chairs, strollers and shopping carts blighting the lawns.

Now the Cantonese Gardens. Even at this hour, a line outside, three deep. Now Manny's Bakery, also jammed, now Zeigler's Dairy, now Congregation Agudah Anshri of Flatbush. Now the Byzantine archway of Maidstone Arms, thirty minutes (30), from Manhattan, convenient to all subways and shopping, still chce. three and three-and-a-half room apts., gas included. Now hedgelocked one- and two-family houses. Lethargic sprinklers. Kids gumming zwieback in wading pools. A profusion of nameplates. *M. Bardash, Dental Surgeon. J. Willis Grunebaum, Podiatrist. Gilbert Frankenthal, M.D., Hrs. 9–11, 3–5. Patents, Contracts, Eugene Himmel—Att'y at Law. By appointment only, Dr. Milton Lee Margolin.*

Suddenly Weiner, in throbbing sepulchral tones, declaimed, "Who knoweth Brooklyn? Stranger, oh, stranger, I answer you. I will answer you that only the hungry-hearted manswarm, the dreamers of dry dreams in the wind-spanned womblocked avenues called Pitkin and Church and Neptune and Ocean and Blake and Rogers and Tilden—" Then his eyes flickered and he smiled wanly. "Gaah, you know what?"

"What?" they cried. "WHAT?"

"Well, it comes to me that instead of turning off Flatbush Avenue Extension, we would have done better going straight and through the park, where, I think, somehow, somehow, you can pick up Ocean Parkway. In short, *chaverim*—"

A groan went round the car.

"—we are a little, little bit *fahrblunged*."

"Our navigator," fumed Levine. "Brooklyn-born and Brooklyn-bred. The boxball champ of Brownsville."

"That's right!" Weiner proclaimed. "But who ever left Brownsville? I was twelve before I—"

"Your fault," Levine flung over his shoulder to Morroe. "It behooved you, it was your, ah, prerogative to obtain detailed instructions."

In an ugly voice Morroe demanded that the car be stopped, that he be put off at the nearest subway station.

He was restrained by Ottensteen, who said, "This, this is America. Here you get lost, thank God you're not in a desert, you don't wander forty years. You stop. You go over, you ask like a *mensch*, you're put on the right track."

"A gas station," Weiner suggested. "With a nice rest-

120

room. Because I don't know about you guys. . . ." And he started to squirm.

"Good, good, I can fill her up," said Levine, relaxing. "But only Amoco," he warned.

In low gear they began to cruise and cruise, and the labor of the engine was like a repeated drawing upon Morroe's heart. His foot had fallen asleep; moving it, he knocked against Ottensteen's shoe. Receiving a knock in return. With interest. His own cry was lost in Weiner's "I wanna go . . . oh . . . oh! I hafta! Honest!" Then, half a block ahead, Morroe glimpsed a gas station.

But Levine refused to stop, saying, "Too small, much too small . . . They don't sell enough. Guck and goo in the pumps . . . Poison to one's valves . . ."

Near an old station wagon he pulled up and lightly beeped his horn at the rosy Germanic-looking lady inside. She had on a narrow fur piece; its little beast jaws gaped open as though from great pain or rage. "Say, oh, say, pardon me," he called, swishing his arm, "but what would be the best way of, ah, reaching Ocean Parkway? Ocean Parkway!"

She stared long at them. And clutched the fur piece like an amulet.

"The Parkway . . . Ocean Parkway . . ." Levine sang, blinking, straining forward his smooth schoolboy face.

Ring-cluttered fingers glinted. And the window was rolled up against them.

"So, so many Hamans," said Ottensteen when they got going. "So many Hamans and only one Purim."

Again now Morroe pointed out a gas station. A big

one, with many pumps, with a truck at that very moment making delivery.

Snippily he was told that he needed a remedial reading course, that they must wait for an Amoco.

"From the same hole in the ground," Morroe replied. "Into the same pipe."

"Murderer!" hissed Weiner despairingly. "Enemy of mankind!"

Grudging and graceless, Levine nevertheless gave in. He downshifted, he signaled with blinker, then profusely with hand, and gently, gently, eased out for the wide U turn.

There was no noise and next to no impact. There was only the taxi looming close, mountainous, shutting out the colors of the day with its hot reds and yellows.

His mouth warped, his eyes immense, demented, Levine began to sigh and whimper and flail his arms like a dreamer. "Ah . . . ah . . ." he brought out. "Fuggin-bastard!"

"That expression," Weiner began to speculate. "Not since junior high. Not since Frankie Esposito—"

To Weiner, Morroe said, "Shhh, shhh." And to Levine, "Holly, naah! Naah, Holly! How are you carrying on? Whoosh! Over what? Nothing happened. You'll get out and you'll see it's nothing."

Levine shut his eyes and pressed the lids as if to blind himself.

A fright went through Morroe, and he considered first a few smacks across Levine's face, then a hard shaking. Instead he put the back of a hand to Levine's forehead and in a little voice he said, "You want me, me to go out, to see and let you know what's what? You want?"

One eye opened, spun helplessly like a wheel in a rut. And Levine spread his arms as though in benediction.

Squeezing and forcing with his shoulders, whacking his head on the windshield, Morroe got himself past Levine and into the street. After him came Ottensteen, who began to stomp around and around the car while he worked them over. "*Der alte* Ottensteen, what does he know? He's stubborn, he's opinionated, he wants only to make trouble. Pay no attention, buy, buy German cars. Oh, boy, he's happy, he's overjoyed. And he says—and *how* he says, 'Good for you, good for you!'"

Quicker and angrier grew his steps as he gave them to understand that even from the grave Hitler would deal them blows, now and forever. And meanwhile Morroe looked over the damage, which could have been worse, but was bad enough. Mercifully, he said, "Whoosh, a dib here and a dab there. One side of the bumper—and what do I know about cars?—you may, may just have to get it straightened. Then the signal light . . . the bulb is gone. That and the left-rear hubcap. The total, the entirety. All in all, how much could it possibly cost?"

A little revived, Levine grunted, "It'll cost. . . . It will cost."

"You should make sure it costs," Ottensteen said, addressing heaven. "You should soak and soak him. A penny, that's all, one penny for every grain of sand in *Eretz Yisroel.*"

Then an enormous quiet settled upon them as the cab driver, taking his time, padded over. He was on the short side, but of broad, stocky build. Gold crowns showed up in his one-sided bite, his hair was plentiful, black and tufted like Persian lamb, and a mishealed scar aggravated the flesh over his button eyes. There was a spring and a weave to his walk, and he held his hands chest-high, as though sheltering himself from punches. Immediately Morroe cast him for the brute order, a foulmouth, a roughhouse artist and a dog in his heart.

Up close he put a dead butt to his lips. Then he slouched against a fender, blew on his knuckles and to nobody in particular said, "You Jewish?"

His legs braced to spring, Morroe answered for all, declaring that he owed him no accounting, that such matters should cause him no loss of sleep.

"Yuhshamed?"

"Find out from me!" shrilled Ottensteen. "From *der alte* Ottensteen!"

"That'sa boy!" the driver cried with a rejoicing smile. "Now lemme tell yuh something." Grave again, he leveled his brows at Levine. "I don't know what kinda Jew you are. Maybe you fast all day Yom Kippur, maybe you don't miss a *Yiskor* for your Mom and Dad. Or maybe you look at it the way I look at it. Yuh figure, wahah, it's all a crockashit. Next to economic factors what caused all the war and made all the hate? Religion. Right? And what's religion? Oi-oi-oi and singsong? Crap, that's crap. It's making the other guy feel nice inside. It's treating him like he's also a person. Right?"

"That's how I look at it," said Morroe.

"Very, very nicely put," said Ottensteen.

"I thought, I had the thought of waxing it yesterday.

124

And something stopped me . . . something . . ." Levine was half-sobbing.

Then the driver lit his butt, saying, "I'll show you my kinda guy. I have a boss, a ginzo—though he speaks a great Jewish. *Ver geharget, shwartzer, baitzim, pupek,* and he even knows "*Eli, Eli*"! So a year and a half he keeps promising, 'I go to Italy, you get a present.' So he goes and I get. Can you see?" He bent forward and a large silver medal swung free of his flecked sport shirt. "Saint Francis. I need it? Like a sty in my eye. You get another person, no character, he'd say, 'That's a helluva *chutzpah.* I don't give you no *Mogen David,* what are you asking me to go against my religion?' My kinda guy—he wears it. He figures, let every day be Brotherhood Week. Not to hurt the next one. That's human feeling and toleration. That's religion. Right?"

"License and registration," exclaimed Levine, stumbling with weakened legs from the car. "License and registration."

Making his face dangerous as he spit away his butt, the driver said, "Jocko, you got *mazel.* Why you got *mazel?* Because I feel good. I feel good, for three reasons." He ticked them off on his rough-skinned fingers. "One, my Milton is gonna bellhop at Scaroon Manor. Where even a busboy comes home with fifteen, eighteen hundred. Two, the next four-and-a-half rooms in my building I absolutely get. Three, my wife gave herself the *Reader's Digest* cancer test and she felt a little lump in her breast. All week we're praying they won't have to cut. Then yesterday we see the biggest man at Mount Sinai. Einfeld. Thirty dollars a first visit. So what? Some-

125

times a penny is a dollar, sometimes a dollar is a penny. Right? He squeezes her once, twice, finished. I kid him, 'Doc, don't enjoy it too much!' In a second he knew. 'Goodbye and good luck,' he tells us. 'It's only a swollen gland.'"

"Never mind, never mind," said Ottensteen. "You did absolutely right, you should watch over a wife."

And Morroe gave out a sound of confirmation, adding, "With things like that you don't kid around."

Meanwhile Levine scribbled and scribbled on old envelopes, growling under his breath the name of the street, the position of traffic lights, the nature of his damage, the time of day. Suddenly he rose on his toes and whistled and hissed with a dry mouth. A patrol car slowed, then dodged around the corner. In a towering rage he cried, "Ah, ah, they certainly saw me! Never mind. I shall call the nearest precinct. Or better—still better!—take this stupid moron down and make a citizen's arrest."

His collar was held and smoothed with mock fastidiousness by the driver. Who, mildly protesting, inquired, "Whaddaya getting steam up? For what? WhaddamI a 'stupid moron'!"

"My nomenclature offends you?" Levine laughed mirthlessly. "That's . . . too . . . fucking . . . bad!"

"Y'hear? Hey!" The driver entered his plea with the others. "I walk over a gentleman. I don't raise my voice, I don't lift my hand. And right away—'fuck'!"

"License and registration . . . license and registration . . ."

"You got time, Jocko. You'll wait."

"Now."

"When I hear apologies, Jocko. When I get some human relations."

Levine, setting his teeth, said, "This minute."

The driver yawned, folded his arms and made muscles bulge.

"Vehicular homicide." Levine's glance wandered off cunningly. "Isn't there, is there not, some such charge on the books?"

At this the driver clicked his tongue. With clasped hands and raised shoulders he parodied confusion. Then awe. Then fear.

"You find this comical?" Levine blared. "You think I'm not serious?"

"What I think?" the driver asked almost mournfully. "What I think is . . . you're a *putz*. *P, U, T, Z!*"

"Gaah! Not nice," cried Weiner, charging out of the car and grabbing hold of them. "One intellectual should call another intellectual a *putz!*"

"Because I'm not a professional," the driver all but wept, "that's why he opens a mouth on me? You wanna go blind in an eye? That's how I wanted to hack. Eighty-eights I got in all my regents, except once—"

"He's nobody's dope," Ottensteen avowed. "I'll bet you, I'll give a guarantee, he wouldn't buy a German automobile."

"The Depression was my fault. Right? I gave my Pop water in the blood. So I shouldn't have it too good. So I should leave school and sell Eskimo Pies up and down Coney Island. So the cops should lay for me under the boardwalk and dump out my dry ice."

Relentless, inflexible, Levine droned, "License and registration . . . license and registration."

"What am I asking? I don't ask sympathy. Only respect. Only that I should be spoken to like I'm a mother's child."

As though spitting hairs Levine said, "I should respect you? You go into me and I should respect you? You are a psychopath—you sonofabitch!"

"He wants a pregnant lip!" the driver cried out, shoving Levine. "He's cruising for a bruising!"

But Weiner stepped forward, drew the driver's arm taut against his side and leaned his weight upon him. "Gaah, don't be a Shmohawk," he muttered up close to his ear. "He has an in with The Syndicate. He runs with the Trilling bunch."

Though he snorted and pulled impressively, the driver reflected on this for a moment. "So what?" he protested finally. "I want, I go into that candy store, I call up Izzy Farina, he comes down in ten minutes—ten minutes. He took on tougher for me. To hell with it. That's not my kinda guy. Like when I had basic at Fort Meade there was this hillbilly, Armbruster. Before he got drafted he didn't know how to flush a toilet even. He knew only he didn't like Jews. He'd call me 'Yankel.' Once is a joke, twice is a joke. The third time I warn him. 'Respect!' The same way I tell your *putz* pal. A buddy I had from New York, he wansa handle him for me. Julie Liss—he used to be a lifeguard. And he was built. Powerful! I tell him, 'Never mind, Julie.' And I wait and I hold myself back till the last night, till we're shipping out. And I say, 'Armbruster, let's go to the latrine, let's take a pee together.' So he gets up, he goes. So I give him a little lesson in human relations. So I nearly tear his head off. You know what I say to him when I finish? I say to him, 'Now I won't get sore. Now you want, anytime now, you can call me Yankel.' "

Then Levine scowled and swaggered and thumped his chest. Then he lowered his brow and drew in his neck and went, "Buh-buh-buh. Buh-buh-buh-buh!"

"Again!" the driver ordered, shouldering Weiner aside. "You should do that once more. Just once more!"

"Ah, buh-buh-buh. And once again, buh-buh-buh-buh," Levine bayed lyrically.

"No communication," brooded Weiner. "Between the arts, no communication."

"Take off the ring." Already the driver was doing a stamping dance and throwing short stage punches.

"You take off, remove, the watch."

"When you take off the ring I take off the watch."

"Holly, hey, Holly!" Morroe sought to distract. "I'm looking at the hubcap again. You know, it's barely, barely touched?"

"The fists, the fists, right away with the fists," said Ottensteen. "Jewish boys . . ."

"You're chickenshit," the driver told Levine.

"Chickenshit. Ah, buh-buh-buh-buh," parried Levine, with a grimace of self-congratulation.

"Take off the ring!"

"You want me to take it off? That is what you want?" And Levine gave it over to Morroe. "All right. All right, ratbastard."

But Weiner heaved against them, saying, "Why not

fight, sort of, with open hands, slapping like. Stomach is five points, face counts for ten, and whoever gets fifty first wins. That's how we did it in P.S. 182."

"Very good, wonderful!" Morroe burst in. "This, now this appeals to me. A little friendly boxing."

It was then the driver struck. A clumsy overhand smash falling high upon the nose of Levine. Who, immediately squirting blood, charged in nonetheless, yelling, "That's the last one he's getting off, from me! *The* last one!" From somewhere inside his jacket there was the sound of a seam splitting, his tie was lashing his face and one shoe had slipped down his heel. Both feinted clumsily. More by accident than skill Levine scored on the driver's cheek; at the wet smack he dropped his hands and gasped, "Pardon me . . ."

"Ibitmytunk," the driver roared huskily.

"Peroxide," Morroe suggested. "One part peroxide to three, make it four parts water. A gargle . . ."

Dead white, the driver blundered against Levine. He said, "In my book you're still *putz*."

Levine made a dumb sign, emitted a noise like gagging and plunged in. He hooked an arm around the driver's neck and kicked and butted with deadly intent, taking fist flurries in the belly. The driver lifted him off the ground, seeking to slam him against the car. Levine hung on as Weiner "heeyahed" and "whoooeed" and pounded an imaginary Stetson. Suddenly his nose gave a short burst of blood. He sniffled and spat and let go. Without much spirit the driver grabbed, held and clinched. He caught at Levine's tie, forcing his head down. While Levine, falling to one knee, hung upon the driver's belt buckle, yanking his pants askew and exposing the wide elastic web of his jockey shorts.

"You cocksucker, let go my belt!" the driver demanded.

To which Levine replied, "Let go my tie, you lousy fuck, I'll let go, release, your belt."

And now Weiner rushed forward. "You had a nice fight. . . . You both looked good. . . . You got it out of your systems. . . . So it's all over. . . . Make nice."

Levine relinquished his hold. The driver followed suit and, doctor-like, touched Levine's nose. "Did we need this?" he chided. "Foowa? For the insurance companies? For monopolated capitalism?"

"Go, go ahead," said Ottensteen. "Who told you stop? Spill some more Jewish blood."

Through the folds of his staining handkerchief, Levine insisted that he had always been an easy bleeder, that, objectively and appearances notwithstanding, he had given, returned, as much, fully as much as he had gotten.

"He's okay, this boy." Along ribs and shoulders and biceps the driver felt Levine. "I got gloves in the house, you'll come over, we'll work out."

And one by one he had them promise that before the summer was out they would arrange to meet, they would take lockers at the handball courts or fish for fluke and flounder in the waters off Sheepshead Bay.

Next he made a ceremonious exchange of license and registration with Levine. He spread out also his army discharge papers, his social security card and a B'nai

B'rith newsletter. He hinted, then he gave absolute guarantee, that from this scrape Levine would lose nothing. Did Levine have a lawyer? A specialist in accident cases? If not, he recommended Coniff, on Court Street. Coniff the *Goniff*. Out of a cracked sidewalk, a rusty nail, a cigarette burn, a piece of bad wiring, he mounted claims for thousands. Let two A & P shopping carts collide and a son went through medical school.

"Heaven and earth—and swindle," said Ottensteen.

"I *was* contemplating a new bumper," mused Levine.

"Moey meets Izzy—" Weiner chuckled and sputtered "—Moey meets Izzy and he says, 'Izzy, hey, Izzy, so how was by you the fire?' And Izzy says, '*Shah, shah,* its tomorrow!' "

His lips thinning, the driver asked, "Whaddaya have to make em Izzy and Moey? That kind you find everywhere. By all races and faiths."

"Poor taste," Morroe hastened to say.

"He's one hundred per cent right," Ottensteen insisted.

"I imagine I should check the wheel alignment," said Levine. "These things can be tricky, unpredictable, they—"

"*Putz,* hey, *putz!*" The driver clasped Levine around the shoulders and gently scrutinized him. "Tomorrow you see Coniff. Let *him* take care. Let *him* aggravate."

Suddenly he threw himself into a trot, launching lefts and rights all the way to the cab. And puffed back brandishing a bottle of Imperial.

"For human relations," he said. "For everybody to be a mother's child."

132

"From your lips to God's ear," said Ottensteen, the first to drink. Next was Weiner, showing off with three long pulls at the bottle. Then Levine. Then Morroe, who silently invoked the name of Leslie and swallowed down his share. And more.

8 ——————————————————————————

THEY WERE NOT yet safely past the hot and heavy traffic of Grand Army Plaza, where three times Levine had stalled, when Weiner began to carry on.

Like one who mounts a pulpit he mounted his seat, tilted crazily out of the open roof and shattered the air with a "*Gevald!*"

So perched, he smiled down upon a Cadillac pink as a healthy scalp and cried, "Love! God is Love!"

The driver, a narrow-faced, florid person, answered him, "Hit the next lamppost, dog!"

"Vomitface, hey, dutyhead!" Weiner rubbed a "Shame . . . shame," on his fingers, staggered and fell back to the seat. With great effort he turned toward Ottensteen and Morroe and whimpered, "We must love one another or die. Die . . . die . . . Yi-dy-diddle-dy . . ."

A numbness over his tongue, a dark confusion in his mind, Morroe nodded and nodded and said, "Our gang . . . Our gang . . ."

While Ottensteen, swaying, slowly swaying, sang:

"Ich bin ah mommeh—
Aber vee iz mein kind?"

"Hey, man," said Weiner, snapping his fingers and bugging his eyes, "dat, dat dere's a *mommeh?*"

"He a *mommeh?"* In an atrocious falsetto Levine responded to cue.

"Dat wot ah heerd him say, *neshoma.*"

"Well, den, you answer me a *kashe,* man."

"Well, den you put it to me, *zeeskait.*"

"Well, ef dat dere's a *mommeh* . . ."

"Dat, dat his contention. . . ."

"Well, den, where his *kind?*"

Then, whoosh!

Ottensteen hiccuped, flinched and burst into shameless tears.

"One Leslie." Ottensteen kissed his fingertips. "One only Labeleh."

"A 'riginal." There was a gummy tension in Morroe's breathing and he was having trouble with his words. "Effthing he came up with, a style, a poynview."

"Definitely, definitely," Levine concurred. "A secondary talent of the highest order."

Ottensteen took Morroe's hand in both his own. He opened it, he studied the palm as though for signs and portents, and he said finally, "In Silver's Baths I warned him. Like a person gets a flashing, an intuition. Like God turns *der alte* Ottensteen into his mouthpiece. I said when we were getting undressed—I said, 'Labeleh, please, please don't take insult if I should tell you something. But I want you to make it your business to go about losing a little bit of weight. The doctors, the experts, warn every time about heart and weight and pressure. And for your size you are carrying around an excess. *Gedenk. Gedenk, gedenk, gedenk!*' "

He put aside Morroe's hand and honked like a goose into his handkerchief.

And Morroe sank back, a daffy smile on his face. The refulgent, open sky burned on him, and he allowed himself to faint a little. His body was at rest, yet he felt as though he had been clubbed to death. His lips were still, yet he felt he was screaming. Against that rancid, sour thing, that abomination rising like smoke in the depths of his breast. The languor that could not be borne, the torpor that was dragging him far out and past all caring.

Leslie, he begged, intercede for me.

I am no big intellect. I am no bargain. I watch too much television. I read, but I do not retain. I am not lost, exactly, but still I am nowhere. I am the servant of no great end. I follow the recommendations of the *Consumer's Research Bulletin.*

But do me this favor, anyway. Keep them off. For they hem me in from all sides now. They wait deep in the dark. They put in my mouth the taste of darkness.

They set grief and despair upon me like savage dogs. They give me queer feelings, they get me all balled up. When I turn my head or open an eye they will rip me with tooth and claw. They will throw me from awful heights. They will drown me in a drop of water. They will put me in a grave.

And then he got a whiff of far-off ocean.

And then a kid cried, "Heygeddaball! Ladymissus, byafut!"

And then a splash of heartburn. Which he welcomed. Which he gave in to utterly, thinking, Let it be my payment, let it forestall worse, let it only dispel what hangs over me. Over us. And he woke himself. And he looked upon the boys, and for an instant felt love, such love that it was beyond sustaining, and something inside broke for them. "Our gang," he muttered again. "Our gang."

But they were busy telling old tales of Leslie.

How on Gandhi's death he had given up meat and sex, then only meat, for two weeks.

How he planted himself before a Sutton Place building and unto the eighteenth story screamed, "Ma, throw me down a nickel! Ma!"

How at a writer's workshop in Utah he had lectured, with copious readings, on *Lorna Doone*.

How he had made them play the Dostoyevsky Game, where they would one by one confess their most shameful and sordid acts.

How he worshiped the White Goddess. How he was immersed in the destructive element. How he would indulge himself with chromatic harmonicas, classical guitars, Borsalino hats, meerschaum pipes, tropical fish, Swiss chocolates, Bing cherries out of season.

And racing deeper and deeper into the heart of the park, they spoke of their last moments with him.

In a fun shop, where he had bought a fake dog turd and a Jimmy Dean mask.

At the Everyman School, where he had lectured on *Celine: The Pornography of the Absolute.*

Up and down the streets of Williamsburg, seeking out Hasidim, who had fled from him as from a plague.

"Hector's . . ." Morroe started to say, then bit his tongue. But he could not hold back the recollection, though it drenched him with shame. Last January or February, whenever it was, Leslie had barged into his office and dragged him down for a long lunch. During his busiest period. During the middle, make it the peak, of the fall campaign, when the fund-raisers followed you into the men's room and hustled you from the stalls. Leslie, between grants, had asked about jobs. But Morroe knew of nothing. That was the truth, the honest truth, though his distracted, peevish air might have seemed a rebuff, the mark of a small spirit. Also, he had insisted, perhaps a little pointedly, on going to Hector's Cafeteria. Figuring he would most likely be stuck with the check. And he had been, too.

"Look, look!" Ottensteen turned on him. *"Der id-yutt!"*

"Shah. Shahshahshahshahshah," Morroe whispered. But under cover of his daffy grin he was saying to Leslie, What did you want and what did you expect?

That you should be the *boulevardier,* the free spirit, the late riser, and I the workhorse of the world? Why? Because I can't write a review or a little story? Did that make you the only one with special needs and moods and a claim against the world?

Whoosh!

He expelled an enormous sigh and his head, sliding along the seat, flopped to an uneasy rest near Ottensteen's shoulder.

"*Nu,* flaming youth!" cried Ottensteen. "Big shot drinker!" Yet he smiled and stirred and gave up an inch or two of comfort.

Now there was a lake, looking cool and green and radiant, as if reflected in enamel.

Now horses galloped and clopped and sent dust mingling with the steam of their dung.

Now the wind carried monkey-house gibber and the ripping snore of lions.

Now children, multitudes beyond tally. And the din, the infernal din. Like an army of beaters, like a stockyard. It punished every part of him, it hampered his breath and made his teeth ache at their roots.

And out of the general tumult some cries came to him as though from the furthest reaches of pain.

"*Harry, he's cheesing, Harry!*"

"*You spit on the bubbee! The bubbee you spit on!*"

"*Make a siss!*"

"*Don't, DON'T DON'T DON'T open a big mouth!*"

"*Go nice to Uncle Al. . . . Nice, Nice!*"

"*Everything by her is no and no and no!*"

"*Walk over and hit him back!*"

Now there was a burst of benches and trees, then only benches, and the park rushed to a sudden end.

"Alert, attention, keep watch everyone," Levine instructed, like a nervous scoutmaster. "Any moment, any block now!"

Ottensteen, with a dour squint, said, "What a section, what faces and types! That one there, the fatso—look, look, at him, the assistant manager of the world!"

But Morroe, broken-backed, dripping sweat, gave a low growl and pointed. And beyond his finger was the chapel, a little diamond of a building, its canopy silky-white, with broad green stripes and fringes like a prayer shawl, its stained glass orange and black and blue like the inside of a flame. Upon the runner of rich red carpet a lion of Judah was embroidered; the copper handles on the double doors were molded like the tablets of the law; even the young maples that lined the street seemed trimmed and pruned to the shape of menorahs.

"Yoi!" rumbled Ottensteen, shedding more tears. "It's a dream, it's a farce, it's make-believe." And coarsely he began to berate God, calling Him old whore, assassin and two-faced hypocrite.

Then Levine sounded his horn and shouted "Whoopee!" For there was a spot, a perfect spot, right in front of the chapel.

While he parked, the others entered. In the half-light of the foyer they beheld only a skinny little man running a damp rag over the mirrors and Venetian blinds. He was far from a youngster, and one eye was clouded by cataracts. Yet he seemed happy for the work; whatever he touched gleamed.

"Is it on already?" Ottensteen asked, shuffling his enormous shoes on the cork floor.

"Too much you didn't miss. I'll show you in by the side, you shouldn't interrupt the rabbi."

Along a curvy corridor he led them, down three steps, three more, then past stacks and stacks of folding chairs. He said, "Where the drapes are, go straight. Otherwise you could end up . . . never mind where."

They walked dumbly on. But suddenly he called them back, waving some black stuff at them. "Here is strictly semiorthodox. Here you have to have a *yarmalke.*"

Imperious, autocratic, Ottensteen replied, "To me it's a nonsense, to my friends it's a nonsense and to the deceased a double nonsense!"

"Reshpec' . . ." Morroe declared.

"I want to see how it looks on him," said Weiner. "Let's see!" He snatched one and mounted it like a college boy's beanie upon Ottensteen's head.

"I have an iron *no!*" Ottensteen informed him, plucking at the *yarmalke.* But Weiner clamped his hand upon it, and they were swaying back and forth as Levine came hurrying up.

"Does anyone have a tissue or a clean handkerchief?" he asked in panic. "I think my nose is bleeding again."

9 ————————————————————————

"GAAH, IT'S SO CROWDED. Did you ever expect such a crowd?"

"They most likely ran a notice in the Yiddish press. And from his family alone . . ."

"Whoosh, I see his father. Isn't that his father?"

"Where do you see?"

"Way, way up front. In the straw hat. Oh, my, oh, hold on to him, hold on, he's going to faint."

Two rows down an elderly gent wearing a white duck jacket twisted around, tapping and tapping his lips. And Morroe mouthed "Excuse . . ."

The rabbi, a large moon-faced man with bifocals and only the smallest of beards, then said, "Please rise, the entire congregation." While he prayed in swift sonorous Hebrew, ushers passed bunches of booklets from pew to pew. Presently the rabbi made a sign to sit. "Open to page four," he instructed, "where the print is big."

He read, "Extolled and hallowed be the name of God throughout the world which He has established according to His will. And may He speedily create His kingdom of righteousness on earth. Amen."

He was answered, "Praised be His glorious name unto all eternity."

Above all others the voice of Ottensteen soared.

"You know who the rabbi must be?" whispered Weiner. "That must be Leslie's cousin. That's Julian Bruckner."

"The math genius?" Levine waved the notion away. "I say yes."

"What are you talking about? From St. Paul?"

"*Schmuck*, they have planes. He—"

"Sharrup!" hissed the elderly gent.

The rabbi now took a step away from his lectern and looked intently at the coffin, as though seeking a cue. He nodded vigorously four or five times, after which he said, "Bereaved family and friends, we live in a time, a generation, a society when it's supposed to be not nice to belly-ache over the pain and trouble of living. Feel, but don't cry, take punishment, but don't show. Keep everything nice, neat, under control. And no details. 'How was the day?' says the wife when you go home. 'A day like a day,' you tell her. Never mind that where you buy the paper every morning you got shortchanged. Never mind that you had a little bit of nastiness with this one

143

or that one in the place which gave you a terrible sour stomach, or on the elevator going down the boss said such a cold good night. Nobody is interested in the routine and the petty. Like in the movies or the television a person might say, 'I feel hungry, I think I'll go eat,' and the next thing you see him smile and take out a cigar and say, 'Oh, what a good meal I had.' Who cares in case he had to wait ten minutes for a table, and who wants to know that he found dirt in the napkin? Or if he's supposed to die, how does he die? I assure you, dear friends, you don't see him in a hospital with tubes sticking up his nose and getting needles and painful tests and doctors coming back and forth for the consultations. He cracks a little joke, he closes his eyes, and goodbye and good luck. Better than that, how many times—how many, many times!—you're walking where there are children and one falls down and with tears runs to the mother. 'Mommy, Mommy, I hurt myself.' Poor thing, what it gets is not a kiss and a cuddle, but a sock across the face. All right, you have to teach not to be a wild Indian and to cross a street looking on both sides. The Talmud says, 'Blessed is the hand, no matter how hard and heavy, which instructs in a good thing.' Except here, what is the mother's purpose and principle? Only to show the kid it should keep everything inside. It should have one tough face for everything. That's today's living, and everybody is a Humphrey Bogart."

"He's making a production," commented Weiner.

"Definitely overblown," murmured Levine.

"A golden mouthpiece," Ottensteen declared.

The rabbi coughed, and in the cough his next few

words were swallowed. ". . . life and death . . ." He hacked and rasped and then, finding breath, continued in a louder voice. "Life and death no one cares about like they used to. I remember once upon a time you celebrated a birth and you mourned a death, and in between you recognized, clear-cut and simple, you were growing older, you were aging and dying every minute. A religious Jew would have his burial cloth, his shroud right next to where he kept his *tallith*. This way he was reminded that he had no written agreement with God, that he couldn't guarantee today what he would be tomorrow. And when he went people would carry on, the oldest and the youngest, and no one was ashamed to make a scene and no one withheld himself. Nowadays—nowadays they can't wait to bury and forget. You dassn't spend an extra second, you dassn't say an extra word. 'Rabbi, please go easy, my wife has sick nerves. . . .' 'Rabbi, you shouldn't be insulted, but do everybody a favor, make it quick, simple and quick. . . .' "

Humbling his back and deeply bowing his head, Morroe fell into thoughts of his mother. He had been roller skating when she died, and they had called him in from the streets. His father, made vicious and a little crazy for the moment, struck out at him because he had been slow to answer. But Uncle Lazar dodged between them, taking the blows upon himself with folded arms. Till his father, shamed, in tears, reeled to the bathroom and bolted the door.

Then Uncle Lazar took his hand and led him to where his mother lay. Neighbor women were wetting her down with sponges and combing and braiding her hair. "Go give a kiss," said Uncle Lazar. Locking his breath and closing his eyes he bent to her, feeling a stir and rise, an emanation under his lips, as though from the last atrocious assault of a pain which had not yet consumed itself. Then he gulped air and opened his eyes just enough to see; and in the blurred moment he saw in the face of his mother the face of a foe.

He had stared and stared, and soon found nothing, really, to surprise him, nothing prodigious occurring in his heart. It was as though he had been made to see her often dead, only now more clearly than at any time before.

They took him next door later and fed him. Each woman ran in and out with different dishes and forced upon him favorites and specialties. There were eggs and onions browned in chicken fat. There were cold pickled fish and sweetbreads and tiny meatballs in sweet-and-sour sauce. There were celery and olives and red and white radishes. There was brisket of beef to which clung onion shreds and barley. There was seltzer and every kind of tonic and soda and boxes of ginger snaps and chocolate wafers and Fig Newtons.

He had eaten and eaten with a gusto hunger alone could not explain. Down to the last strand of soup green. Sucking the centers out of the marrow bones. But what a thing to recall! What a stupid thing! When the name of their old street escaped him, even the cemetery in which his mother lay!

"And the body is telling you every second how you have it too good."

The rabbi's voice prodded the edges of his thought.

"Did you look a little too long and with too much pleasure at the grandchildren? Take a few palpitations. Did the wife pick up a nice bedspread and covers for the couch? Let her have a low back pain. Did you get a particularly first-class haircut from the barber? Here, here's a cavity, or a little piece off the bridgework. Did you get a perfect fit in a cheap suit right off the rack? Pay for it with acid in the stomach and a trifle too much albumen and sugar in the blood. Did the father-in-law send a postal from Miami and a box of mixed fruits? Give him a stone in the kidney, a swelling in the prostate."

Saying this, the rabbi meditated silently for a while, pressing and grinding against the lectern in a way that must have been brutal against his bones.

He pulled a handful of tissues from somewhere in his sagging pocket, patted his mouth and said further, "Talk to the body and you talk to an enemy. Argue and back-talk with the cop on the beat and the good God in heaven, with the hoodlum who wants your money and the murderer who wants your life. Kid it along a little. Promise how you'll take better care of it, staying out of drafts, no lifting and bending, avoiding spicy foods. You'll cut down and you'll build up. You won't go in on Saturday, you'll take more taxis, you'll think a hundred and ten times before you raise your voice or climb a little flight. Plead with it. Tell it how you're special and unique, a person who likes one soap and not another, who has to get himself into a certain posture before you fall asleep and can't bear if the newspaper isn't folded your particular way. Never mind, never mind, says the body. I'm not interested. With me you cut no ice, with me you're only a bad blood vessel, a deficiency in the heart, a spot on the lung, a swelling on a gland, an abscess they can't heal. When I get impatient, when I get irritated and give the say-so you'll be only a thing. I'll push, you'll fall. And where you fall you'll lie. . . ."

Weiner smirked.

Levine giggled.

Ottensteen clicked and clicked with his tongue.

"Felix, can you see?" said Morroe. "From where you are? By the coffin, on the right—is that Inez?"

His voice waning, his intonation altered, the rabbi said, "*In* the commentary of Rabbi Menahem *ben* Solomon Ha-Meiri he tells us that even though—*even* though punishment full and final is handed out in the world to come, *still* in all every person *and* individual gets a taste and sniff of his punishment *in* this world, in this life. Why does he say punishment and not reward? He says punishment because all who are *born* are born to die *and* all who die are called up to a judg*ment*. Whether you like it or not, nobody asks. For *every* little action and every little thought, also for what you didn't do *and* didn't think the Almighty *will* weigh *and* measure. *In* this world, in this life. You have to expect it, you have to live with it, on top of your other troubles. *That* on the Day of Judgment *in* the Valley of Jehoshaphat you'll be called up. *Either* to everlasting life *or* to such a shaming there's no imagining *how* terrible."

Morroe softly asked, "Can you see? Can you make out? Is that Inez?"

"Leave me alone," said Ottensteen, wiping tears away. "With my sick eyes."

148

Item by item, the rabbi listed the punishments of the sinner. The long-dead and the unborn would have nothing to do with him. He would seek to confess his wickedness, but he would grow dumb. At the gates of Gehenna imps would afflict him, as well as vast armies of demons who would pull him from the right and from the left. They would turn him into a snake and cause him to shed his skin. He would become as a leaf, shivering in the wind. In his heart would be unbridled desire, but no way to appease it. Thirty times thirty times would his seed be cursed. By kin and next of kin unto thirty times thirty generations, who would chant the Chapter of Curses. He would be sent forth as a dybbuk, and his name added to the Book of Evil. All this and a lot more through eternity, till the end of days, and only after the battle of Armageddon, when the ram's horn would blow and there would be drums and dancing in the street for the Messiah.

"For such reasons and others which this is not the place to go into it's common sense that a man ought to do whatever he can to get everlasting life. He has to please God, and there's no one way of pleasing God— because what kind of God would it be that you pleased in only one way? Some do it by teaching, some do it by learning, another by fasting and still another by eating. Which is why the zaddik of Lublin used to say, 'Everyone should see what way his heart draws him to, and then he should choose this way with all his might.' Bereaved family and friends, in my opinion—and I don't say it because it's the occasion—the too-recently departed was such a person."

"Hey, man," murmured Weiner, "duz you go 'long wid de za-deek ob Lo-oh-balin?"

Behind a handkerchief Levine replied, "Uh-*uh*. Ah pussonally follows de teachins ob de ma-ha-geed ob Vilna."

And the rabbi continued, "He had very high moral and intellectual qualities which gave him an interest in everything and in everything a desire to ex-cel. Where there was a subject he came across he would read up— this I myself testify. About certain parts of Jewish custom and history he forgot more than I'll maybe ever know. In any argument he could hold his own. His father tells me he used to write away to all the congressmen for pamphlets and little packets of seeds, and that he once got a letter signed by Senator La Follette and a special pass he could use when he wanted to come to Washington, D.C. From nothing he made little airplanes. Before *bar mitzvah* he went into a newspaper contest on why we need the League of Nations and he won one of the top prizes. There was even a scandal; they found out his age, that he was such a kid, and they didn't believe. His parents had to make a special trip with him down to the office and sign statements he was the author and he got absolutely no help. In the libraries he became a terrible nuisance. They kept him because of rules only in the children's section and he would pester grownups they should get him books he really wasn't permitted. From what I understand he also had an interest in chess, a high talent, and if he had developed it he might have made a name—"

But he had no grounding in the social sciences, Morroe was thinking. Philosophy he was very strong on, especially logic, and literature goes without saying. But in history I could buy and sell him.

"We shouldn't think of him as only a book reader. He was a New York boy, an American boy, a boy from our century, and being such means Babe Ruth and the Katzenjammer Kids and Tar-*zan* of the Apes and chewing gum and bad marks in conduct and talking fresh and not paying attention. When he wanted he had a marvelous head for Talmud Torah, except that he very seldom wanted and gave the *rebbe* trouble. He would get moods and not want to dress up, though his parents provided him the finest clothes. Instead of carrying a briefcase he would tie around his books with an old belt, and he lost expensive fountain pens, special compasses for arithmetic, mufflers and gloves. Things like that. He reached a time when nothing his parents did pleased. Particularly when it came to the father, whose feelings he hurt by his criticism of everything. They would have fights because his father got enjoyment from reading the *News* and the *Mirror* and wasn't happy that the unions got into his shop—"

Whoosh, come on, what shop? Morroe wrinkled his face at this. They always have to embroider a little. He peddled buttons, threads and trimmings, the old man. I know, I remember, because Etta gave him an order. And he worked right out of his house.

"—bear in mind that he was in knickers yet. One time his father told him, '*Boichick,* if I'm an exploiter then what are you, since you eat and drink from my exploiting?' The result—the result was for two days he took in his mouth nothing but pretzel sticks and water. Till the father, being a father, naturally couldn't stand it and went and brought him home records and a really expensive set of—"

"Murderers!" From up front there was commotion and a shrill rising pitch. "He's breathing! What are you doing to him, murderers?"

"No, no, no," the rabbi said, rapping lightly on the lectern a few times. "You mustn't, I, I tell you you dassn't. You wet his grave, you don't let him rest easy." Even so, a sob cracked his next sentence. "He had—" He took time to blow his nose and fiddle with his *yarmalke*. "He had a clear mind, and maybe too clear. There was nothing he would let pass, nothing he would be deceived by. In a minute he could make people think they didn't know who they were, that they didn't tell the truth or show their true feelings or try to live in a worth-while way. He wanted they should be . . . critical, they should look to see from where their feet grew. He was an underminer. It's a special power which in a way he would have been better off not having. Because it's not appreciated and can do harm. 'Hey, hey,' people would tell him, 'what do you want from us, what do you expect from us? Leave us alone. We can barely lift our feet and you're telling us to be Nijinskys. We're grateful they don't throw stones at us and you're telling us to go start revolutions. We whisper *shah* and you bellow *gevald*. We say yes and you say no. Leave us alone. Go away. Realize who you're dealing with. Bear in mind we're *kleyner menschen* who have nerve only to ask for small things. Our God is the God of *kleyner menschen*, a civil service

God, a God of professionals. Our concerns are his concerns. That the apartment should be painted every few years. That the slipcovers should fit. That we should be able to furnish homes for our daughters and offices for the sons. That when we cut velvets they shouldn't order cottons. Leave us alone. We don't want trouble, we don't want to know too much. . . ."

Levine sniffled, squirmed and mumbled, "Kch-kch—"

Weiner answered with the dry barking sound of a seal.

"I'm trying to fight it," said Levine, tittering. "I'm trying, I'm trying!"

"Don't give in!"

"Burning, burning," Levine muttered ferociously. "Jug Jug . . . Da dayadhvan . . . Stately plump Buck Mulligan . . ."

"Good, good! Gaah! Fight it, *bubbele!*"

"It's going away. . . . It's going away. . . . It's passing now. . . ."

"All gone, *bubbele?*"

"Almost, almost . . . I'll tell you when. . . ."

"Now?"

"Thank God. Now . . ."

Then Weiner, softly, sneakily, muttered, "Choopie-bar-choopie . . . Choopie-bar-choopie . . ."

The bench began to rock.

"C-c-c-carp," went Weiner. And, "S-s-s-sable."

A noise like gentle gargling came out of Levine. He pinched his cheeks and bit down on his tongue. His body jerked ecstatically. "Rat bastard!" he wheezed, while Weiner, with clasped hands, played dumb. "Big stink! Lousy fuck!"

"Quiet down!" said Morroe, as loudly as he dared. A little stream of laughter inside him welled, bubbled. He strove against it with black thoughts. Of the school nurse who had sent him home because of nits. Of tribes who slit the heels and tendons of the dead, that they should not rise and run from the grave. Of the ancient condom his father had spotted in his wallet. Of the *Titanic* sinking and the *Hindenburg* aflame. Of Lowenthal, his dentist, whom he did not fully trust. Slowly, slowly he was composing himself. When Weiner fractured him with a "Choopie-bar-choopie!"

Two or three faces turned toward them. Then an usher padded over. Then Morroe felt itching and burning and a throbbing, dreadful pain on his cheek, or his neck—he wasn't sure which. His eyes rolled up into his head; in a moment, another moment he would pass out. "Enough?" said Ottensteen, his fingers crunched like a trap on Morroe's right ear. "Beast, savage animal!"

A small, almost infantile groan escaped Morroe. His glasses slipped down and teetered at the tip of his nose. He wailed softly, "Felix . . . They're falling, Felix . . . Felix, heylookatheybreak . . ."

"Get blind," replied Ottensteen. "*And* dumb." He administered one more protracted pinch and let go. As Levine, swollen with mirth, quietly rolled from side to side.

The rabbi meanwhile rumbled on, saying, "The average individual doesn't learn how to see or to be curious. Things go into his mind just so far, just so much, to such and such a point and place and there it finishes.

He doesn't like to be surprised by life or have his habits upset. Tell him you're Jack the Ripper, show him your big knife and he'll answer, 'Mister, pardon me, I get off the next stop.' However, with the departed who we now remember you had a great, a remarkable interest in people and phenomenon. I recall very fondly how some years ago I met him by the library when we both had a little time to spare and how we walked around and then went for a bite. What a delight it was, what a pleasure! The way he saw the city, the streets, the way he had himself opened to the least little thing! Here he saw a tree, he knew it by name. There he noticed a woman walking with a funny dog and he pats and plays with the animal and before we walk away finds out whatever there is to find out about the breed, how smart they are, what they like to eat. In no time he was her best friend. And that wasn't all. I'm with him maybe two hours and what we didn't talk about, what ground we didn't cover! The different type elevators they have. The way big buildings are made so they are able to take the shocks from subway trains. Where you go if you want to get books rebound at a reasonable price. How you should break in a pipe. What to look for in a pair of new shoes. The swollen profits in drug supplies. Also the way Jews lived under the Romans. Also the inventing of clocks. Also the greatness of Winston Churchill, and his feelings about Jews. Also Joe Louis, Fatty Arbuckle, Bertrand Russell and I think the future of Israel. We went then to eat. A place I never noticed though I used to be in the neighborhood three times a week. Everyone—everyone there knew him and he knew everyone. The counterman, when he saw him walk over, must have gained ten pounds. We, we wanted to order the corned beef, but he gives us a wink and makes a motion toward the brisket. And he put together a pair of healthy sandwiches that if the boss saw him he could have been fired then and there. With potato salad I don't think he punched out on the check, plus sour pickles—"

"I am hungry," Levine proclaimed.

"I could go some Chinks," Weiner replied.

"Ain' dair sumpin else you'd pre-fer, *neshoma?*"

"What dat be, man?"

"W-w-w-whitefish!"

Short high giggles were pried through their lips.

"Was he doing it for show?" The rabbi made the words softly. "I would personally doubt it. I would say he had a temperament that was a giving temperament and believed that giving returns giving and love returns love. Of course, it isn't such a desirable thing in business, and from such an approach he didn't exactly swell up his practice—"

What does he mean by that *practice*, Morroe wondered? Unless, the practice of literature. And why doesn't he mention something, a few words about the writing? He certainly should. . . .

"—like for no reason at all he starts a conversation with the cashier. He was buying a pack of cigarettes and when she hands him the matches he says to her, 'Isn't it strange—isn't it strange how I should buy a pack of cigarettes in New York, in Manhattan, and I should get

156

with it a matchbook from a bank in Chicago?' Now, whether because there was a line of customers, or whether because she thought he was getting fresh, she didn't answer and I felt hurt for him. Because here also he was trying to give, and like with so many things in his life he didn't know where or when. He, he wanted to be part of her existence, to leave her with a deep idea, but he probably only upset her and threw off her figuring."

"Oh, oh, positively!" Morroe was saying to himself. " 'Leave her with a deep idea!' Right away!"

The rabbi meanwhile turned the pages of a large pad, moistening two fingers on his tongue. After a long instant of thought he said, "I have already talked more than I wanted to and maybe more than I should. But I notice here how I had a few important, significant points to bring out which would give us a better understanding of this fine person to who we pay hom-age. *Children and family* I have written down. An item I should cover. All right. In my profession I go into quite a lot of houses and I can't get used to what I see. Parents have children and expect the children to fail and disappoint them. Parent doesn't know child, child doesn't know parent. Whatever you do for them is wrong. If you blew on their baby cereal, that was no good. You gave them too much protection. If you held back and didn't blow they also blame you. Because they'd burn a tongue. What you want from them is never what you get from them. You're afraid to command and they don't want to obey. You ask from them everything and nothing, and what you ask for is never what you want. You put on them the necessary oil and talcum, you train them to habits of personal cleanliness—"

"Do you really feel for Chinks?" Levine wistfully asked.

"I could go some egg foo yun," replied Weiner. "I could go some *good* moo goo gai pan."

"Because there are four of us, and with four people . . ."

"Gaah, we order different dishes, each one different, then we mix . . ."

"His wife, his good wife told me something which sheds very nice light on the man and father he was. When his older girl was three or four she got into rages for almost no reason. You couldn't stop her, you couldn't control or discipline her, and they were afraid she would do herself harm. One day—one day she carried on worse than ever. For no reason. He tells his wife to go bring blankets. 'What for?' 'Go bring.' Then he takes the *maydele* in his arms and carries her up to the roof. He puts the blanket around them both, he cuddles, he caresses. He says, 'You'll make a yell and I'll make a yell. Let's see. Let's see who can do louder.' So the *maydele* starts in and he starts in. She makes a yell and he makes a worse yell. She kicks and slaps, he pretends to kick and slap. She runs wild around the roof, he runs wild after her. She begin to sniffle, he sniffles. She makes a funny face, he makes a funnier face. And ut-ut-ut, she laughs. A little bit of a laugh. He hears, but he pretends he doesn't hear. The *maydele* gives him a little hit, as if to say, 'Notice me, pay attention!' So he hugs her. He gives her a love bite while she laughs and cries, although more laughs. They climb under the blanket and they make believe it's a tent, a castle, an automobile, a magic airplane. 'Look, look,' he says to the *maydele*, 'see the sun, see how nice. Let's both together breathe the sun down, down into our tummies.' How is that possible? How do you breathe the sun down? She wants to know, the *maydele*. By throwing out the chest, he instructs. By closing the eyes. By saying, Sun come into me, sun let me swallow you. By pretending you never knew before what it is to breathe, that now is the first time. She obeys, she enjoys. Next, he and the *maydele* breathe down a cloud, and another cloud, and a wind that's blowing. Then he tells a story and she tells a story. He makes up a sun song, she makes up a sun song. She wants a kiss, he wants a kiss. She says, 'I love you,' he says, 'I love you.' She goes to sleep and he goes to sleep. Together on the roof, under one blanket. This was the kind of man and father he was."

Once more the rabbi searched his pad, telling the people this: "I had written down here a certain quotation with a very important point which I can't seem to locate. How he for who we hold such high regard was like in a certain story where the hero is walking and he sees that a little animal is being mistreated and he stops off to give a hand. It turns out, of course, that the creature is what they call a genie, and this genie rewards him—a ring, a locket, a charm—making him free from what you and I are not free from. That is, cash, the getting of cash, and the hardness of the getting. Also material things, property, strict obedience to the authorities and satisfaction with what life is supposed to provide, even when it isn't enough. Like I mentioned before, this made him a special case and didn't necessarily endear him to one and all. But if we have no room in the world or in our hearts for special cases, then whose fault is it? That's all I think I'm going to say."

He next instructed all present to rise, and he recited: "Praised *and* glorified be the name of the Holy One, *though* He be *above* all the praises which we can utter. Our guide *is* He in life and our redeemer *through* all eternity."

He was answered: "Our help cometh from *Him*, the creator of heaven and earth."

Now fierce hot light washed the chapel.

Now organ notes soured the air.

Now lines were formed, then one line only, and the many ungainly steps jiggled the coffin on its wooden stand.

Do they show more than the face, Morroe was thinking? Probably just the face. And what do they need so many flowers? And perfume, I'll swear they're piping in perfume. Unless . . . in this weather . . . the odor.

"Look at that tie," someone ahead commented. "Who picked out that tie for him?"

Piercing the heart, Morroe recollected. Only where did I read it? How before burial a doctor would come and he would pierce the heart with some instrument and draw a few drops of blood. For what? Against vampires, maybe, or werewolves.

And so he neared the coffin, resolving not to look, but looking anyway. At the tie, with its foolish stripes of

160

many colors. At the little flecks of pure white powder on the chin and in the creases of the neck. At the delicate way the head rested against the satin cushion. Then, then first Morroe sensed the beginning of tears; he leaned forward, peering and peering into the coffin, into the face which wore an expression of gentle courtesy, as though in excuse for causing grief and inconvenience. It was only when Weiner had whispered *"Schmuck!"* and *"Schmuck!"* again that Morroe recoiled and saw that he, the dead man, the corpse, was not Leslie.

10 ────────────────────

WITH A "WHOOSH!" Morroe plunged into the crowd and was carried along. Above the dim notes of the organ he heard his name. He played dumb, though some woman from behind kept pointing and motioning and giving him baffled looks. Then he spotted a men's room and bulled his way through. It was choked with people; he couldn't even get near the sinks. Suddenly a booth opened up and Morroe, without asking, marched right in, banging the latch and flushing the bowl again and again till the growls of anger and abuse abated. Much longer than he needed to, he perched on the alien toilet seat, his head back against a curve of cold pipe, his hands turned downward, his knees stretching his pants out of shape.

Half in turmoil, half numb, he caught all kinds of conversation.

"*He's got his hand out all the time. You ask him to say a Yiskor for you, it's fifty dollars.*"

"*When he comes over, when he apologizes to me before people, that's when I'll ride out to the cemetery with him in one car.*"

"*He was never a normal personality. A normal personality is not going to set fire to his mother's bathroom curtains when he's a big boy already.*"

"*. . . and I don't like a doctor who doesn't listen. Instead of hearing me out he keeps saying, 'Frankly, I'm puzzled; frankly, I'm puzzled.' . . .*"

"*They themselves use those expressions to each other. Like you could call me a kike and I wouldn't take offense. Listen to our Charlotte some time, you'll hear how every other word out of her mouth is 'That nigger.' . . .*"

"*I dreamed about birds, and birds are always unlucky for me.*"

"*I was trying to get free service? Since when? I spoke to him like a friend, I said, 'Counselor, you think there's any point in starting a case?' 'Ask your lawyer,' he snaps. 'Ask your lawyer.' So I very politely tell him: 'Oi, bist du a chuchim!' *"

"*Everybody respected his learning, and if it wasn't that he couldn't relate to people, the members were all set to vote him their rabbi for life.*"

"*This polly is flying around the house, fast, crazy, and it's much bigger than it should be and we're all scared and your Aunt Sylvia . . .*"

Suddenly Morroe was aware of an eye filling a chink in the door and transfixing his own eye like a spear. A rattling began, and drops of water and green liquid soap splattered him. "*Bubbele,* hurry up, make it snappy!" Three or four balls of toilet tissue floated down. "We'll wait for you outside, *bubbele.* Outside!"

Girding himself, with only a skimpy rinsing of his hands, Morroe went forth amid the still-dense crowd. Up the flights and down the flights, once more through the zigzag corridor, around the draperies, past the stacks and stacks of folding chairs. An old lady screamed, gagged, fainted as he blundered by. "Pull down her skirt!" someone yelled, and the yell was joined by wailing and by the hollow whir of the loudspeaker system and over it a lush singsong: "Will the immediate family go gather at limousine number one the chauffeur is waiting just immediate family will you please only the immediate family." At length he entered the chaos of the foyer and beheld the boys. Under the banked Israeli flags, by the double doors, where there was no avoiding them. With eyes cast humbly down he came forward.

"Hi, guy," said Levine.

"Welcome, stranger," said Weiner.

"He's smiling," Ottensteen grunted. "He's enjoying himself, *der idyutt!*"

Then Weiner showed a fist and Levine showed a fist. "Odds," said Weiner. "Evens," said Levine. And circling, slowly circling Morroe, they gave him mean two-fingered smacks on the back of his head.

"That hurts," said Morroe. "You know you can hurt someone that way?"

"It's an ancient ceremony," Weiner explained. "It's the exorcism of the *schmuck*."

"I'm a *schmuck?*"

"You are the archetypal, quintessential *schmuck*, the homonunculus of all *schmucks*."

"If I'm a *schmuck* . . . if I'm a *schmuck*, you're a moral hypocrite."

Other words stirred within him and warred for a place on his tongue. But Ottensteen waved his arms about, compelling silence, and said, "So? So where do we go and what do we do?"

"We should make some calls," said Weiner. "Isn't there somebody we can call?"

"By all means and definitely," Ottensteen returned blissfully. "Try—try number one New York."

Then Morroe lumbered in again with, "I'm a *schmuck*. Sure." He tried to show how strongly he was in charge of himself, but his face kept playing him false. "Don't think it hasn't reached me that at one time your favorite name for me was Morroe *Schmuck*. That's right. You're hot-shot intellectuals, you publish here and you publish there, but you could take lessons in . . . insight. To pinpoint, to pigeonhole—that you know how to do, you're really good at that stuff. You get hold of one viewpoint, one attitude about a person and you crucify him." He stared into his palms as though seeking stigmata.

Weiner exploded a "Gaah!"

Ottensteen said, "You misled and you misdirected. You fixed us up."

"Furthermore, it was no accident," Levine ventured.

"As the Marxists were fond of saying, *it was no accident.*"

"No? No, what then?" cried Morroe, his heart picking up a rough beat. "Tell me, I want to hear your brilliant point, the way—the way you structure this. Because a statement like that, it's significant, it's pregnant, it probes the quality of experience. As the New Critics are fond of saying." His injured gaze held steady.

Levine, with a total neutrality of expression, observed, "We know, from Fenichel, of the varied and ingenious mechanisms operative in the expiation of acute hostility. The original impulse must, ah, be subverted, warded off. How? By an unconsciously purposeful forgetting, by a peculiar characteristic vagueness in relation to time and place. Mind you, I deliberately eschew all moral judgment, all effort—"

"Bravo. Yippee." Morroe softly applauded. "Not just plain hostility, but *acute* hostility. You first-class shit! I did more for Leslie, shahresinpeas, than all of you put together. Anytime. He wasn't afraid to come to me because he realized, he knew, he would find an open hand and an open heart." Up into his injured gaze multitudes seemed to swim, myriads, swarms and legions marched from all the ages and kingdoms of man, carrying off his books, his good ball-point pens, his records, his after-shave lotions in their fine stone jugs, giving him post-dated checks and notes to cosign, coveting, using, hinting, taking advantage, *shnorring.*

Though he winked conspicuously to the others, Levine said nothing.

"Furthermore," Morroe muttered, "I would say you're

in the wrong kind of analysis. Yes, I would say you'd be getting greater benefits from urinalysis."

I'm a slow starter, Morroe thought, his scalp prickling with pleasure, but if I have to I can give one for one. And he was preparing another shaft when an usher appeared, saying, "Don't block the door fellows, please, be nice, the fire inspectors are handing summonses right and left." Grudgingly they moved into the street, Morroe hanging back a little, declaiming, "Acute hostility. Sure. Purposeful forgetting. That's right. But what can you expect from one who didn't happen to regard the Progressive Party as a vital center, a third force? Who, ah, failed, to perceive, ah, that Henry Wallace represented—what was that brilliant, terrific phrase?—'the, ah, fructifying conscience of the intellectual.' "

"A complete distortion, a pathetic invention," Levine snorted over his shoulder. "Which I shall take from whence it comes. From whence it comes!"

Ottensteen, meanwhile, shied away from them and latched on to a policeman who was directing traffic with a long flashlight. Were there other chapels, parlors in the neighborhood, the vicinity? For he had to meet his sister, a highly nervous, sickly person, and deliver into her hands a forgotten envelope containing important prescriptions and railroad tickets.

No, sir, the policeman couldn't say; this section was all new to him. Old, paunched, short-winded and stiff, he explained that he himself lived in Staten Island, that he was from a private outfit, not the city. A relief man, paid by the hour, called when he was needed.

Swishing around, Ottensteen aimed for three very

old men with beards and sidelocks and sable-trimmed satin coats, dark and crabbed like Hebrew letters. Them he told, in a swift sputter of Yiddish, that his burial society, long unhappy in its dealings here, had instructed him to look around, to see if he could get a better price, a more convenient location. Could they suggest and recommend?

One hid his eyes in a handkerchief. One suffered a coughing spasm. One spat three times.

He next spoke to a chauffeur, a Negro with the height and reach of a Watusi warrior. Who would not hear out his tale of a misdelivered steamer basket. Who turned sharp-eyed and testy and said, "Din see no basket, doan need no fuckin fruit."

The peanut man knew of nothing.

A young couple could not help. Though the husband claimed to have once been Ottensteen's waiter at Tiawanga Lodge. Long since burned down and rebuilt.

A girl from the office pointed out the director. But he, bawling out the ushers for their arrangement of flowers, their placing of ropes and stanchions, was in no mood for Ottensteen.

Whereupon Ottensteen waddled to the nearest limousine, flung open a door and bade all passengers to shift over, scrunch in and make a place.

Before the boys had moved he was straddling the running board like a Keystone cop.

By the time they got near he was one hand and half a foot inside the limousine. He was thrusting children from laps. He was sprawling upon thighs and flanks and bellies.

He was spilling change. He was moaning, and over the moans voices chimed:

"Who sent for him?"

"Take a train, you nutsy you!"

"Keep hands from the next one's child!"

"Goodbye and good luck my stockings!"

Then the boys leaned their weight on him and pulled him in slow stages from the limousine.

"Only for the ride," Ottensteen begged. "Only to the cemetery for the *kaddish*."

But they grabbed and hoisted and drew him along on scuffing heels.

"All Jews—all Jews are brothers!" bawled Ottensteen.

"We'll look for a phone," said Weiner.

"We'll go through the *Classified*," said Levine. "Under parlors, chapels, halls."

"A vital center, that's right. A third force, sure," said Morroe.

"*Yisgodol, vyiskodosh*," chanted Ottensteen. "A funeral is a funeral!"

In this fashion they crossed the street and entered what was open. A small candy store with boxes of empties piled everywhere, with globes of colored gumballs, a penny scale, gauze-covered chocolates and fixtures and displays from the year one. Kids were lounging around, big, smooth, fair, overdeveloped lumps spending heavy on frappés, charlotte russes, jelly apples, fudgicles and other rich stuff. And, in Morroe's view, acting awfully nervy, taking too many liberties; using the magazine rack for a public library; walking blithely behind the counter and

169

helping themselves to seltzer, to cracked ice and match-books; talking smut; piling three and four into a phone booth on one call; sending the owner, with her fat-hampered feet, to sweeten and unsweeten, to add sprinkles, bring straws, wipe away. His father would have used fists on them, even the ammonia-filled water gun hidden against holdups.

They sat Ottensteen down at a round wooden table and catered to him. Weiner massaged his scalp, fetching overjoyed shivers and throat noises. Morroe, with paper napkins, applied a passable cold compress—though Ottensteen called him golem, *yolt* and humanity's menace. Levine went for aspirins, and when Ottensteen had swallowed them Weiner said, "Take something else in your mouth, Felix. Build up strength."

"I had a very, very bitter and tragic life. They put it on television, it would crack the tube."

"Let me order, let it be my treat. A malted. Gaah, not just a *malted*, but a float. With a Melorol on top."

"Miss-tah." The candy-store lady leaned over her fountain. "Go fifteen years back. Go twenty. Find me President Roosevelt and what I once had in strength, I'll sell you Melorols."

"Two sisters HIAS could trace to Warsaw, then *fartig*. Another one got cholera whom I didn't hardly know, although I keep dreaming she's calling up from the Bronx to ask about Momma's lavalier. That was Chinkele. My little brother Itche Mate I was close to, in fact, the only one he would let feed him. Because I didn't watch him better he got scared by a big dog that belonged in the next village. And he died of fits. . . ."

170

"You want, Miss-tah, I think I have Eskimo Pies. But I don't recommend in a malted. I'm not trying to sell."

"My wife had only one pleasure, to write away for soap samples. A girdle you couldn't get her to wear, and she wasn't normal in her monthlies. She used to put oilcloth on the table and then newspaper over the oilcloth. Where there was a bank she hid an account from me. The calendars still come. She took in a girl three times a week, but the refrigerator smelled bad. If it had only one scallion she still wouldn't defrost. . . ."

"Today salesmen do you a favor to write an order. Plus everything is twice the price and half the size."

"My son takes from me like a blind horse. He never carries his own cigarettes. In camp I don't think he won a medal. The way Catherine the Great took lovers he takes courses. He's twenty-seven and I think he plays with himself."

And Ottensteen let a tear fall atop the fountain suggestions.

"Gaah, an egg cream, Felix. To please me."

"Maybe—maybe with a cookie."

They ordered egg creams all around. The candy-store lady, after her fourth trip, lingered by the table, twisting a chocolate-stained rag. She eventually said, "When you take at the fountain an egg cream, is regular twelve cents. When you want at the table, I got to charge fifteen-cent minimal. Otherwise I have a hangout, not a store." She flopped the rag at some kids. "They sit and don't spend."

"Principle is principle," said Ottensteen, drinking heartily.

171

"But just try, you'll see how for the three cents, I put in extra milk."

"Someone who has integrity." A belch stretched out Ottensteen's last syllable. "Very nice."

"It's my character. I wish I could be like some business people in this neighborhood, on this block. From the piece of wax paper they try not to give you they buy apartment houses."

"You have to look far and wide for integrity."

"You might never come into my store again, but it's in my character to act to you like I would act to a steady customer."

"You take today's cleaners," Ottensteen rose, helped himself to a Mallomar. "They don't go inside the cuffs. Barbers, the average kind, never learn their trade. The butchers hide grinders in back so you can't see what's in your chop meat—"

"Osher," Levine called out, cracking the spine of a *Classified*, "affiliated with M. Joseph Weber. Pettit Funeral Home, out, Pettuci, no, Pillser Brothers, a possible, *Q* has nothing, Rabinovitch, M., on Dayhill Road, Rabinowitz, Hiram, Kings Highway, Rabbinowitz and Sattler Funeral Services, four addresses, Regis, Saint, definitely out, ah, Reitch, Morton, nonsectarian—"

"Stay with *O*," said Morroe. "I think it's the *O* family."

"—Ober, Olfine, Ollatoroff—"

"Otts-otts-otts," said the candy-store lady. "We have time to know from these concerns."

"—Osher we had—"

"I think the *goyim* live longer in general."

172

Then Morroe, studying his glass as if for signs and portents, said, "Miss, maybe you could give us an idea. Or put us on the right track."

"Still, still, stay buried!" instructed Ottensteen. And he trapped the candy-store lady's hands in his hands and he related how many years back there had been a young cigar maker, a burning socialist. His boss, respecting his work, had one night singled him out, asking if he would mind staying later in the loft to fill special orders. He gladly obliged. The hours passed, the work went nicely. So, stretching out on the bench, he grabbed a quick snooze. When something troubled his sleep. He shuddered, he woke himself, and got the shock of his life. For dripping blood all over his bench stood Milk Eye, the gangster. He who was tender to pigeons and dreadful to people. "Hide me," says Milk Eye. "Where have I got to hide?" For answer, Milk Eye picks up a knife. One, he will murder. Two, he will mutilate. Three, he will murder *and* mutilate. Long after Milk Eye's "Two," yet a breath before his "Three," an idea. Too shaky to talk, he points. Where he points is the open fire-escape door with two mattresses airing. Sweating bitter lemons, he lays Milk Eye between them, a sandwich. Then he lays himself over the sandwich. Taking a relaxed attitude. The next minute they come. Two overgrown Irish gangsters. Who beat his face like a tambourine. Who suddenly beg his pardon: he should please, please excuse their roughness and gruffness; it was their way of showing affection. Let him point, only point, to where Milk Eye hides and he would get handsome presents. Temptation shakes up his socialist youth heart.

173

What is Milk Eye, and who needs him? But something, something inside cries, Whore, hypocrite, sellout artist. Since when—since when is human life not precious? And he gives a firm, though courteous, No. Whereupon blows fall. All his forces fail him. Back on his sick feet, he washes away Milk Eye's blood and does what he can with old Mercurochrome. At last, at last, exit Milk Eye. Passes a week to ten days. Sure enough, he who gets no mail gets a lawyer letter. Present yourself to a certain custom tailor for high-class suits. Next, another lawyer saying, Come sign papers. You will be nicely taken care of, the lawyer tells him, you can look forward to great expectations. Passes eight months to a year. Checks. More years, more checks. Now from his newspaper desk the young cigar maker gets rumors, but only rumors, about a new Milk Eye. That he has become devout. That he has moved to Flatbush. Then, then the young cigar maker goes to Atlantic City, New Jersey, to write up a highly important conference. Where he reads in a newspaper a small-print item: "The officers and board of Goldzweig Institute mourn their beloved associate. . . ." Immediately, immediately he sets out for the funeral. Over parkways and under tunnels the special limousine rushes. Brooklyn, Flatbush. All right, where to? The world stops while he carries on a hopeless search for the small-print item. (By nature an organized person, he has, alas, forgotten to jot down where the services are set.) He tries stores and stands, tramping the immense avenue blocks. But no appeal, no amount, will get him the edition he seeks. *Finis. Fartig.* The story ends. Only for one finishing touch. If she has so far not surmised, let the candy-store lady now meet the young cigar maker. He, himself, Felix Ottensteen, staff member of *Yetzt*.

"You are that Ottensteen?" The candy-store lady positively blushed.

"Also N. J. Felix in the magazine section."

"You write very, very nice little articles. Interesting. Especially when you knock."

"Today what's to boost?"

And Morroe, with a fixed flat voice, said, "The more I think, the more I'm positive. We should stick within the *O*—"

"*Schmuck*," whispered Weiner. "*Schmuckschmuck-schmuck*."

"—family."

"Your Milk Eye had children?" the candy-store lady inquired.

"Only a crippled wife. An intelligent, highly learned woman who kept a strictly kosher home."

"Otts-otts-otts," went the candy-store lady as she stomped off to sell and serve. Returning, she brought back halvah and haunted eyes, saying, "It's no good. I take to heart too much."

Ottensteen's sigh fluttered over every living thing.

"Like with Phillie the cake man. He delivers me the last one and if I tell him, Phillie, Phillie, I need service, I'll cancel by you, he tells me what he pays to keep his boy in a retarded home. It's no good."

Ottensteen went on record that in business heart was a hindrance.

"You look at my counter, you see boxes and jars for every disease. God spare us, I have no room for stock."

175

Ottensteen hoped her counter would be so crowded for the next hundred and twenty years.

"I think of the crippled wife, I get aggravated. It's no good. It's why I'm on a salt-free diet." The candy-store lady extracted from her apron a crumbly cracker. "After sweet halvah I take plain Uneeda biscuit," she shyly confessed, then said, "You asked across the street?"

They had definitely asked.

"I would try then Nostrand Memorial on Nostrand Avenue. How you go is you go to Nostrand, down Nostrand, down till you come to Kings Highway. You come to Kings Highway you turn, you look, you notice a Barton's—"

"Write down!" Ottensteen glowered at Morroe. "I want to see you making notes!"

"—you watch for an appetizing store, where if you want you can take home their potato salad in an insulated bag. Then, two doors away, Nostrand Memorial. Can't miss."

Levine rose, a hand stretched toward Morroe. Who, preparing a smile, a few kidding words, got set in friendship's name to grasp. "I shall call ahead," Levine acidly said. "I shall want a dime from you."

Though incensed, Morroe came up with change. Thinking: I wish on you what you wish on me.

"They buried my brother-in-law, God spare us, that's how I come to know the place. In your life you never saw a brother-in-law and sister-in-law should be so close. Every day in the morning he called me like clockwork. 'Hello, Princess, how are you, Princess?'" The candy-store lady's stomach suddenly issued a statement of sorrow.

"I start thinking about him, right away I have to take Tums. It's no good."

He, himself, *der alte* Ottensteen, believed in and lived on Tums.

Weiner cited the human condition.

"Information," Levine was saying, "one moment, Information. Your purpose, your, ah, function is not to correct my pronunciation. Nostrand is of Dutch origin and I gave it the long Dutch *o*."

"In two and a half weeks, God spare us, he'll have his *yahrzeit*, and we made up that the whole family should get together whatever it costs and take a special *New York Times* notice. They had in mind a professional to write it up, but I figured let me try, let me do it and have the pleasure because I loved him, I was special to him, I was his princess. You want, I'll recite, you can criticize."

It would be their pleasure, their pleasure and privilege.

The candy-store lady climbed out of the drapes and loops of her apron and, after a few silent seconds said, "Goes like this: Poretz, Mandel Hirsch. One long sad year without you. Words are inadequate to express what is in our hearts. Each day brings thoughts of you. We miss you and live on in your dear, dear memory." She entered her apron again. "Tell me, Mr, Ottensteen, if you think I should drop out one 'dear.' You I'll listen to."

Ottensteen kissed his fingertips.

Weiner begged for a copy.

"I realize that, sir." Levine cupped and stroked the phone's mouthpiece. "Sir, sir, I am *not* trying to give you a hard—"

"I had *some* fight over it with my cousin Ida. It's not fancy enough. It should say, instead of 'in your *dear dear* memory,' 'in your *green* memory.' So she's bowing out and is having them plant a tree for him in Israel."

"—B, R, A, V, E, R, M, A, N, Leslie, and I am grateful."

"Spite work, pure and simple. You look at families, you don't have to wonder why there's war in the world."

"Whoo, whoo hoo hoo," Levine yapped at them from the booth. "Underway . . . finishing up . . . calling somebody over . . ."

Weiner slid from his chair. "If it's Inez put me on. Don't forget. Don't hang up. Let me say hello."

His teeth clicked. His chest rose. His eyes filled with love and fear. He reached toward the phone, but Levine snapped the door shut and wedged his behind against it.

"Come on!" Weiner flung himself against the booth. "Pummeonasec!"

Levine blithely gestured and talked away.

"Otts-otts-otts," went the candy-store lady.

"Open up. Oppenuppasec and don't fu—— kid around!"

"Miss-tah, don't start me trouble with the phone people!"

"*Doucement!*" yelled Levine, with the door half-open. "I happen to have Minerva Turtletaub on the line."

A light seemed to switch off behind Weiner's face. He seated himself and to an empty glass said, "Skinny Minnie, that's a fine howdoyoudo. Since when, gaah, since when was she such a good friend to Inez?"

"Why I gave an argument," the candy-store lady said,

178

"is I get arguments. They sent a mechanic who claims I mistreat the equipment. *Ah Poilisheh.*"

"Furthermore, wasn't there some story that they were supposed to be on the outs on account of when Minnie went to Europe she wouldn't bring back a Swedish cuticle scissors for Inez?"

It was an Italian sewing machine, Morroe ached to say. Or an English bike. In any case, some difference!

"I'm sure she's a Stalinist—the bone structure, the complexion, the general way she carries herself. Gaah, maybe not a Stalinist, but certainly Stalinoid."

Then Levine danced out of the booth and gleefully announced that all had been arranged. Easily, flawlessly, but with fanatic attention to detail. If they hurried, it was not at all impossible to make the service, or a portion thereof. If traffic slowed or trouble came and they could not make the service, the procession would definitely be held up for them. If they did not make the service and the procession dared delay no longer, it could nevertheless be joined at certain clearly designated streets. If they could not make the service, missed the procession and blundered among strange streets, a look-out would be posted near the big cemetery gate. If they could not make the service, missed the procession, blundered among strange streets, turned at the wrong gate, let them seek out the plot and the grave. If they could not make the service, missed the procession, blundered among strange streets, turned into the wrong gate, came upon the plot but found all mourners long or lately gone, they were to assemble, with selected nearest and dearest, at the apartment of Inez. Stopping first, since it was on their way and they must pass, to bring two pizzas, large, from Donadio's. One all cheese, one cheese and anchovy.

They rose and made a path through kids and empties. Morroe, to avoid a kid, skidded on an empty. When he dragged himself up he felt a hunk of silver floating like a dead fish in his mouth. Slowly, slowly he tested. Whoosh! The fragment of a filling, no older than the month. Only God can help me, he reflected and, though mortally tired, he got set to lunge, smash through any obstacle, and sprint to a subway. But Ottensteen checked him at the door.

"Buy something. I want to see you buy and give her business."

He bought: Jujubes, Charms, Sight Savers, Mary Janes, Hopjes and a soap eraser. His change he fed into a cerebral palsy box.

The candy-store lady then shucked off her apron and said gently to Ottensteen, "Next time we come together let it be for celebrations."

To which Ottensteen made reply: "Let it be a world for all Jewish children."

"Let Israel be strong and have it good."

"Let the rich get a little poorer and the poor get a little holier."

"Let there be a Roosevelt and a La Guardia to take care of our enemies."

"Let there be one key for every lock."

"Let it be we should never, never need, but what we need, God should give us."

She was still talking as they left the store and fell in

step behind Levine. Who glowed with plans of how, to the pizzas, they might well add black olives and head cheese, red peppers and prosciutto—a half pound, sliced thin, would be sufficient—and whatever else was suited to the preparation, the essential fixings and makings of an antipasto.

Ottensteen proposed a good coffee cake, saying, "When I come, I come like a sport."

Morroe, his tongue immersed in pollution and decay, began to limp.

Weiner, popeyed and nearly gagging on the words, said, "Gaah, all of a sudden she's an ass-hole buddy to Inez, all of a sudden she's in charge of arrangements." And he blurted out the story of what once befell Inez at the hands, though not exactly the hands, of Skinny Minnie. How on a night when Inez, six and a half months gone, was at a natural childbirth class, Skinny Minnie had paid Leslie a visit; how she had found him with the page proofs of a hotsy-totsy *Naysayer* piece—"The Containment of Politics"; how she had caught three grievous typos; how Leslie, from a sense of obligation, an onrush of gratitude, had put a hand or two under blouse and skirt; how Minnie, true-blue, and palsy-walsy, had begun for his benefit the performance of certain labial labors; how in the midst of these labors a rude and aggressive outcry had been forthcoming from Inez, early by twenty-five minutes; how Leslie, springing up, working fast, had fashioned a bludgeon from his page proofs; how with this bludgeon he had smashed Skinny Minnie again and again over the head; how with each smash he had hissed, "What are you *doing*, you dirty thing?"

"A marvelous boy," said Ottensteen. "A power and a force."

In the car, a heat rash suddenly burning his forehead, Weiner let it be known that no part or process of Skinny Minnie was without affliction. That three times foreign bodies had been found in her Fallopian tubes. That her nipples were inverted. That her septum was deviated, her sinuses clogged, her ankles pronated. That the wealth and strength of her body hair defied electrolysis. That her breath could sour pickles.

"Pish-posh," said Levine, negotiating a scrupulous U-turn.

Then Weiner maintained that Skinny Minnie was basically bad ball.

"Bad ball, buh-buh-buh," remarked Levine.

Red now behind both ears, Weiner cited her fantastic economies. She would steal aspirins from a friend's medicine chest, sugar cubes and napkins from restaurant tables. She went to special stores for day-old bread. She bought damaged canned goods at discount. She got her newspapers from subway seats. She used the cheapest cuts of meat.

"Never you mind," said Ottensteen. Who happened to think she was a cute little individual, a wit and a wise-acre, one who could give a tease and handle a tease. And though modern in all else, a highly religious girl, a strict keeper of the Sabbath.

"In this, I must concur with Felix." A sweetness settled over Levine. "Her orthodoxy, at any rate. Which almost, ah, burned us both alive. You see, it was her mother's *yahrzeit* and somehow the candle tipped over on our sheet. . . ."

"Well, well, well," said Weiner, clearing a rough spot in his voice, scratching away at eye, ear, nose and throat.

". . . and there were certain times, certain special holidays, when she made herself absolutely taboo. But on, ah, Simchas Torah, there were definite compensations."

"Well, well, well. No wonder the girls eat you up at one greedy gobble. I mean, gaah, the formidable combination of popular-culture expert and cocksmith." Weiner bared his teeth like a Mexican bandit. "But in one thing—one thing I'm understandably curious. Are you the biggest cocksmith by the popular-culture experts or the biggest popular-culture expert by the cocksmiths?"

Levine invited contrast with Weiner in either area or field of endeavor.

And, trembling a little, Weiner demanded the name of the Phantom's dog.

"Would that be—" Levine pretended to ponder "—ah, Wolf?"

"The Shadow's girl friend," Weiner shot back.

"Heh, heh," laughed Levine. "Margo."

"We're with the Shadow, we'll stay with the Shadow. I am after, I am waiting for the name of the little fellow who drove him around."

"That was Moey from Brooklyn. He was always being asked to report. 'Report! The Shadow hissed sibilantly.' "

"Baseball Joe. He was left-handed or he was right-handed?"

Levine, in a mellow mood, said, "A worth-while question, *mon vieux*, albeit revealing you as a somewhat stealthy little rascal. For Baseball Joe, as all perceptive students of the mass arts bear witness, was, ah, a switch-hitter."

"Richard Wentworth. To a chosen few, to an intrepid little band he was known as . . ."

"The Spider. Whom I tend to think of as the forerunner, the progenitor, of the hero as apocalyptic redeemer."

"We'll go to best friends. Who had a best friend Wrangler?"

"Tom Mix," said Levine, as though it were a benediction.

"Who had a best friend Black Barney?"

"No doubt you are expecting me to say Buck Rogers. Then I will say Buck Rogers. But under protest. Because long, well before Black Barney entered the scene, Dr. Huer was on hand. As a matter of fact he, he's the one who rescued Buck Rogers from a state of suspended animation, then fixed him up with a flying belt. And if you had rescued me from a state of suspended animation I would consider you my best friend."

"You are so wrong—so wrong about the flying belt that I am shaken up." By a slight quiver Weiner showed that he was shaken up. "But I have broad shoulders, let it pass. Let it be radio. Let it be Hop Harrigan time. Hop Harrigan. He's coming in, he's zooming down, he's getting ready to land, but he first has to radio the announcer. What does he have to radio the announcer?"

184

"Pilot to navigator," murmured Levine, "ah, pilot to navigator. This is Hop Harrigan . . . coming in."

"Coming *in!* Coming *in!*" Weiner grated. "Gaah, with expression! With *tahm!* With total immolation of self!" His voice took on a venomous, wheedling tone. "Now the Thimble Theatre. Popeye. He had the Goon named Alice and the Jeep named . . . ?"

Levine, his face under stress, was silent.

"I'll give a hint, a real clue." In the whites of Weiner's eyes a faint purple tinge spread. "It's the same name as a certain *schwartze* action painter what kicked, literally kicked, Minnie out of bed because she wanted him to do the windows."

"Action painter! Buh-buh-buh!" remarked Levine.

"Yagivupp?"

Levine demanded that his old bias against Popeye be taken into account, his inability to relate to the Thimble Theatre.

"Right now!" cried Weiner. "Right now if I called my mother up and she dragged herself over to the phone with her hip, which they got metal spikes in, and I said to her, 'Momma, God bless you, what was the name of Popeye's Jeep?' the answer would flow from her lips. I bet even—" his hand pounced on Morroe's thigh—"even *bubbele* here would know."

Morroe's reply was, "A *schmuck* can not be expected to know the name of Popeye's Jeep."

Then Levine issued his challenge. "Bogart."

"Bogart," affirmed Weiner.

At Nostrand Avenue Weiner had named fourteen

movies wherein Bogart had been featured but not starred.

By the intersection of Nostrand and Church Avenues he had named the horses of Tom Tyler, Bob Steele, George O'Brien, Hoot Gibson, Ken Maynard and Buck Jones; nine books by Albert Payson Terhune; the four Boy Allies; the three Battle Aces of G-8; and five more movies wherein Bogart had been featured but not starred.

By the intersection of Nostrand and Newkirk Avenues Weiner had named seven books by H. Rider Haggard; fourteen by Edgar Rice Burroughs, exclusive of the Tarzan series; and eleven movies wherein Porter Hall had been featured but not starred.

By the intersection of Nostrand Avenue and Kings Highway he had named twenty-seven Mickey Rooney movies exclusive of the Andy Hardy series; nine movies wherein Harold Huber had been featured but not starred; and hummed the themes of "Myrt and Marge," "Lum and Abner" and "Vic and Sade."

By the Barton's he had named the original Dead End Kids.

By the appetizing store he had named eight movies wherein Warren Hymer had been featured but not starred. And at the chapel, where two full blocks of cars waited and the air shook from the turning of all their motors, he had named the eight greatest stage shows of the New York Paramount, the role Bebe Daniels had taken in *Forty-second Street,* and the technical advisor for *Hell's Angels.*

11 ———————————————————

HE COULD OFFER no proof and there was little point
mentioning the fact, but Morroe was convinced that the
Inez he had last laid eyes on wore taffeta, not silk, open
toes, not pumps. The next minute, though, as he began
to tally and take stock of the other mourners who milled
around the cemetery gate in muted meeting and greeting,
he was confounded by greater peculiarities. So that he
cried to himself "Ye Gods!" and "Whoosh!"

There was dark Milton Ragner, Milton the unworldly,
who had slashed his wrists in a tub of warm water because he could think of no way to get rid of an old
mattress.

There was Ozzie Waldman, Ozzie the *kvetch*. For his

favor you could die. He gave away nothing, not even a piece of information. Meet him after a visit to his mother, ask him, "Ozzie, where were you?" and he would say, "I saw a woman."

There was Ethel Landsberger, big and shapely and elegant, from the Landsberger Parking System people. She hunted with falcons, she was hot for writers and spent thousands to print her terrible verse. Always in upper case. REMEMBER NO SUCH THING AS IT IS/ FORGET WHAT IS ONLY AT ALL.

There was Gideon Pfeffer, the big Latin America specialist. He knew five or six languages, he made special trips for the State Department, he could hold his own against Sidney Hook. But he was without charm. He blew matches out under your unlighted cigarette and never bothered introducing you to people.

There was Edgar Segal, Edgar the *macher*. Where there was a magazine, he was on the free list. Where there was a forum, he was on the platform, filling the water glasses. Where there were two, he made the third.

There was Maurice Salomon, the editor of *Second Thoughts*, with his Robespierre profile. He had the air of the oldest of men, as if he had been through the Hundred Years' War, taken down Sacco and Vanzetti's last words and seen all movements turn into failure and fiasco. He would be twenty-nine, make it thirty, on his next birthday.

There was Arabelle Talbot Harrington, looking as if she should be fingering a rosary or stamping library cards. Oh, Leslie had a great story about her: how late, late one night at the Devereaux Colony, she paraded nude around the grounds and screamed up into the main guest house, "Will one of you please come down and fuck me!"

There was Cordell Nash. His family had streets named after them and got private audiences with the Pope. Yet all his friends were Jewish. He loved to make jokes like, "Pour me a *goyische kopp* of coffee."

There was Irving Sklare thumping along in his space shoes. They called him "Irving Development" because he was a city planner. Every third word out of his mouth was "environment."

There was Leslie's sister Amelia, fatter than ever, and Lemkuhl the druggist, and there were Colin Bewley the translator and Selma Raab the juvenile editor and Portnoy the veterinarian and Mordecai Roth of *The Naysayer* and Horace Spiro of *Portent* and Inez' old maid Margo and Danny Sherman the gagwriter and Harvey Korn the sociologist and many others Morroe knew barely or not at all. Momma, what a crew, what a collection! Who had summoned such numbers so late? Where do you reach them? And by what means? Were there six Inezes working the switchboard of the world? I am in the presence of mystery, Morroe thought, and his gums began to torment him. For a wild moment he had a flash of Inez, a lightly leaping bird shrilling, "Come, come, come!" from window to window, or dancing up the city and down the city, tooting Leslie's old recorder.

Ottensteen, on his right, was lecturing Selma Raab, the juvenile editor. "*Chaval Al De'ovidim.*" Three times he repeated the phrase. "You'll see it on a lot of Jewish stones. To translate—to translate I would say, 'Alas,

189

maybe woe or sorrow for the lost who are never forgotten.' "

Weiner, behind him, had hold of Cordell Nash. Whose choked laugh was already beginning to burst quietly. "And the pool is emptied out, completely empty. And he's soaking and splashing, splashing and soaking. And the manager tippy-toes over and he says, 'How are you, Mr. Shmollowitz, and is everything to your liking?' And he answers him, '*Vun*-derful, *vun*-derful. Now if I only had some money!' "

And Levine, in front, had linked arms with Maurice Salomon and was saying, "I see, then, not a piece which would definitely pigeonhole Leslie—though the, ah, cultural configurations have a critical bearing—but a kind of retrospective reappraisal. In the way that all reappraisals are retrospective. 'Leslie Braverman: the Comic Vision,' or 'The Comic Vision of Leslie Braverman.' "

Kronk!

Creaking and swaying, crunching gravel, with pale radiance of lowbeam the hearse, from a devious path, intercepted their path and lumbered ahead at walking pace. Showing the blunt end of the fine wood coffin. Laminated like a scroll. Silver handles and silver screws. Where my friend is laid. Who could polish off, at one sitting, six bialystocken and a half-pound of Novia Scotia lox.

Whoosh!

A fat raindrop spattered one lens. Another exploded in his hair. Storm or sun shower; the day had lacked only this. He saw three clouds move upon each other, collide and merge. To become a bust of Goethe. A dogfight between angry little Spads. An Etruscan warrior. Officer Pupp getting set with his club. Then only the club. Then the sun renewed its thrust.

A squeeze at his armpit. A scent of camphor stick and lilac water. Sandra Luboff. Miss Social Welfare. Vigorous her step, determined her look. Like a protest marcher. But a great body, and beautiful that long thick dangle of Indian-black hair. He had had her, very nearly had her. In the Biblical sense.

"Isawimonlylarswake," she said.

"Sawfultuffdeel," he answered.

Leslie's living room lighted by candle stubs in colored glass. A party of parties, by its own right a being and a becoming. Where no drink went stale, yet none were seen drunk. Where no ashtray was out of reach. Where platters of marzipan cookies shone with a toytown brilliance and fresh bowls of potato chips and salted peanuts were magically generated. Where all seemed of one kind and one heart, yet each was what he himself wished to be: warmer, wiser, wittier, calmer, surer, more playful, capable, energetic, potent, attractive, straightforward and sensible than in life. Where scholars who had mastered Kant and Hegel, dour young poets and senior fellows in schools of letters recited dirty limericks, sang the ballads of Bessie Smith and imitated James Cagney, Charles Laughton and Bette Davis. Where the heavy-footed danced flamenco and the poorest of singers sustained impossible notes.

Then Leslie had cried, "*Lummir aller tanzen!*"

And Inez had cried, "*Tanzen, tanzen!*"

Some went "Bim-bom-bim" and some went "Day-doi-

doi." Some put foul or foolish words to the melody. Some paired off and some stood alone. Some unhooked and some unzipped and some kicked off shoes. Some pranced like cheerleaders, some like goats and centaurs. Some seemed to be pulling fish nets, some to be treading grapes. Some formed a circle and he, Morroe, with galloping heart and soaring spirit, was of this circle.

Then Leslie had cried, "Give! Be open! Be whole! Make contact! Kiss, kiss!"

And Inez had cried, "Kiss, kiss, kiss!"

Out went the candles. He called, "Etta, oh, Etta!" in mock Dagwood Bumstead tones, and by the last light he beheld his Etta going down gladly upon a strange lap. He felt: not rage, but righteousness. He thought: All right for you my girl, all right. Goose and gander, tit and tat. An eye for an eye, a feel for a feel. Let your whoopee sanctify my whoopee. So he whirled, both arms flung out as if awakened from innocent sleep. Embracing first Deena Adler. Then Sandra.

Although with highest hopes, how presume that she would swing her body into the embrace? That from 'prune' and 'prism' pecks she would unleash a kiss to burst shoelaces? How imagine that she would lead and he dumbly follow outside, upstairs, to the roof? Kissing and grabbing, ducking clotheslines, skirting sprinklers and ventilators and other hazards.

Excitement boiling up in him, Morroe made ready for a night's small fun: a bunny-swift entrance, a coupling and a gracious uncoupling. Followed by a few words of humble gratitude, maybe the sharing of a cigarette. He

192

would within the week send out a gift: an Oscar Williams anthology or a ceramic medallion bearing the inscription "*Honi soit qui mal y pense.*" On the card one bold letter, underscored: "M."

So making free with her ungirdled behind, he had cautiously suggested here and now.

She went along with the now, but balked at the here.

A hotel?

She was not strongly for hotels.

Would she be averse to her place?

In Queens, at the end of the line. And on the premises a mother with bladder trouble.

He had somewhere spotted a baby blanket. This, plus his jacket could serve.

Since puberty's onset she was allergic to wool.

Then, then an act of God: the wind which buffeted and chilled blew suddenly against their legs an abundance of newssheets. Making haste, Morroe scooped them up, spread them out and on hands and knees coaxed Sandra to his side. She knelt, while he whispered thickly, "*I like my body when it is with your body/ It is so quite . . .*" She broke into a nervous giggle and drew away. Had he offended? No, he was very sweet, but in the kneeling she had torn her garter belt.

He promised another. And began again, "*I like my body when it is with your body/ It is so quite new a thing/ Muscles better and nerves. . . .*"

He had weighted her skimpy panties with clothespins and was seeking her when the sound of heavy steps shriveled him. The iron door inch by dreadful inch opened, spattered weak light on them. A figure came forward, breathing vapor—a man. Sandra whimpered; Morroe, frontier midwife, gave her a clothespin to bite. He pictured: some terrible-tempered janitor; a tatooed arm (blue anchors and red roses) swinging a mop handle; a kick in the ass from an army surplus boot. Or wait, wait—he broke into a hot, then a cold, sweat—a cuter prospect! No janitor this, but the first of many from Leslie's living room. The whole thundering herd dancing onto the roof. At their head Leslie begging, "Don't stop for us!" Coarse laughter in the wings.

"Rieff! Rieff, Rieff, Rieff, Rieff!"

A little dog sniffled him. "Curse you, you bitch!" whispered Morroe as it presented fluffy rump and broke wind a foot from his face. He prayed it would do no worse, but it did. On top of which the man was stamping around and around in the pitch-dark, holding endless conversations with himself. Saying things like: "Gentlemen, please remove my name from your mailing list. . . . I am an old and desirable tenant. . . . Beyond question an injustice is being perpetrated. . . . They deliberately cook cabbage and cauliflower so that the smell will drive me out. . . . Despite everything I held the door for them when they carried bundles. . . ."

Also he sang:

"This is the Symphony
That Schubert wrote but never finished. . . ."

And

"Oh, wild rose, MacDowell knows
You're the sweetest flower. . . ."

He was bawling out a low-flying plane ("Climb, fool! Pull up, I say, up, up, up!") as they fled. Near Leslie's door they stood quietly for a while. Till Sandra told him that though she had lost a garter belt she had nevertheless gained a friend.

He was glad.

Would he in the foreseeable future call?

He would certainly call.

Because what had been between them had been lovely and spontaneous and, in its way, the highest kind of chastity.

Chaste it had been.

Let him take her number at the office.

On a piece of scrap he doodled seven matchstick men.

Her office had two Sandras. Let him be sure to ask for the one from Queens.

On one matchstick head he doodled a crown.

In the cab later he and Etta had wordlessly engaged each other like two gladiators, then like children playing doctor; in the elevator she was already loosening her clothes and fumbling at his; in the hall he crooned obscene promises; in bed she gave him no time to keep them.

"ThankGodnorain," Sandra now said.

"Salweedneed," Morroe answered.

And craftily, imperceptibly, he copped a feel of himself.

Woe.

Woe and whoosh!

You are a swine, he told himself, you are abnormal and definitely off your rocker.

Then to trick his blood, to divert its current, he emptied his mind of everything and he let only the vastest concepts filter back. Power, State, Society, Creator, Preserver, Universal, Silurian, Mesozoic, Jurassic, Commonwealth, Empire, Republic, Pain, Terror, Mob, Legion, Caste, Class, Labor, Rome, Egypt, Byzantine, Arctic. But he could not entirely hold off Slap and Tickle, Soft and Downy, Small and Tight, Bibble and Bobble, Whip and Feather, Armpit and Navel.

"How are you walking?" Ottensteen's hand was between his shoulders, poking his back. "It's a revulsion to watch you walk, you walk like a sick elephant."

"Down, boy!" and "Mercy, mercy!" Morroe whispered. And he concentrated his gaze on headstones, vaults, crypts, monuments, markers, mausoleums, his thoughts on the dead. To them, them, he made silent address.

He said, What can I tell you and what do I know? Your certainty, my problems. We got over the Depression, we got over Hitler. Skeezix is married and has hands full with the kids. My life isn't really connected to anything. Discount houses are very big lately. Likewise mutual funds. Likewise paperback books. Likewise tolerance, brotherhood, human relations, intergroup harmony. Your names and mine at the foot of one page. Now whole families can charter special planes for Israel. We're beginning to see Jewish faces in banks, though not so many. I get very little personal mail. Either people are more nervous lately or there is more to get on their nerves. We are losing India. Black princes from Africa eat at the Automat. I can imagine the day of my death, but not the day after. Everybody seems to have good taste. Bus drivers are becoming more vicious. Macy's has gone downhill. Likewise the big movie houses, the Modern Library series, wrapping paper, pencil sharpeners, kitchen matches, Nedick's orange drink. I have as much in common with the men who rule me as I have with the Gracchi. Big names appear for Jewish causes. Somewhere I read that it costs $3,500 a year to be poor. Comedians are very sad and keep breaking in with, "Seriously, though, folks, seriously . . ." Smilin' Jack is married. Warner Baxter, Richard Dix and Warren William died. Jack Benny is still big. No one talks anymore about Winchell. I don't think you missed too much. Honestly . . .

A dark silent relief enclosed him.

A bird worrying a worm delighted him.

A shimmer of green poplars, make it evergreens, filled him with reverence.

To a fat fly he gave the freedom of his temple.

To a ragged line of ants he yielded right of way.

To Leslie he promised, I'll cry for you. How I'll cry! I'll turn your insults into anecdotes, your *mishugass* into myth. I'll write off the hundred and thirty-seven dollars. Likewise that badger shaving brush and the Miriam Beard *History of the Business Man,* out of print and very scarce.

He altered his gait to a sturdy martial rhythm.

He opened the bottom button of his jacket.

He tuned in to the boys.

To Ottensteen, who was saying to Selma Raab, "More than you realize he took to heart. Once, once on a Sunday

197

he looked pale and green and very strange to me. It was hurting him, he was personally suffering because that minute and that second one-third of the country was watching Ed Sullivan."

To Levine, who was saying to Maurice Salomon, "We must first determine whether we want memoir or critique. If memoir, it behooves us to go easy on the bold and baroque, on his cafeteria-and-dexedrine period. If critique, it behooves us then, or it then behooves us, to find in his work what I like to think of as, ah, the double image—that which is, at once, symbolic expression of our time and tragic protest against it. *Moi-même*, I favor the memoir-critique. The former lending tension to the latter, the latter lending irony to the former."

To Weiner, who was saying to Cordell Nash, "He loved my mother's split-pea soup. True, he didn't mind her sweet and sour cabbage and he was partial to her honey cake. But he *loved* her split pea soup. Every Thursday my mother sent along the jar, the big jar for him, and every Thursday he would walk in. First he would look. Then he would handle it, like it was the Holy Grail. Then he would turn the cap, soft, slow, easy, thread by thread, and he would sing a little. *Boi-boi-bimboi-biddle-bamboi.* Gaah, soft, slow, sweet, easy he'd pour it in the pot, he'd make sure it didn't overheat, it didn't boil away. And he would sing a little. *Boi-boi-boi-tzickle-dickle-bim-bam.* And he would eat and while he ate he would explain to me. That food, good food was the warp and woof, the blood and bone, the spirit and substance, the very essence of Judaism. Then if there was time we'd go out and look for pussy."

And Morroe continued his reflections, and his mind gave birth to warm feelings, good impulses, worth-while projects. He would keep in touch with Inez and take her to the best, make it good restaurants for lunch. He would fix her up with somebody from the office, a decent, modest, genuine person like Morty Shulman who would dote on her, take pleasure in her strange ways and go gently with her into a pleasant menopause. He would show an interest in the little girls, treat them to Radio City, the Statue of Liberty, the Hayden Planetarium and F. A. O. Schwarz toys on birthdays and special occasions.

If it please God he would be, he would try to be . . . a true *mensch*.

But then he went *Ah! Ah! Ah!*

And *Fuck! Shit! Pee!*

He hopped, heavily hopped.

Pain.

Exquisite pain between his toes.

From pebble, shoe nail or wrinkled sock.

He left the path, stepping over a thick flower bed, momentarily oppressed at the accidental murder of a few blossoms. With his hands he instructed the boys to bear with him, to seek no explanation now, to trust his judgment, to rest assured that he would soon catch up. After which he trod gently among the too many graves and plopped on a low marble bench, grateful to the giver. ("*A true friend and life-long adherent of the ideals and aspirations of the Workmen's Circle,*" said the stained scroll. "*One who was happy to serve his departed brothers and sisters as Secretary-Treasurer, then as President. Anonymous.*")

There, shaking out a shoe, amid miscellaneous birds, cluttering weeds, moved by the moving wind and the blue and vacant sky, his sighs fogging his glasses, Morroe fell in love.

With Goldie Bromberg.

Barely thirty. Dead these thousands and thousands of days. Gone in a more mortal time. Outlived by half a depression, a whole war.

Who, he asked himself, falls in love with a dead girl?

The boys are right, one hundred per cent right. You really must be a *schmuck*.

Yet he pushed his face to perhaps a yard from her chipped little gravestone and stained his eyes on the tinted snapshot (fading, it seemed, even while he watched). Dark, dark was Goldie Bromberg, the hair pulled back in a bun, though a few lively ringlets had escaped, a nose long enough but made passable by a tilt, a pair of old-baby eyes heavy with reproach, full lips parted and somewhat insolent (a big mouth, a tough tongue, had once called her mother "old bitch"). He invented for her weak teeth (the shoddy work of dispensary dentists), hefty hips (she was sensitive about them), an overdeveloped chest (at fifteen she had outgrown a rich aunt's brassieres), a tendency to sweating (two and three times a day she changed her undies).

What might have been Morroe made memory. Crossing gloomy years he landed in Siberia (Prince M——, redeeming her harlot's soul like a pawn ticket), then Vilna (a wonder-working rabbi ordering out her dybbuk), then Auschwitz (she sneaked him SS slops to keep his pitiful bones together), then settled, reluctantly, for the

Catskills. For five days and nights at Blau's Star House, limousine service from Times Square, modified American plan, a good place for friendly professionals. He, a substitute in the junior high school system—three times a glottal *g* had cost him a permanent's license—she, fresh from commercial courses, keeping books (two sets) for the manager. (A dirty slob, had peeped at her in the outside shower.) On the first night they exchanged brief resumés of childhood times and sang songs of social significance till dawn, which they greeted with love's first kiss. On the second night he tried out some verse (*I like my body when it is with your body* . . .) and instructed her in political economy; she quickly grasped the labor theory of value. On the third night his hands got sexy, but her "Please don't . . ." nearly stopped his heart. On the fourth night she made him sign what she had that afternoon typed: "*I, Morroe Rieff, do promise Goldie Bromberg faithfully that if, as and when she lets me do what only one boy did before I will see her in the city;*" and allowed him ten minutes of free play with a breast. On the fifth night he begged for satisfaction, she for time. To sublimate, they sang till his last possible limousine. Before boarding he gave her *Engels on Capital;* she gave him her red and white graduation album. (*First comes love/ Next comes marriage/ Then comes Goldie with a baby carriage.*) Five minutes in the city he called person-to-person, talking to her for two dollars and seventy-seven cents. Come Friday, her mother was serving him cold soup and warm soda, her father had ears only for the radio, her kid brother beat him at hand wrestling. A long nine weeks later, the wedding.

(It took him three embarrassing tries to smash the wine-glass underfoot.) The caterer charged him for three empty tables. The waiters kept back half a case of whiskey. A fat cousin from Cleveland made a speech, told jokes. ("I got here a special telegram to the groom. The telegram says, and I quote, 'I didn't get in last week. Stop. You should only have better luck tonight. Stop. Signed, Alfred Landon.' ") Alone at last, Goldie fled his embrace. The ceremony's excitement, she explained, or a misreading of the calendar; the same thing had happened to her mother. Ten, make it eleven months hence, their son Seymour was born. A breech birth, ass-backward as he would be in all things. He cried when Morroe went near, he ruined Goldie's breasts, he retained too much water and his first teeth gave promise of costly orthodontia. But sweets he loved, also fatty foods. (A thyroid condition, the doctor pooh-poohed.) At age two they put him on a pony for a picture; he fainted. At age four he hit and spit, feared dogs, birds and bicycles, suffered nightmares, but could tell time and rattle off the Pledge of Allegiance. At age six he was breaking both arms, chipping an anklebone, reading 3B readers. His little poems were the talk of the school. (*As I went in the street one day/ I saw some children play/ To play with them I thought will be/ The nicest thing that ever can be.*) At age eight he made three BMs a week, tipped the scales at seventy-one pounds, bungled his kites, could not skate even on one skate, but spelled *disestablishmentarianism* and *feign*. Shortly after *bar-mitzvah* (he wrote his own speech) he drowned in rough Rockaway water. (Irony of ironies: Seymour could swim with the best!) Goldie ate out her heart, grew sick from the diet. (A little bicarb and get someone for the windows, the doctor pooh-poohed.) After the first exploratory she dreamed often of dead Seymour; he was in the street calling, "Throw me down a cruller!" or with Mrs. Roosevelt in the White House, showing off his Palmer penmanship. After the second—so it shouldn't be a total loss they removed her appendix—he bought Goldie a quilted bed jacket, he told her how clean he kept the house, how nicely he took care of his meals and needs, how in two weeks' time they would be watching Kay Francis and John Boles. When her pain permitted, they sang radio songs. (*"Ramona/ The mission bells are calling you/ Ramona . . ."* and *"Every night I hear her croon/ A Russian lullaby . . ."*) He read to her *Lorna Doone* and *Bleak House*, skipping big chunks. On the rainy day before she died he wrote out and signed what she dictated: *"I, Morroe Rieff, do promise Goldie faithfully that if, as and when, without hurting my health, I will miss her and always think about her."* Five, make it seven months later, he married an assistant principal; they lived on his salary and banked hers.

With a sob, Morroe stirred, crammed his foot into his shoe and rose unsteadily. Then he squatted, and slowly, systematically got to work. He pulled up handfuls of weed and grass from around Goldie's grave. He gathered twigs, and with the sharp end of one twig speared leaves. He arranged and rearranged the pebbles so that they might spell her name; at *D* he ran out. He used the teeth of a tiny pocket comb on bird droppings and his handkerchief on her poor snapshot. Although the stooping posture fired an old neuritis and spots like giant sperm bombarded his eyes, Morroe went on laboring for his love. Barehanded, he stripped away moss and mildew. With blunt, tireless strokes he tamped down Goldie's shabby coat of earth and beheaded a last wretched weed. The marble bench he lifted off the ground and carried five steps away; let it not rest so heavy on her feet. What was left of his comb he scraped and scraped against a lousy kid's scrawl. What was left of his handkerchief he flicked at a vagrant grub, sending it elsewhere to turn butterfly.

He bade goodbye to Goldie: Goldie, goodbye. Goodbye, Goldie. Likewise, Seymour.

Then he took a short run and sprang over the flower bed, nearly breaking his ass. Back on the path he looked right and left, high and low, even shooting a glance at the top of a tall tree, but saw only cemetery. He began to walk, picking out the freshest set of tire marks to follow; near the main gate he finally caught up with an ice cream truck doing good business. Making haste, he struck out along a new path, altogether empty and so quiet he heard his own choppy steps and the wash of his blood, deep, dangerous, as if an animal spoke through his skin. A squadron of geese (crows? ravens?) dove out of the sun and honked him: *Schmuck! Schmuck! Schmuckschmuck schmuckschmuck!* Whereupon he broke into a jog, then a trot, then a gallop, and it seemed to him, while he covered ground and went nowhere, that his hair was thinning, his cells altering, his forces failing, that the world was aging and turning cold, that somewhere an assassin had moved to the center of a crowd, a child been born to punish the race. For a foolish moment he considered setting fire to leaves and sending smoke signals, but he had no matches, let alone blanket. When his roundabout route brought him past Goldie's plot he froze and a little cry leaped out. And with his whole spirit Morroe called upon the *Ribono Shel Olam,* constructing an arthritic old man with his Uncle Lazar's face. Enough! More than enough! he half-pleaded, half-commanded. Let him only see the end of this day and he would dedicate himself to a life of service and good deeds; he would pay the balance on his U.J.A. pledge, plus a fresh ten dollars.

Although awaiting the bleeding of a rock, the flowering of a dead twig, he finally made do with a wind-blown tissue. Where the hot little gust took it he went, till the path parted ways. Instinct said go left, Morroe disregarded the advice. A few gnats (mosquitoes? wasps?) immediately rushed him, raising a beautiful blister on the fat part of his lip. He scaled a railing, pushed through a straggly shrub and took shelter near the granite pedestal of a bronze-tinted statue. David plucking a lyre for half a dozen frisky lambs. One of which gave Morroe a nasal *"Shalom."*

He cringed, sucked air, and was on the the verge of prostrating himself. When from around the pedestal limped a big sloppy stoop-shouldered woman wearing a ravelly coat sweater and a peaked hat made of old newspapers. She scanned him with the dark-red gaze of an abused bear.

At last, she cleared her throat and wheezed, "Hahbrukken beskitt."

Morroe mildly told her that she must have the wrong party, that he had done her no injury. Further, such language was unsuited to one so high in her descending years.

Bobbing her head and with finger commanding attention, she pantomimed stooping, the pain of stooping, lifting, the impossibility of lifting.

He turned out his pockets to show no change, but she wouldn't take notice. *"Vei iz mir,"* she mumbled, *"mir iz vei,"* and clasped one of his hands between her own, coaxing him slowly along. On the other side of the pedestal he saw a big wicker basket loaded with golden-brown salt-dotted pretzels. He made up his mind not to buy and waved her off. Wailing, *"Gottenyu!"* she sold him on another look at the basket. "This?" He pointed to the cane handle, split on one end and torn from its glue and nails. "This is where all the trouble is? The *tzoo-riss?"*

"Hahbrukken beskitt," she said, all smiles.

He patiently explained that the handle was hopeless, beyond repair, a lost cause. *"Nisht kenn ficksen."*

She grasped the basket by the width, then by the length. She tugged with one hand, then with both, and when it wouldn't budge she whimpered and tottered.

"Ah, ah-hah," Morroe cried. He now understood.

"Without a handle no good. No grip, no . . . purchase. Too *schwer*."

"*Schwer*."

"You want, you want me to lift it up for you? *Ich zoll liften?*"

"*Rachmaniss.*"

He grabbed and yanked and almost lost his balance. Pretzels spilled off the wooden pegs. A splinter pierced his palm. His eyes ran. His joints cracked like gun shots. His body shook like a wet dog. He tried three different grips, he put forth all his strength, but the basket was unbelieveably heavy. As if it lay undersea, fathoms deep.

"Lady," he cried, "lady, what is in here?"

She said, "*Tzooriss*" and broke into sobbing.

He dried his hands.

He spread his legs.

He sank his knees.

He tipped the basket against the platform of his left hip.

He worked the handle across his back and shoulders and under his right armpit.

He braced, he sank his knees a little more, he rocked, he slowly rose, and the basket rose with him.

"Here," he rasped, "here."

With mouth and brows he signified to the old girl that this was the limit of his good nature, that while he wished her only the best she must now take over.

But she had already turned away, limping fast.

He stumbled after, in a husky voice calling, "Whoosh, whoosh, lady. *Dei. Dir. Eich!*"

He got a kiss off her fingertips.

"Hoo, yoo-hoo," he bellowed, using up the rest of his voice. "Come take. Take! *Nemt!*"

She shed upon him a look full of love.

Cursing her in his heart, Morroe wavered into motion again. After a few steps sweat trickled down his forehead and beneath his arms. After a few more he had a parched throat and butchered ribs from the bumping basket. Three, then four strides ahead, the old girl paced him, making good time. Dust billowed up behind her, causing him to sneeze a great wracking sneeze.

He was about to tell her that she could at least reach into his pocket for tissues, but the Yiddish fled his mind. Anyway, he soon had other troubles.

For under the right armpit he was itchy, and the fingers of his left hand were puffy and red.

Then he heard the sound of cracking wood.

Then he felt the handle very slowly slip its mooring.

Then in a tormenting arc the basket swayed one way and the other.

Then he walked into a railing and his moan brought the old girl scuttling back.

"*Mazeltov,*" she cackled mirthlessly.

Morroe's impulse was to cast a coin and try a fast getaway. But half a good turn, he estimated, made him less than a *mensch*. So he restacked pretzels and tried coming to an understanding with the old girl.

He brought out that he stood ready anytime to do a favor.

"Jewshartz," she beamed.

He was, though, neither truck nor horse. "Hatruck-horse."

"*Fehrt*," she corrected hoarsely.

He believed that two sets of hands were needed here, at the very least. "*Tzvei*."

"*Ah kronkeh* kidney."

He was not in the best of health either.

To her he looked fine.

At this he wished her a cordial "*Gut yontiff*" and took off.

She wrestled him back.

"Habedboy!" she upbraided.

Though she kept pinching and squeezing his fingers he firmly refused to go through life a cripple. They must work together. "*Tzuzammen*."

She wet him with tears, but conceded.

At his "Whoosh!" they lifted the basket from opposite sides; it rankled him to see how smoothly and swiftly her side was airborne. When he had used up his second wind she was still on her first. And the limp, where was her limp? She who had been lame as a Turk had all of a sudden speed to burn.

He asked how far he must yet go, how long he must be thus burdened. "*Vie lahng?*"

"*Zum* train."

Hadn't he seen a nearby bus? He had seen such a bus. "Hahbus."

With such a load they would close doors in her face. "*Antehsemiten*."

Then she put on speed.

Then he matched her pace.

Then he could no longer match it.

Then he dropped into a panting walk, thinking, This isn't fair; after all, she's got sneakers.

Then she too slowed down, for they were among people.

And Morroe met himself in the mournful quietude of many eyes. And comments from all sides rained in his face.

"When she dies he won't have to feel guilty."

"He's doing the right thing."

"My Ronnie would also be so devoted!"

"I respect him for it."

"Keep a mother with you how long you can."

"To look at him he doesn't even look Jewish."

In no time the old girl was set up and selling.

"Hadime!" she cried. "Take fahadime!"

Morroe, at his end, made it three for a quarter.

"How about a bag?" a woman asked. "Put in a bag."

He told her no bags.

Another customer claimed she had said one but he had given three.

"*Vei iz mir,*" he wailed softly. "*Mir iz vei.*"

There were mutterings by some that the pretzels were dry and old and had his flavor.

"*Rachmaniss,*" he moaned.

He was requested to name what it was that had soured the smell of one pretzel.

He said, with a thick tongue, "*Tzooris.*"

Soon he lacked nickels.

After another flurry of customers he needed pennies and dimes.

Minutes later he was altogether without silver.

He turned to ask the old girl for change. "Change!"

While she was counting and recounting Morroe just happened to notice a fat baldy sticking his nose among the pretzels and squeezing the life out of them. Before he could open a mouth the nervy character had mangled two pretzels, sampled from another and, without buying, blithely walked off.

Incensed, Morroe gave chase, hissing *"Goniff!"* and *"Chutzpah!"* and scanning the ground for something to hurl, though the walks were crowded and he had a wild arm. For twenty yards, make it twenty-two, he kept the cranium in sight. But he had suddenly to stop. To blink. To shut his eyes as it came straight at him: a dazzle, an unholy radiance, a burning bush. A long second and a few blinks later he squeezed into focus two Yeshivah students, maybe young rabbis, caressing, embracing, while sun played on a pair of glossy red beards.

But then he spotted the cranium and was on his way again, chuckling a dirty chuckle, burping from the murderous excitement of what he planned for this character. How he would sting him, strip him of dignity, bring him low, put him down with a strident, "Hey, Baldy!" He zigzagged, he closed in fast and stretched out a hand like a cop stopping traffic.

When he was yanked by the coat tail and hauled back, one leg widowed in the air.

As best he could Morroe turned himself around. And there stood Ottensteen. Likewise, Levine and Weiner.

"Constraint," said Weiner.

"Forbearance," said Levine.

"*Schweig*," said Ottensteen.

Morroe heard himself say a dreamy "Oh, hi . . ."

"I'm not interested and I don't want to know." Ottensteen eased up on the coattail. "But if I was interested—"

And Ottensteen flung him to Levine, who flung him to Weiner, who flung him back to Ottensteen, who started him walking with soft little punches to his behind.

"—and didn't mind some aggravation I would ask how, how it is that you are my own personal *Moloch Hamoviss*. I would try to find out why you decided Felix Ottensteen is in your way and shouldn't remain on earth. I would be also a trifle curious to hear where you were that you are so dirty and what exactly you were doing that you are so out of breath and red in the face. Then . . ."

"When you're getting a hernia," Morroe softly said, walking with an awful hobbling motion, "how do you tell?"

". . . then I wouldn't wish you harm. Everything should be all right, everything should be very nice and the way you like it. With maybe one exception . . ."

"To go back," said Levine, "is it two lefts, left and right?"

"Left, left again at the Horwitz plot, but *half*-right at Kaplan," said Weiner.

". . . you should start to roll a little bit. And once you start rolling you shouldn't be able to stop. You should have to go from bed to . . ."

"A pretzel?" said Levine. "I am enamored of those pretzels."

"Who can get near on that line?" said Weiner.

". . . bed and from house to house, from street to street, from town to town, from lakes to rivers and rivers to seas, from up the hills and down the hills, from around the mountains and between the mountains, from cold places to hot places . . ."

"*Vei iz mir!*" Morroe started to say, but changed instead to "Wait and hear!"

". . . from every wood and every field, from where they have only night to where they have only day, from the hands of Pharaoh to the hands of Titus, from where you'll twitter like a bird to where you'll bark like a dog, from where you'll be fatter than a barrel to where you wouldn't even have a shadow, from world to world and between worlds. . . ." Ottensteen snuffled grimly and sighed as though he had been weeping for hours. Then he said, "*Nu*, what happened?"

"What happened?" Morroe halted in mid-step. "You want to hear what happened. . . ."

Levine said, "It's Horowitz, not Horwitz."

Weiner said, "Call me *pisher* for an *o*."

"Well, what happened was . . ." There were ups and downs in Morroe's voice, and he shivered like a somnambulist shocked out of sleep. In slow motion he searched his pockets, came up with *Sight Savers*, peeled one off and began to expressively clean his glasses, as if to say, 'See, I am coming up with a *Sight Saver*, I am peeling one off, I am cleaning my glasses.' He next worked dental floss between each and every tooth; on the third time around a barefaced lie flew into his mind.

And limping forward, one arm cleaving the air, the other frozen over his heart, Morroe told all that had lately befallen him. How while only a moment and a step away from his fellow mourners—he had even hissed and snapped fingers to catch their eyes—a funny thing happened to him. How he had been hailed and halted. How an old man, no taller than five feet, had tipped his worn black bowler at him. How the little fellow had tremblingly inquired if he was Jewish. How he had next put to him other questions: Was his father alive, and his mother? Did he live with his father? Did he see him and visit him? Was his father one who knew his way around a synagogue and how to wear a tallith? Had his father—to whom he sent regards—taught him the meaning of *mitzvoth?* Morroe next told how the little fellow, looking like he was internally bleeding, whispered his shame and sorrow. How for the unveiling of Klonsky's stone the Society was lacking one to make a *minyan.* How he, himself, the recording secretary, had sent out postcards where he needed letters and letters where he needed telegrams. How for five, make it ten minutes of next-to-no trouble, nine pairs of lips would recite Morroe's merits into God's ear.

And Morroe told further how he had given way to the little fellow, how where there were nine he had made the holy tenth. How with the baring of the stone he had begged nine pardons, but friends would be wondering. How a shopping bag had materialized, and how from this shopping bag slivovitz and honey cake were taken. How he was put on strict notice that nine sets of feelings would be hurt if he refused a sip and a snip. How with plenty, make it enough time, he had scooted off. How *en route, in medias res,* from the rancid sip or the sun-spoiled snip, he had suffered a dizziness, a wooziness, an upset in his stomach. How a kindly caretaker had turned over his john. How there he relieved himself of all he had that day eaten, and more. How feeling, even so, as miserable as man has ever felt, yet worried for the worries of his friends, he had ventured out. How in this state he had been set upon and ill-used.

For quite some time the boys gave Morroe rapt attention, and though he looked passable he felt a vague presentiment of panic. But just when he revised one or two details—the little fellow sprouting a few inches, the hat a regular fedora, at most a brown derby—Levine spoke up.

"Don't, ah, don't disregard the likelihood of a virus."

And Weiner, arching the back of a hand around Morroe's brow, "A definite hundred-and-a-half, a possible hundred-and-one."

"You stop off at a fruit store," Ottensteen put in, "you buy a bag of Sunkists, you bring home, you stuff yourself with citrus.'"

Morroe's spirit expanded.

In his shy and goofy way, under his lashes, he gazed at the boys.

He was that minute ready to die for them. Or at least to do them big favors.

He thought, They may not respect me, but they like me.

He also thought, They wish me no great good, but they wouldn't want harm to come to me.

And then they went up a little rise.

And then they went down a little incline.

And they bore right.

And they bore half-left.

And the fine warm spray of an alabaster fountain was blown upon them.

And there was a children's plot with little sun dials and a soft blue ark and stone beasts and birds and fishes in the grass, and they passed beyond this.

And there were family plots for Blaustein, Engel, Danzig, Applebome, Barchoff, Schneierson, Nass, Lowey, Diamond, Kratter, and they passed beyond these.

And one was for Braverman, and this one they entered.

And Morroe moistened his lips and braced his shoulders and took down some deep stiff breaths.

And it came to him that so he had often entered Leslie's living room.

And then Levine ran a finger over the flap of Morroe's left pocket and over his left sleeve.

And Levine said to him, "What is this stuff, this substance?"

And Levine further said, "It, ah, feels like, it has the consistency of . . ."

And Levine touched finger to mouth and softly spoke this word: "Salt."

First called up to the graveside was Maurice Salomon, who had this to say: that Leslie's mind and temperament were sternly moral; that it had been his role, his unique function in both fiction and criticism to deal with matters and circumstances which the American character—pluralistic, fragmented and debauched by commercialism—

would not readily admit to consciousness; that he had confronted life not with the armor of bias or the cant of dogma, but with a simple openness to the multiplicity of experience; that he undertook to tell us what it was for the individual to be alive at this moment in history; that he had conceded nothing to the times, but had over and again borne personal testimony that IT IS and I AM; that because of the vigor, the purity and passion of this testimony—the moral thrust—he claimed our attention.

Next spoke Arabelle Talbot Harrington, and she lauded Leslie as teacher, as one who delighted in instructing and who instructed by action and example. It gave her great pleasure to remember now that some years back she had been entering a cafeteria with Leslie; and suddenly there had stepped forward a derelict, an outcast, a human discard, a representative of the urban underbelly: a bum. He had begun to exhort them with his whiskey-ruined voice. No, not for a handout, but a loan to be paid back in proper course and due time. You see, Mac, Lady . . . a dishwashing job . . . a week's work . . . put him on his feet again . . . served in the last one, Mac, Lady. Thereupon Leslie had handed over a quarter. And with gravity and gentle ceremony he had proffered an old bill stub bearing his name and address and advised that he would look for payment in an early mail. Arabelle had later chided him. Why the pretense? The farce? Was he so new to the City, to such small swindles? Having been fool for the quarter, must he make himself more fool with the bill stub?

And Leslie had said this, and this is what Leslie had said: "With the quarter I found my own humanness; with the bill stub I restored his."

Next called was Ottensteen. His arms folded, his head low, his gaze turned inward, he said that though he was just now too filled up he would anyway do his best for his dear and very good friend. And he reminded all present, in case they didn't know, that in the Passover Hagadah, when it told in one section about how much God gave the Children of Israel in forty years on the desert, there was after every single item the word *Dayenu:* It would have been sufficient. If, for example, God had just sent manna but didn't bother handing out the Ten Commandments—*Dayenu.* If He handed out the Ten Commandments but didn't see to their drinking water—*Dayenu.* And similar, and such. This word, this *Dayenu* now stood written on his mind. So . . . if Leslie had been only a highly intelligent person and not a writer—*Dayenu.* If he had been only a writer of stories and didn't bother with his articles—again, *Dayenu.* If he had written his articles and didn't have his outstanding personality—once again, *Dayenu.* If he had this personality and didn't like people—again and again, *Dayenu.* If he had just liked people and didn't have on them an influence—*Dayenu* and sufficient. If he had just had an influence and not been sincere with people—sufficient and *Dayenu.* If he had been sincere, sincere but not sweet—

And many minutes later, though he was choking on a *Dayenu,* Ottensteen was eased, gently eased away from the graveside, and there came forward the folksinger, Leroy Gillman. Who said that though he was non-Jewish, though he was a Negro and not too familiar with the observances, he felt it properly right to sing; because that was the way of his people and he knew no better way to let a heart speak. What he would sing had been meant as a farewell, a goodbye for a certain prince hundreds of years back; it was now fittingly natural for this prince of a guy. He accordingly sang:

"Bonnie Charlie's now awa'
Safely owre the friendly main;
Mony a heart will break in twa,
Should he no come back again.
Will ye no come back again?
Will ye no come back again?
Better lo'ed ye cannot be,
Will ye no come back again?"

Even after Leroy's last note went pining upward; even after the coffin was rough-handled by the four diggers; even after they had set it on that evil-looking contraption and jacked it up, and it hung and then slid into the pit; even after he flung his handful of dirt; even after the shovels flashed and chipped and smoothed; even after Leslie's little father shouted out, "No man should live to bury a son!"; and even after Ottensteen, Weiner and Levine bawled openly, Morroe held back. Shithead, he labeled himself, horse's ass, peculiar creature. You could cry when the planes shot King Kong off the Empire State Building. You could cry when

219

Wallace Beery slapped Jackie Cooper and then punished his hand. You could cry when Lew Ayres reached for that butterfly.

But even so, nothing wet came from his eyes.

From somewhere a glass pitcher was produced and Ottensteen took charge.

"Rinse, *shlimazel*. A Jew mustn't go from the cemetery unless he washes off."

The water he dispensed sloshed over Morroe's cupped palms and miserably wet down a trouser leg and one sock. Morroe ground his teeth but muttered only a mild "Whoosh"; small penance for Klonsky and the nine. Anyway, the trousers at least were drip-dry. So he blotted his hands on his tie, then discreetly peeled off the soaked sock and gave it a burial under his heel. While thus engaged his eye chanced to fall on Inez, who seemed to be acting in a mysterious way.

She was cutting in and out and back and forth across the plot. She was bounding from one group to another. She was winking and blinking at Hal Essrig even as Phil Houseman had her arms trapped. She was flashing a significant look at Leo Munich even as Gary Lehrer whisked grass from her hem. She was putting her lips to Pearl Frey's ear even as she rumpled Millie Penn's hair. She was tapping her shoe against Jack Marrin's shoe even as she hugged and squeezed Norman Falk. She was using Francine Zober's lipstick even as she mouthed a secret syllable for Arabelle Harrington. She was kissing and being kissed by Stanley Fertig even as she shot out three fingers, make it a whole hand at Jim Newman.

And then, though Morroe momentarily lost sight of her and would have sworn that when last seen she had been ten graves away, Inez was standing before him and the boys.

To him she said, "Why didn't you bring Ellen, baby? I was looking for Ellen."

To the boys she said, "You boys are like family, so I don't have to ask. Do I have to ask? Will I see you at the house? I'll see you!"

"I would love to," Ottensteen said, "and I was looking forward . . ."

"Don't tell Maurice. He asks where you're going, you're going to Otto Popkin and you're going to get the key he has to Jane Finkel's cellar and you're going to take Leslie's old volley ball set over to Al Zackerblud."

". . . but certain parties saw to it, they made sure I should have to walk and get swollen feet and shooting pains and right now all I can tell you is . . ."

"Forget about the pizza, sweetie, we're not going to have pizza. We're not *not* having pizza, but we're not having *pizza* pizza. I have marinara sauce, I'll take the marinara sauce, I'll put it on English muffins, it'll be good, good, good!"

". . . I'm *oysgamitched*."

And Weiner said he was pooped.

And Levine said he was fatigued.

And Morroe said nothing, only opening and closing fingers to indicate that the decision was not in his hands.

221

But by and by they had it all settled, and with the help of Inez they had worked out these arangements: let Ottensteen feel better on his feet and he would telephone Weiner. Let Weiner hear from his mother that all was well and get Ottensteen's call then he must telephone Levine. Let Levine find a quick and easy parking space and thus be home to answer then he must telephone Morroe. Let Morroe have no fever, then he must telephone Inez. Let Inez find herself without English muffins, then she must remind Morroe to buy and bring. Let Morroe, having no fever and getting no reminder from Inez, play it safe and pick up English muffins anyway.

Then with a "Good! Good! Good!" and a "Fine! Fine! Fine!" Inez was on her way again. Morroe, caught by an impulse, bolted after her.

"Listen, Inez," he said. "Inez, listen. If tonight I can't . . . if we don't . . . I'll definitely call . . . be over . . . coming week."

She hollered back that she would make a dinner. And warned that he would be unwelcome, that he would be thrown out and on her shit list forever if he arrived without Eileen.

As they neared the main gate Levine's eyes turned glassy.

A white spot appeared on the tip of his nose, a fine dew of perspiration on his brow.

He stamped his feet.

He kicked at a pebble, but missed.

He walked around in tiny circles.

He went "Umumumum," and "Ahahahah." He escaped

Weiner's grasp, then Morroe's and after a short run skidded to a stop alongside a green Chevrolet.

Addressing the running board he said, "Sir . . . ah, fellah . . . friend . . ."

It took some time to unlock Levine's bumpers from the Chevy's bumpers, and in the process Morroe got himself a beautiful cut from a rusted license plate. He was dabbing it with his last tissue and squeezing to bring blood when the pretzel lady passed by. From what he could see she was practically sold out.

12 ———————————

IN A SECOND-RUN HOUSE off Times Square Morroe ate
pretzels while watching a revival of *King Solomon's
Mines*. Suddenly Leslie, wearing a pith helmet and short
pants, *shlumped* out of the jungle.

Hey, hey, what are you doing there? Morroe wanted
to know.

Here? Here I'm the white hunter.

Am I mistaken or don't you look shorter? How come
you look so short?

How come? How come is I said *schmuck* to a witch
doctor!

He sprang from his seat to follow Leslie into the
brush, but found himself in *The Informer*. After betray-

ing Leslie he treated half of Dublin to egg creams. The rest of his twenty quid he tossed to herself, Inez, then had second thoughts. But she wouldn't give back the money. They struggled; while they struggled Seymour huffed and puffed out of the fog. Rollerskating kids pursued, chanting "Fat, fat, the water rat. Fifty bullets in his cap." He chased the chasers, yelling "*Antehsemiten*" and awakened to Ottensteen's huge voice in his ear.

"Your grandma should one night pine for you and decide to come down and pay a visit from heaven, and she should want to kiss you and you should drool and dribble on her the way you drooled and dribbled on me."

"Eifelsleep," Morroe said through his yawn.

"You're old enough to never wake up," Ottensteen retorted. "Plenty old enough!"

Levine, beeping the horn, cried, "Ah ah, here now, for goodness sake. I deem that definitely out of order."

Weiner put in a "Gaah!" and in a breathy voice said, "Felix*el,* not nice, Felix*el!* Considering the circumstances. . . . Where we come from. . . ."

"I was very tired," Morroe burbled. "I was very tired and the engine noise must have relaxed me, plus with the top open it's quite pleasant, and I dozed off, which shows you how I must have been tired for me to doze off like that, because in trains, in the most comfortable berths and roomettes I barely close an eye, I come away a wreck, and insofar as I dribbled and drooled that shows how I had to be very tired, since whenever I'm tired I sleep with an open mouth, and if I happen to be laying toward my right side I tend to salivate through a gap, an opening in the bottom molars. You can see. You want to see . . . ?"

Twisting his mouth, he introduced a finger among his teeth. He waited till Ottensteen had taken a leery look, then said, "The glands—the salivary glands are very highly overactive. My dentist maintains that in all his practice he never saw anything like it. He calls me The Gusher."

With one hand Ottensteen slowly stroked and knuckled Morroe's neck; the other he rolled at Levine and Weiner in a gesture of mutual faith and hearty fellowship. "You should know already—" He cleared up a huskiness in his throat. "It's not since yesterday you are dealing with *der alte* Ottensteen. You should realize he can't be honey to one and to another vinegar. He is far, very far from perfect, but this he is: he is true-blue. He can't play a role. He's not two-faced. He doesn't split himself in parts. He tries to be a whole man, not a sch-sch—"

"Schizoid," ventured Morroe.

"—schemer. He opens a mouth, he falls on people, he makes them feel like two cents. He's not happy doing it, but he does it. And if he opens a mouth on the person, the person should be able to see that *der alte* Ottensteen is driving at something, making in his special way a point. And what is his special way? His special way is to hit and bark, to bark and hit. And the person should be able to understand that the hit is a love tap and the bark is a blessing. He should understand and appreciate."

"You don't have to worry, Felix. I see these things. I'm aware." Knuckle by knuckle and finger by finger Morroe slowly broke Ottensteen's grip on his neck. "You would be surprised at how I know what goes on, how nothing gets by me. All right, I won't say *nothing*. But I think I can objectively say I miss very little. Really." He repeated the "Really," holding it on his tongue like a Lifesaver, staring and staring into the rear-view mirror till he had trapped Levine's, then Weiner's eyes.

"A big mouth—definitely. A mean mouth—possibly. A spiteful mouth—maybe. But a dirty mouth—" a handkerchief flitted around Ottensteen's eyes—"a dirty mouth *der alte* Ottensteen doesn't have. You don't hear him broadcast to the world that he can get it going and keep it going even when it's after change of life. He tries to behave with a delicacy, a niceness, a . . . *finekeit*. And there's plenty people his age and younger who don't have *finekeit*. Take for an instance a certain Yiddish poet, a highly, *highly* eminent, you could say a genuine giant. This is a big name and you don't need to hear it for the purposes of this conversation. Nahum Bimberger—"

"Bridge or tunnel?" asked Levine.

Looking kindly across at him, Weiner answered, "Gaah, Holly, who cares? It's where you prefer. Whichever suits you, your convenience."

"I have *ab*solutely no preference, Barn."

"In that case," reasoned Weiner, "I say take the bridge. Take the bridge and save the quarter."

"You are being silly, Barn, and I am surprised at you. Did anyone hear me mention anything about money? Don't mention the thirty-five cents as a factor and do not get me angry."

"Who says money is a factor? What I'm saying—I

am saying do only what's best for you. Never mind going out of your way. I don't want to take you out—"

"Barn, bridge or tunnel, tunnel or bridge, I shall be happy. Tell me the route you, ah, chaps prefer. Tell me!"

"There's two for downtown and two for uptown, so— so, speaking as one of the uptowns I'll cast a deciding vote. I'll say tunnel. Tunnel!" And Morroe was hanging over Levine's seat and waving a dollar. "Here." He let the wind blow the bill near Levine's face. "Please." He tried to slide it into Levine's shirt pocket, but there was no pocket. "Take." He began to tease and tickle Levine's fingers with it. "Please . . . My pleasure . . . Courtesy of the road."

"NO! No and no."

"I feel like it. Holly, if I didn't feel like it—" Morroe was tunneling through to Levine's palm.

"Don't, do not get me angry, Morroe."

"I'll let go and it will fly, fly away. One . . . two . . . two and a half . . ."

"Ah, ah, now I am getting angry."

"Use it in good health."

Slowly, in a kind of tropism, Levine's hand opened, then closed about the bill.

"In the *best* of health."

"I am taking it because you are pestering and distracting me and are therefore liable to cause an accident—"

"God forbid!" Morroe gasped.

"—but you are going to get change. I charge you, Barn, you . . . Your responsibility . . . Change . . . You must remind me."

"Oh, oh! Whoosh! I am veh-eh-eh-ry worried about

228

the change!" Morroe slapped himself on the cheeks and made believe he was gnawing his fingers.

Silence followed.

Then Ottensteen, using his lowest voice, said, "Maybe you'll let *der alte* Ottensteen finish up Bimberger?"

"Absolutely. All ears," said Morroe, looking avidly into Ottensteen's mouth.

"I am listening, Felix," Levine sang out. "*J'attends.*"

"Gaah, go, go ahead," Weiner rushed in. "Finish him up. . . . Bimberger."

With tiny, almost imperceptible wiggles Ottensteen was freeing his jacket from Morroe's behind. "For a long, long period *der alte* Ottensteen didn't bother with Bimberger. How come? Because one night he came over the house, he ate a dinner and after the dinner *der alte* Ottensteen excuses himself. He takes an aspirin and a little snooze. Suddenly—all of a sudden a *geshrei,* a *gevald!* A pogrom in the living room. On bare feet and sick feet *der alte* Ottensteen runs over and he sees— he sees Bimberger has a hold of his late wife and is feeling her and carrying her in all her weight to the sofa." He momentarily glanced down as his last snip of jacket emerged. " 'Hello, friend Felix.' 'I am not your friend.' 'Why are you not my friend?' 'Because you are a pig, a louse and a slob and you are behaving along dirty lines.' 'Define a little your terms.' 'How should I define when you don't even stop when I'm talking?' 'Why should I stop when what I'm doing I'm doing only because I'm a good Jew?' 'How does what you are doing make you a good Jew, you pig, you louse and you slob?' " Ottensteen dug around and under Morroe and plucked out a button.

" 'Friend Felix, you don't remember what the great Rabbi Isaac said? Said Rabbi Isaac: From the day when they destroyed the Temple, from that day a good Jew can get pleasure from sexy intercourse only when he commits a sin.' " Working thumb and forefinger between Morroe's hip and thigh, he deftly withdrew a thread. " 'For years, bad blood. The room and the restaurant Bimberger went into *der alte* Ottensteen left. Until finally and eventually *der alte* Ottensteen went over, he put out a hand and he said—he said: 'I don't make up with Nahum Bimberger the pig, the louse and the slob. I make up with Nahum Bimberger the man, the master, the mind who gave the world once *Meine Gruener Betler.*' "

"You did the right thing," said Morroe.

"Life is far too short," said Levine.

"You sometimes have to look away," said Weiner.

Minutes went by. There was skimpy conversation: Levine, his manner anchored solidly in humanity and warmth, wondered if Weiner might stick a warning, a cautionary hand out to facilitate the changing of lanes, and Weiner wondered if Morroe might not take upon himself the task of checking the rear, and Morroe wondered if Levine might not put aside his sweet but stubborn yen to accommodate and deposit the boys at some place central and convenient. From Ottensteen generous comments sprang out: What the *Deutscher* wanted to build they knew how to build. . . . For the person who wanted a nice little automobile it was a nice little automobile. . . . Where you needed support the seats gave support. . . . He understood there were plenty, plenty around in Israel.

230

And then he came down with a fist on his knees.

And then he put his head in his hands.

And then he flung his head away from his hands, like a thing of little worth.

And then through a full nose he caroled, "Oi-boi-boi-boi-boi-boi-boi-doi-yoi-boi-boi!"

And Morroe chimed in with a "Whoosh-oosh-oosh-oosh-oosh-oosh!"

And Weiner unloosed a, "Gaah, vah-tah-tah-tah-tah-vah-gaah!"

And Levine went, "*Merde*-ah, *merde, merde, merde, merde, merde alors.*"

Ottensteen said, "Should I tell you a secret? Let *der alte* Ottensteen let you in on a big secret. The whole existence is a joke and doesn't pay. *It . . . does . . . not . . . pay!*"

Morroe said, "I wonder sometimes how people are able to get up in the morning."

Weiner said, "Why is life like a glass of tea? *Nu,* so it's *not* like a glass of tea."

Levine said, "*La*, ah, *vida es sueño y los sueños sueños son.*"

Various postures were assumed: Ottensteen slumped in a way that made his suit seem three or four sizes too big; Weiner fought a limited war near his crotch; Levine worked his nostrils as though smelling smoke; Morroe stroked an invisible beard, then a neat little goatee.

"Maurice Salomon told me—" Levine had to stop and deal with a shakiness in his voice. "Maurie mentioned that he would like to make the next *Second Thoughts* an all-Braverman issue."

"Wonderful. Wonderful, wonderful," said Morroe.

"How can they go wrong?" Ottensteen wanted to know. "Far wrong they can not go."

Weiner endorsed the idea with a "Gaah!" and, nodding and nodding, said, "I'm not too hot on *Second Thoughts*. I mean, I'm as good a *realpolitiker* as Maurie —Christ, I broke with the Trotskyites when I was fourteen. Fourteen! Before I even got laid—so I don't need him to tell me, that little *kahnackeh*, that atom bombs are dangerous. But . . . for Leslie . . . for Leslie I'd write for them. Sort of a biographical piece, but not a biographical piece. In a way an assessment, but not—"

"—ah, Barn, that, ah, Barn, has already been spoken for. One might say . . . committed."

"—altogether an assessment."

"You, ah, might do well to try it out on the *Mizrakh Monthly*. Personally, I see it, I very *def*initely see it in the *Mizrakh Monthly*. The lead piece. I have only to call or drop a quick note to Rabbi Lippman and you are all set. Virtually in print!"

"Let me. Let *der alte* Ottensteen make the call and drop the note." Ottensteen held up two fingers, one twisted so hard around the other that blood left both. "Here is how we are, Lippman and me, one to the other. To my say-so he pays strict attention."

"The *Mizrakh Monthly*," Weiner whispered, his words all furry. "Who reads the *Mizrakh Monthly?* I think once in my chiropodist's office—"

"It is very widely read. Let me assure you, Barn, in certain circles and many quarters it is influential and well regarded."

Weiner answered nothing.

And some moments later Ottensteen spoke, "Now no more Leslie. No more Labeleh. No more postcards: 'Dear Mr. President, when you are making up your cabinet on me don't count.' No more rush-rush to where they are playing the Marx Brothers. No more Toilet Thoughts."

"You remember those, gaah? He would carry in a notebook, a little blue notebook and a pencil whenever he had to go. . . ."

"Whoosh, wonderful stuff. Wonderful, wonderful."

"The comings and goings, the tos and fros, the back and forth of his mind. The stray thought pinned on a point in time. Myself, I recall with affection this one: 'The agonies of Auschwitz and Buchenwald were fore-shadowed when the first Jewish housewife laid hands upon the neck of the first pullet.' "

"From his Taft Cafeteria period," Weiner reflected. "He did his best work in the Taft john."

"Or the poignancy, the power *and* poignancy of: 'I feel sometimes like a bird who has not migrated in time.' "

"My favorite, you forgot my favorite one," Weiner chided sadly. " 'I like *shiksas*, but I don't like their brothers.' "

"That's good, that's quite good, Barn." Levine cackled a bit. "But I happen to prefer 'God, ah, grant me the compassion, when I see a small man, to lean over and whisper to him.' "

"Take a guess where he produced that. From where the inspiration came. On *der alte* Ottensteen's—"

But Morroe, holding up his hand like a schoolboy, broke through with, "Excuse me, only I don't get it."

"WHAT?" Weiner swung a grumpy glance at him. "What don't you get?"

"Never mind," Morroe countered, heavyhearted. "Forget I—"

"You don't be afraid! He wants to snap, he'll have dealings with *der alte* Ottensteen."

"I *snapped?*" Weiner whimpered.

"What then—*I* snapped?"

"Here, here!" and "Now, now!" Levine said, with authority. "As far as I could make out, Barn, you did not snap. Still, there was to your tone a, ah, peremptory quality, a rather truculent edge which might well have given Felix the impression of a nature somewhat less than affable."

"See!'" cried Weiner. "You see, Felix?"

"Meanwhile," Levine was saying, "I believe Morroe had a point. Let us hear now from Morroe."

"Tiss, whoosh . . ." Morroe tried for light laughter, but it came out sinister snicker. "I forgot, practically," he lied. "Oh, well . . . It was the pullet one. That one I don't get, or if I get it . . ."

"What's to get?" Weiner demanded.

"What's to get—" Morroe was aggressively aloof— "I don't get."

"So, so?"

"*Nu*, that wasn't a snap?"

"The point I'm making is this. Thi-hiss is my point. . . ." Morroe had a sudden moment of pure absolute mindlessness; he stopped to watch his thumbs beat each other. Next he thought, for no good reason, that Latin, Latin would be in order; and he wavered between *coitus interruptus* and *nolo contendere* before making do with *non sequitur*.

"It's a *non sequitur*."

"Not nice!" Ottensteen cried out. "Shouldn't say!"

"As a matter of fact," Morroe grabbed at an insight, "It's not only a *non sequitur*, it doesn't even follow."

"Where Leslie wanted it to go it went!" Ottensteen all but wept.

His hands mounted on his thighs, his eyes grown big, Morroe said, "How can you compare, liken what a Jewish housewife does to a pullet to what *they* did in the camps? You're going to tell me Leslie went through a little vegetarian phase. Okay. But . . . chickens and men, whoosh!" Morroe made as though to rest his case, then added, "And after all, since when is a kitchen sink a crematorium?"

That, that was good, he thought. The way I was able to drive in with that last point.

From Ottensteen he got a nip on the cheek.

From Levine a "Well played! Well played!"

From Weiner, a gracious "Gaah!"

A good half-minute went by before he said, "You don't think I was being too negative?"

They were surprised at the suggestion.

"Because I think it wouldn't be at all a bad idea— it would be a terrific idea!—if they could put into that issue ten, make it twelve of his Toilet Thoughts—only with a different title—as a special boxed feature. Wait, wait *a* minute! Who has to box it? A column rule all around, and each one set off with a two-line initial. And maybe this is not the time and I'm not such a marvelous expert on layout, but if Maurie wants—only if he wants—let him call and I'll give him a little idea about the typography. But only if he wants. . . ."

"A column rule, ah-hah." Levine nodded toward Weiner and Weiner nodded toward Morroe. "*And* two-line initials." He nodded to himself and paused, seeming dazed by the windfall.

And Morroe was all ready to inquire if anyone wanted a Hopje when Ottensteen said heavily, "What—what is the answer?"

To which Weiner made reply, "You know, that's a good question." He giggled and lowered his head as though expecting to be kissed by Ottensteen. "A good question," he repeated, but Ottensteen had his hands teetering over them, shaping destinies. "Boys," he was saying, "Boys . . ."

He was met by strict attention.

"For Leslie—for Labeleh we would want to do, only we cannot do."

Small sounds of sorrow rippled through the car.

"If I asked you, 'Boys—boys, cut off for our good friend a few of your years, donate a piece of your health—' "

He would not have to ask twice.

"So what is it we would want to do that we can do? We would want to do what we can do for the wife who is become a widow, for the children who are become orphans . . ."

236

"The older one is a little snotty," said Weiner.

". . . so *der alte* Ottensteen has come up with and conceived an idea. Not an idea—say, a plan. All right, more than an idea and less than a plan. To understand, you need to understand the principles from which *der alte* Ottensteen operates. His principle is this—this is his principle: That where you go you have to go. . . ." He gestured at Morroe like a band leader. "Let's hear how you have to go!"

"You have to go," Morroe told him, "like a sport."

"Nicely put. So . . . the plan is a fund. The fund should be for the girls. For later on. For an education. For an out-of-town school. For their little expenses when they get older. For the bottle toilet water. For the pink-and-white stationery. For a good-looking valise to carry. You don't know—you do not know how important a valise is to a young person. But *der alte* Ottensteen—" he had out his handkerchief—"knows. He—he remembers how he walked through his young years without a valise. How at age eleven and a half Jacob Riis sent him to a camp for sinus and he had to knock on the neighbors' doors they should please do him a favor, maybe they have a shopping bag not in use. Without printing. You hear that? Without . . . *printing!*" Submerging under his handkerchief he blew, blotted and came up all business. "If a fund is going to be a fund calls for a name. Remember —requires number one it carries mention of a fund; number two, it carries mention of a particular person; number three, it carries mention of a particular purpose. Therefore I got in mind to call it—" He raised his palms at Morroe. "Let me hear what I got in mind to call it!"

"We should call it," Morroe told him, "The Braverman Memorial Fund!"

"Correction, correction please," Ottensteen brightly said as he made love to Morroe's shoulder. "The *Leslie* Braverman Memorial Fund."

Levine beeped the horn: two longs and a short.

Weiner clapped hands.

Ottensteen spoke again. "If a fund is a fund calls for one more thing. One more thing is vital and essential. What am I talking about? In what particular thing is *der alte* Ottensteen interested?"

"The particular thing is . . ." And warily Morroe spoke the word: "Money."

"*Gelt!*" Ottensteen's eyes moved and glittered as though following a dancing dollar sign. "Capital!"

Weiner said, "Good thinking, Felix."

And Levine said, "No funds without capital, Felix."

Then Ottensteen came back with, "So far—then so far *der alte* Ottensteen can safely say a . . ."

He got two "so goods" and a "wonderful."

Then Ottensteen alternately moaned and chuckled, and over his head a balloon seemed to rise, to hover, and in the balloon bulbs glowed and asterisks were ingested by question marks. He hummed "Cocktails for Two" and made it something cantorial. He hummed something cantorial and made it "Cocktails for Two."

And Morroe was somehow not surprised when Ottensteen said, "Into five hundred, four goes how many times?"

And he was not surprised when a silence developed.

And he was not surprised when Levine filled it with, "It's, ah, not the money, Felix . . ." and Weiner with, "Gaah, it's the money, it's the money!"

And he was not surprised when Ottensteen put him down for the first hundred and twenty-five dollars.

But his heart rose and sank, flooded and emptied when Ottensteen said, "Next week has to go out a special mailing. Dear Friend—Dear Friend of Leslie Braverman, we who compose and represent a special committee, an interested group, beh-meh-shmeh, and so forth. Has to go!"

With a throb in his throat Morroe said, "Felix always writes a good letter. Always! Even his postcards have—"

"And what about releases?" Weiner was asking Levine.

"Ah, ah," said Levine feebly. "But they, alas, require a highly special skill in the writing, a sense of the essential, a grasp of the fact as fact. And for such as we, engaged as we are in criticism, in another discipline . . ."

"Not so-ho-oh special. Honest, with a little common sense anyone . . . all right, not *anyone* . . ." Morroe's arms closed in to encompass only half the world.

"Brochures?" Weiner speculated.

"One, *one* brochure!" burst out Morroe. "And one even you don't really—"

"Stationery?" Weiner was asking Levine.

"By that you have in mind. . . ?"

"Paper, Holly."

"To *hondle* with the suppliers, to go around to the printers—is that for *der alte* Ottensteen and his sick feet?"

Weiner said, "Lists."

"Letterheads." Levine's sigh could have snuffed out candles.

"The compiling of lists . . ."

"The designing of letterheads . . ."

"The choice of a type face . . . Bodoni . . . Delphian . . . Century Expa-ann-ded . . . Futura . . . Futura BOLD!"

"The myriad colors, the myriad *of* colors! Nassau Blue . . . Deep Madder . . . Peacock Green . . ."

"Peacock Green? The day you use Peacock Green is the day you wave bye-bye to *der alte*—"

"Black, black, black's the best thing! A nice neutral black!" Morroe practically rose in his seat. "Maybe, *maybe* a reflex black!"

"Let me tell you people—" Ottensteen pressed Morroe against his side—"we got here an iron head."

Through his teeth Levine said, "While we were fumbling and fluttering—"

"—he gets it first try! Thwuck!" Weiner punished the air with a judo chop.

"Whoosh-ure!"

"One has the impress of a perception fine-tuned, a—"

"Right away!"

"—sensibility at ease in the market of the commonplace."

"Oh, every day. Every day!"

"And how about that he has a good heart?"

Accompanying himself with an imaginary fiddle, Morroe hummed "Hearts and Flowers."

"*Ah guten neshoma . . .*"

"Yar-dar dar-dar yar-*dar* . . ."

And fifteen, make it twenty minutes later, while he grinned his shy and goofy grin, Morroe promised the boys that within a week the first solicitation letter and the first release would be in the mails; that within ten days he would line up an executive committee, and the second letters and second set of releases would be in the mails; that before the end of the second week he would write and plant small notices in the Sunday book sections, in a selected list of the journals and quarterlies, and a follow-up letter would be in the mails; that in the middle of the third week a final follow-up and a thank-you to the first contributors would be in the mails; that if direct mail proved a disappointment by the fourth week they might well give thought to a per-plate dinner.

Not that it's a craft, his mind told him, but you know your craft.

It also told him, You are being had.

So I'm being had.

You are being snowed and put on.

So I'm being snowed and put on.

You need it?

It's my nature.

But still in all, when Levine took the bridge and made no mention of his dollar, Morroe was sore, he was a little bit sore.

Coming out of the phone booth Weiner's lip trembled, and one side of his face, a nostril and an ear were tinged apricot.

With gravity, with utmost yearning and sorrow, he announced, "I rang and I rang and . . ."

Like a bullet-gutted movie gangster clinging, but just barely, to life, he fell into the car.

". . . I rang."

"She could be where she couldn't answer on the minute," Ottensteen cheerily said.

"A son is only a son," Levine comforted, "but a call from Mother Nature . . ."

"Momma would answer," Weiner said. "*She* would answer." In his far-off gaze he seemed to be watching her leap from operating tables, vault subway turnstiles, jimmy locks, scale fire-escape ladders.

"She ran down for something. She realized she needed a container of milk, a quarter of a pound of butter, wax paper. She ran down and in that minute—in that second, whoosh!"

Weiner shook his head.

"Cold cuts, a roll? It's Sunday, it's hot, she didn't feel like cooking, preparing. . . ."

"*She* didn't feel like cooking? *She* didn't feel like preparing?"

"Then I'll still say milk. Can a person—a person can *never* have too much milk in the house.

"In 1938—" Weiner's apricot tinge heightened, subsided, heightened, stayed heightened—"in 1938 she ran out of ketchup. But, all right. It's modern times. Automation, nuclear power, she couldn't carry, they forgot to send. She's having a good day on her hip, she'll go down. She wants to pick up an item. So where? There is, gaah, Irving Number One and there is Irving Number Two. Irving Number One, who kisses her hands when she walks in, is closed on Sunday. But Irving Number Two—Irving Number Two who is open even on Yom Kippur she wouldn't go into if he gave her a million dollars *and* a jar of instant coffee. Because, gaah, though she went to his daughter's honor roll party, though she rang bells to send him customers, though I used to have to take home his jumbo brown eggs, though he'd knock on his window if she forgot to give him a Hello Irving, though he visited her three times when she was in traction, he sinned. He failed her. There is a store full of customers, she walks in with two deposit bottles, he picks one up, he says to her, 'This one I will positively identify as not my bottle!' Since then . . . from that day . . . gaah . . ."

Ottensteen said she had had a right to spit in his face.

Morroe wanted to know if the bottle had definitely been Irving's bottle.

Levine said *das Ewig Weibliche*.

Then Weiner sat a moment longer.

Then he made an effort to rise.

Then he abandoned the effort.

Then he clamped a hand over his mouth, as though restraining an impulse to vomit.

"She went to a neighbor," Morroe began again. "She realized she was out of milk, she went to a neighbor and just that second, just those few minutes . . ." He sighed, implying vast ironies and coincidences.

"She's looking for the super," said Ottensteen. "Till

you find out where they are, till they come to a door, till they put away the bottle—you know when you have to deal with the *schwartzes* . . ."

"Heh-heh," went Levine. "You *could* have been all along misdialing. I recall that, ah, Ruddick, in a fairly recent paper, cited the fantastic prolix of lapses to which the ego succumbs under the impress of extreme anxiety. Sometimes, ah, not even extreme . . ."

"Who is anxious?" Weiner cried. "I'm just understandably curious." He put a finger on the windshield and traced a cross, then converted the cross into a shaky *Mogen David*.

"Naturally, naturally." Levine started the engine. "But now for home. Home, old sport."

"The best place. You'll go upstairs, you'll squeeze yourself a citrus—"

"—and I am willing to bet by that time—whoosh!"

"—by that time—" Weiner was converting the *Mogen David* into something phallic—"she'll be reaching me. She'll be burning up the wires."

But three, make it four blocks from his building, he began to fidget, to scratch madly at his face.

And within a half-block of his building he had panicked Levine into a short hard stop, had made for the inside of a bar, had emerged moaning "Gaahsoutoforder!" and had broken across the street for another bar.

Then his face, big, red, scrawled with joy, was moments later filling the sun roof.

"I'm getting a busy signal!"

Then he was moving leisurely against traffic.

244

Then he was inside the bar.

Then he was waving and whistling, waving and screaming, "Busy . . . still . . ."

Then he was back in the bar.

Then he was over the sun roof, his loving glance lighting upon each in turn.

"You know what?"

He got two "whats?" and a "*comment?*"

"She was by Irving Number Two."

"Am I smart," demanded Morroe, "or am I smart?"

"They made up."

"In that respect she's like *der alte* Ottensteen. He also can't hold a grudge."

"She has eggs for me. *And* pot cheese."

"The pot cheese around my way—whoosh-echh!"

"I'll bring. A pound for you, a pound for Felix, a pound for Holly. You'll all have. And as long as I'm bringing . . ." Weiner hung back for only a second. ". . . I'll have her make her split pea and barley soup."

They hated to impose.

"What kind of impose? I'll tell you what. I'll . . . tell . . . you . . . what!" He gestured as though offering a toast. "On Thursday the Griffith is starting their Randolph Scott festival. *Coroner Creek* and *Frontier Marshal.* We'll make a night of it. First we can have the soup, or we can go first and *then*, gaah, have the soup."

Either way would suit all.

"So it's definite?"

All asserted that it was definite.

Yet Weiner had taken no more than six steps from

the car before he turned and spoke through the mega-
phone of his hands.

"Should I check anyway?"

Three times Levine beeped the horn, and three times
more.

On the way to Ottensteen's Morroe mumbled that
they had made excellent time, that he had been wrong in
advocating the tunnel, that by taking the bridge they had
saved themselves money *and* time. But Levine played
dumb about his dollar.

One hand stroking the other, his face acknowledging
sad truths, Ottensteen crooned, softly crooned:

"Rai-rai-rai-rai-rai
Rai-rai-rai-rai-rai
Rai-zai-banjo on my knee."

And he took hold of Morroe's sleeve and Levine's
collar before saying, "Boys—boys, it's no good. It's
definitely not good."

"In a way," said Morroe, "it's the system."

"Vuss fahr ah system?"

"The nervous system," Morroe foolishly cracked, "the
transit system . . ."

But Levine diverted Ottensteen with, "All things are
water." He added, "Ah, according to Thales."

"You don't say? That's what he said? That's how he
put it? All . . . thing . . . are . . . water!" And Ottensteen cried, "All things are gall! All things are acid! All
things are . . . *pishachts!*"

Then, treading down Morroe's shoes and his own cuffs,

246

teetering on the running board, Ottensteen was out of the car. He slammed the door and used the same sweep of hand to flick a finger at Morroe.

"You are going to soon make a certain stop. That stop is going to be—where is it going to be?"

"That stop is going to be at a store."

"You're going to buy in the store an item. That item—"

"—will be a nice citrus."

"And with the citrus you'll do what? With the citrus—"

"I'll squeeze juice, or I'll eat it as is."

And without a goodbye, Ottensteen turned. Paunch upthrust, thumbs linked in the small of his back, with crisp short steps he entered the hotel. He could be seen all the way to the elevator, where he stood facing the rear; when last seen he was still facing the rear.

"Whoosh," said Morroe, seating himself finally alongside Levine. "To stop at a store . . . to buy a few cents' worth of citrus . . . can I ask them to change twenty?"

"Ah," Levine waved down his scruples, "definitely, definitely."

"I'd say come up," Morroe told Levine, "but . . . "

. . . my wife can't stand you, he silently declared.

"I couldn't, ah, anyway." Levine's intonation was charged with the irony of one plainly intended for better things.

"Were you here since we fixed up? Did you see what we did. . . ?"

". . . spacious. *And* all rooms off the foyer."

". . . to the closets. Where do you *get* closets like that in the Village?"

"Never, never."

"I ran wiring in myself for lights and for a little fan that goes on when you open, automatically. Myself! Not that I'm so terribly handy, but when you start with the electricians . . . twelve-fifty just to ring your bell. . . ." Look, see how bored he is, Morroe thought, he's practically turning black. Oh, oh, my, that little twitch of fatigue, that petulance on the lips. Screw you, *mon vieux*, tough shit, old sport! And he droned, deliberately droned, "When it gets cooler I plan scraping the floors myself. They have those places where you rent the machine and all the attachments. Lately, I even service my own air-conditioner. The manual that comes with it gives you all the instructions, so I don't have to be at the mercy of those . . . yuks. I pull it out, where it says oil I give it two drops of oil, I vacuum the filter and the coils, along the window I put fresh weather stripping and that special insulating stuff, and there—there's your servicing for the year."

"Well, now," said Levine cheerily, "I think I envy you. *And* your air-conditioner." A second later he said, "I, ah, wish I myself might be so easily serviced."

"Hmmmmmm?" With base pleasure Morroe dissembled confusion.

"Serviced. . . . The biological usage."

"Titter, titter," said Morroe. And, "Guffaw, guffaw."

Nothing further was said by either of them. Morroe, sniffing in, sniffing out, groped for something more subtle, something implacably malign, a word that would poison, an exchange that would paralyze. But beyond another "Titter" he could not go.

Then Levine said something he did not catch.

"... didn't catch."

"... perturbed, fellah. Because I do owe you ... you know ..."

"Whoosh ... put it away ... forget ..."

"... apology."

Morroe attempted a noncommital cough.

"I was behaving in a manner that was essentially ... reprehensible."

"Ohhhhh." Morroe grinned his shy and goofy grin. "Reprehensible? Maybe a little pricky, but not reprehensible."

"There are—were—of course, complex personal factors. Reasons ..."

"Whoosh-ure! What, then? *Without* reasons?"

But Levine, clearly bent on earnestness, answered, "My analysis is—" he fluttered fingers—"shaky."

Tough shit *and* tough titty, Morroe reflected.

"In the best of analyses, in the most solidly established transferences it is far from easy when the therapist takes a holiday. . . ."

Though his "Sure . . ." registered just the right tone of compassion, compassion and pain for the pain of others, Morroe was thinking, Yeah, yeah, not every man is blessed with your sorrows.

"One needs, one is entitled to a holiday. Even an analyst . . ."

"Oh, especially, *especially* an analyst. The types they get, what they have to listen to. Day in, day out. Hour after hour after hour. Whatever they make it's not an enviable livelihood." Morroe considered a pointed look at Levine, then reconsidered.

"I might say, I can say that there are other factors."

Now Morroe fluttered fingers, a sign that nothing human was alien to him.

"You can't, can not imagine the emotional outlay, the constant expense of, ah, spirit in the teaching of writing. It takes its toll, it grinds one down." As though to emphasize his last words, Levine slumped a little over the wheel.

"Well, I'll bet it does. I can imagine. I say *imagine* because, naturally, I'm not speaking firsthand." Nodding and blinking, Morroe was tempted to offer an exchange: his best day in the office for Levine's worst in the classroom. Anytime!

"Her hard young breasts . . ."

"Where?"

"I *cupped* her hard young breasts. In my classes they will never squeeze."

"Yes, well that I can *see*. That definitely could work on your nerves."

"And, of course, the nipples. There are, ah, the nipples. They . . . These *butt* or *jut* into the hand. On occasion they may . . . *spring!*"

"Ucch!"

Gradually, gradually, with the air of one too far gone to even calculate his risk, Levine turned his eyes into Morroe's eyes. "Lately, of late, I think my own work, my output has begun to suffer. I have this piece on Auden, I *must* get it out. But—ennui. Ennui and anxiety.

Then, too, what, precisely what at this late date can one find to say about Auden?"

"Say something nice. . . ."

"I sit and sit at the typewriter and I put down, ah, *tradition*. I put down . . . *moral*. I put down . . . *truth*."

"That doesn't sound bad."

". . . *commitment*."

"*Commitment* is fine. . . ."

". . . *century* . . . *tragic* . . . *condition* . . ."

". . . the right track."

"And then, then it will happen. One by one the words die. I noticed it first with *moral*. It looked mean and gray, somewhat . . . ailing on the page. And two weeks ago, with the best will, I was unable to pull it through. Dead!"

"I had something similar," Morroe informed him. "*Parallel*. I couldn't bear, I was getting almost sick from those two *l*'s after the second *a*."

"*Commitment* went. . . . *Desiccation* went. . . . *Tragic* is, ah, one might say on the critical list. *Alienation*—"

"And also *basic*. The *c*—whoosh!"

"—failing, failing. One more article, at most, the very most, two omnibus reviews."

"I'm sorry." Morroe heard real emotion in his voice.

"I have stopped reading. Oh, I know, naturally, what is going on in *Partisan*—I *have* to keep abreast—but reading, Real Reading . . . It would be no great exaggeration to maintain—" Levine seemed to be checking the rear-view mirror—"no *very* great exaggeration to maintain that since, almost since . . . that I have enjoyed nothing so much as . . . heh-heh . . . *Bob, Son of Battle.*"

"Hey, hey, listen!" cried Morroe. "You remember? That ending, that ending!"

"Ah, ah. Red Wull as antihero . . . the dogs bringing him in . . . the inevitability, the sense of uncontrollable forces fulfilling the what-must-be. . . ."

"It was a terrific dog story, too."

"Perhaps if I should ever give a regional lit course—" Levine glanced covertly at the rear-view mirror. "I am, ah, keeping you."

"You're not, you're not *keeping* me." So Levine would see that he was a free agent Morroe opened the door and put a foot on the curb.

"Anyway, at any rate, I want you to know . . ."

"Forget. It's forgotten. And I got in my share, at least my share of needles. So now the air is . . ."

"*As in water face answereth to face, so the heart of man to man.*"

"Sure." Morroe gripped Levine's hand; he shook and shook it, then used it to help boost himself out of the car. "You don't have to wait for an invitation," he said. "When you're in the neighborhood . . . Even if you're not in the neighborhood."

Now Levine gripped his hand, saying, "Of course, he will be back in four weeks, and I do have confidence in him. We are near, I *feel* we are near the breakthrough."

"If you *feel* you're near, you can't be so far. . . ."

"The end of that negative transference phase. When we see *that* through . . ." Releasing Morroe's hand, Levine worked hard at grinning. "Then . . . then, ah, who knows? Was it not Leslie who said, 'Everything these days is provisional; and our only certainty is the provisional?' "

"As a matter of fact, it wasn't. Not that—"

But Levine had already started the engine and was asking him to listen for a grinding, a possible chatter in reverse. "Nothing, Holly. I honestly can't hear . . ." Then, after he had helped Levine maneuver away from the curb, after he had guided his U-turn, he called, "So don't be a stranger!"

"Going up!"

The elevator remained at seven.

"HelloHEYHOWABOUTIT?"

He saw the cables and weights rise. He saw also, by the indicator, that the car was stopping at six. And at five. And at four. And at three it stayed put. Spite work: someone pressing all the buttons and at each stop holding back the door.

He tapped with his key against the porthole.

He tapped again with his key and banged with the flat of his hand.

He readied himself to ring in one minute, in one second, the super's bell.

At last, at last the porthole showed a dying bulb and the elevator door sprang open.

"Well, thank you, thank you very-y-y-y much," he said, deliberately pushing in before the other party could step out, deliberately keeping his eyes down.

But by the fruit-stained swim trunks he recognized Toego.

"Mr. Rieff, do you know the Hollanders?"

Their mailbox was next to his.

"They had visitors last night. The little brownies. *Mira, Mira!* Two little brownies broke in and carried out a twenty-four-inch TV. On Saturday night, when there's comings and goings and activity. But they're smart, they are smarter and bolder than we think. They came down on the elevator, they had little caps on and they made noise. There was nothing to notice. Repairmen pulling a set. *Mira, mira!* Smart, smart! They even held the door for Mrs. Stock, 7-J—."

That, that was more than some people in the building would do.

"The police won't bother to look. One detective told me as much. He rang my bell, but he didn't write down a word."

They mustn't hold the elevator.

"I'll ride with you, Mr. Rieff. I'm going up, anyway."

He appreciated the company.

And all the way up, between tics, Toego was chuckling, chuckling and going, "*Mira! Mira! Mira! Mira!*"

"I'm home. Honey, I'm home," he told Etta, moving down beside her on the bed.

"Are you sorry?"

"You didn't make me juice and I should be sorry!"

"I made you Jell-O."

"I feel for Jell-O."

"If you'd called—why didn't you call? I could have told you get bananas."

"I'll do without bananas. I can live without bananas in

my Jell-O. And believe me, take my word for it, I couldn't call." He got out of his jacket, his tie and shirt and belt. He began to unzip his pants, stretching them out of shape because he had not first removed his shoes. And because he saw, or thought he saw, a mosquito, he took from the night table a stick of insect repellent and rubbed it all over himself and began to rub it all over Etta; and he said to her, while he worked the sticky stuff over her naked legs and her flanks and over the hem and ribbing of her nightgown and near her nose and cheeks and neck, and into the light pinkness where her hair was parted, he said to her, "Listen, listen, you don't know what a day I had, you don't know. I'll tell you something . . ."

And a long breaking breath.

And whoosh, a tear.

And another, and another, from the mother and father of all sorrows.

And he began to cry freely and quietly.

DATE DUE